Exposed

By Suzana Thompson

Chapter 1

My enemy had seen me naked.

He was holding the proof right before my eyes, and my stomach lurched sickeningly. I ran to the bathroom and remained kneeling in misery after throwing up in the toilet for the second time that morning.

"Seems like you had too much to drink last night," he remarked in that condescending tone he always used with me.

I looked up at him as he stood watching me from the doorway with his attitude of superiority. It was too much—the nausea, him witnessing me puking, his possession of that terrible picture. In that moment of weakness, I actually tried to plead with him. "Please. I've never done anything to you. Please."

"Begging me on your knees. That's a good start."

Dread turned my clammy skin cold. Mason Sumner hated my guts, and he would have no compassion for me. This was bad. This was really, really bad.

"Clean yourself up," he commanded. "In fact, take a shower. I don't want you getting in my car smelling like crap."

"Your car?" I asked in confusion, not understanding why he would allow me into his car. That was the last thing I would have expected from him.

"I'll take you with me since I'm here," he explained, "but you'll have to find your own way home."

"From where?" I questioned warily.

"My house," he replied. "You're going to clean it. Every week," he added.

I was beginning to comprehend that he was blackmailing me into doing this, and I felt relieved at first. It meant that he couldn't show the picture to anyone if he wanted me to comply with his demands. I had been terrified of him putting it out there for everyone to see.

"Get up and get in the shower," he snapped. "I'm not waiting around for you all day.

I pushed myself up to stand on my feet and awkwardly waited for him to leave the bathroom.

"What the hell are you waiting for?" he demanded.

A horrible realization sank in, and my voice trembled when I spoke. "I can't do it with you here."

"You'll do whatever I tell you to," he said. "But I don't have to be in here to see you naked." He held up his phone to emphasize his point. "So I'll let you get undressed alone. Your uniform will be on the bed."

"Uniform?"

"Just put it on," he told me impatiently and walked out of the bathroom.

I closed the door behind him and pushed the toilet lid down to sit wearily with my head in my hands. Despair washed over me as I thought about my sudden, inescapable predicament. Why had I drunk so much? Because Addison had prodded me to keep drinking. It was just the two of us here having a good time. Best friends. Laughing and dancing around to the music she had put on, drinking and cutting loose.

Addison had betrayed me. She had let Mason Sumner in here while I was intoxicated and apparently passed out, and he had taken a picture of me after someone removed all my clothes. I had been naked when I stumbled out of bed this morning and puked my guts out in the toilet, and she had been standing in the hallway afterwards and solemnly told me to get dressed.

"Why did I take my clothes off?" I had asked. "Did I throw up on them?"

"Mason is here," she said instead of answering me. "He wants to talk to you."

I immediately thought of Mason Sumner, but she couldn't be talking about him. He wasn't part of her social circle, and he certainly wouldn't come to her house to seek me out. "Mason who?" I asked.

"Sumner," she replied. "Hurry up and get dressed. He knows you're awake, and I could barely get him to wait five minutes."

I gaped at her, but she gave me a desperate shove. "Now, Ella! He'll be coming out here in a minute."

I hurried back into her room to throw my clothes on as a whirlwind of questions swirled in my mind. I heard Addison holding him off outside in the hallway as she pleaded with him to give me another minute.

"What's the difference? I already saw everything last night," he said.

I fumbled with the clasp on my bra as my heart seized up. It couldn't be true. He couldn't possibly have seen me undress. Yet I didn't know when he had arrived or why he was even here. Why had Addison let him inside her house while I was in the state I was in? How did he even know Addison well enough to be coming over her house?

I had just pulled on my shorts when he came barging into the room. With a shriek, I grabbed my shirt and held it in front of my chest. His striking silver-gray eyes regarded me coldly. "It's a little late for that. You sure weren't modest last night."

He showed me the picture on his phone. It was me sprawled out naked on the bed with my legs spread open to reveal a part of my body that no boy had ever seen before. Mason Sumner was the first, and now he could show it to all his friends, to the whole school even. He certainly hated me enough to humiliate me like that.

I had dropped the shirt and run to the bathroom to vomit again. I was still a pathetic mess sitting here on the toilet in my bra and shorts. I hadn't been able to find my panties in my haste to get dressed.

I jumped at the sudden sound of pounding on the door. "What are you doing?" Mason demanded. "Get in the damn shower or I'm coming in there."

I sprang up and quickly turned on the water in the shower. I hesitated to take my clothes off, not trusting him not to walk in anyway, but taking too long would guarantee that he would. So I stepped out of my shorts and took off my bra before hurrying into the shower and the privacy afforded by the shower curtain.

Washing away the clammy sweat from my skin made me feel a little better, and I rallied a bit. Anger started to course through me. I had never hated Mason before, but what he had done was despicable. And Addison...

What she had done was even worse. She had been my friend, and she had stabbed me in the back. How could she do this to me, I thought bitterly. My suspicion was that it had to do with her desire for popularity. I had told her that they weren't worth it, that the popular crowd was shallow and mean, but she still watched them with envy in her eyes. Mason must have promised her entry into their group if she got me drunk and let him take a nude picture of me.

Tears of shame and hurt welled up in my eyes, and I cried uncontrollably. What was I going to do? Mason was going to make my life hell with that horrible picture. I had just lost my best friend, and I had no one to help me.

My sob turned into a gasp when the water shut off and the curtain was yanked open. I flung one arm across my breasts and thrust my other hand down between my legs to cover my privates. Mason's eyes lingered on my body before taking in my teary face.

"Get out and dry off," he commanded, holding a towel toward me.

Reaching for it would require exposing myself to him. "Put it on the vanity," I said.

He complied and then crossed his arms as he planted his feet firmly in place. "Come out and get it."

"Leave. Please," I added grudgingly.

"If you'd rather have me watch you touch yourself, that's fine with me."

My face flamed with heat, and he used it against me. "Is that one of your fantasies?" he enquired. "Is that why you undressed for me last night? Do you want to follow in your mother's footsteps?"

It was like he had dumped a cold bucket of water over my head. All of my life I strove to be the opposite of my mother. I looked so much like her that people sometimes mistook us for sisters, so I did everything I could not to act like her—until last night. It was a mistake that had cost me dearly.

I stiffened and looked him in the eye. "I'm nothing like her."

Stepping carefully out of the tub while trying to keep all my privates covered, I moved my arm from my breasts to snatch the towel. I held it against me and finally moved my hand off the juncture between my legs to wrap the towel around me.

"Of course you are," Mason told me. "You've got the body to be a stripper too."

He smiled viciously at my surprised expression. "Yes, I know all about her illustrious past. With her good genes, you've got a great career ahead of you."

"Fuck you," I swore angrily, hating him even more for his condescending attitude.

"No thanks," he said. "Your friend already did last night and this morning. She's my girlfriend now. That was the deal."

With that bombshell, he opened the door. "Come on. You've got work to do."

Chapter 2

I stared at the maid's uniform, if you could call it that. "I'm not wearing that."

"Yes, you are," Mason retorted. "If you don't, I'll send that picture out to all my friends, and you can be sure that someone will post it online."

My heart constricted at the thought of that happening, but I couldn't abide by his plans for me either. "I'm not going to let you use me for sex."

"I never said anything about sex. I told you that Addison already took care of that."

I looked at him warily. "Then why do you want me to wear that skimpy thing?"

"I'm just trying to help you get a head start on your career as a stripper."

My heart began pounding, and I shook my head in desperation. "I can't...I can't strip for you."

He stepped intimidatingly close. "You'll do anything I tell you to do," he warned. "So don't argue with me, or I really will make you strip for me. Now put it on and get your ass downstairs."

He strode out of the room and shut the door. I felt grateful for the privacy and then angry that I was feeling grateful for something I was entitled to. My anger surged when my eyes fell once again on the "uniform" on the bed. It was actually lingerie designed to look like a sexy French maid uniform. The black material that covered the breasts was sheer, so I went back in the bathroom and picked my bra up off the floor. I grabbed my shorts too and put them on over the black panties that had been provided with my uniform.

Mason scowled when he saw me, but I spoke before he could. "I'll get arrested for indecent exposure if I go out in this without a bra."

"What is she wearing?" Addison demanded sharply. "What the hell, Mason? *I'm* your girlfriend."

"Which is how I'll introduce you at my party tonight," he replied. "That's why my maid has to clean my house and get it ready."

"You're not going to be screwing her behind my back," Addison insisted vehemently. "I won't put up with it. I had to wait a whole damn year for you to acknowledge me as your girlfriend, and you're not going to have her as your dirty little secret now."

A year. I reeled with the realization that she had been seeing him behind my back for the duration of our friendship. She was the only friend I'd had that he hadn't chased off, and now I knew why. "You've been planning this for a whole year?" I questioned him in disbelief.

"Brilliant, isn't it?" he bragged. "I had to be so patient this time. I had to give her time to earn to your trust."

My gaze shifted to Addison. "So, you were never my friend?" I asked dejectedly.

She scoffed. "Who wants to be friends with you? Anyone can see from a mile away that you're a boyfriend stealer."

Her perception of me was bewildering. "What? I've never stolen anyone's boyfriend."

She glanced down at my outfit and gave me a pointed look.

It triggered my outrage, and I went off on her. "You think I want to wear this? You put me in this shit, you stupid bitch! How could you do this to me?" I finished in anguish, almost breaking down in tears again.

Her expression hardened. "Like you would give a shit about me if Mason hadn't kept you from being popular."

"I never tried to be popular," I insisted. "You know I can't stand those people."

"Girl fights are no fun unless you're ripping each other's clothes off, so let's go," Mason said.

I turned my ire on him. "You are such an asshole. I can't believe you want him to be your boyfriend," I told Addison.

"Every girl wants me," Mason stated like it was a fact.

Sadly, it was true. They looked no further than his gorgeous face and social status as one of the most popular guys at school. His personality certainly had nothing to do with it. He was arrogant, and apparently sexist, and ruthless as I now knew.

"C'mon maid," he commanded. "It's time to do your job."

"You better not fuck her," Addison said in a tone that sounded more panicked than threatening.

His cold gaze was fixed on me as he replied to her. "I don't associate with my inferiors. She's just a servant, and trash. The skank doesn't fall far from the skank tree."

"Yeah," I retorted, "that's why Addison should be worried. Like father, like son."

Mason stiffened. If I thought his gaze was cold before, it was glacial now. He had the pitiless, cold-blooded stare of a predator. His silver-gray eyes always held an animal magnetism, and they now looked like wolf eyes stalking prey.

I took an involuntary step back from him, my heart stuttering like that of a scared rabbit. I actually jumped when he snapped at me, his terse tone cutting across my taut nerves, and I scurried out to his car like he commanded.

He came striding out as I tried to take a breath, not giving me time to compose myself before being trapped with him in his car. He was coiled tight with anger, making the atmosphere in that enclosed space almost unbearably tense. I clutched my knee as I kept my left elbow pressed against my side to keep it off the armrest and as far away from him as possible.

He didn't say a word until we arrived at his house. It was similar to mine, a Colonial style home that was a dream come true for me. "This is where I live now," he said in a harsh, disparaging tone.

"It's nice," I replied timidly, still cowed by the tension emanating from him.

His head turned toward me, and I regretted speaking. "Nice," he repeated in scorn. "Maybe for trailer trash like you. I grew up on an estate that was in my family for generations."

I remembered the place. I had felt like Cinderella at the royal palace during the short time I had lived there—before my mother got us kicked out. I hadn't met Mason, because he had been away at boarding school. I had seen pictures of him though, and I had dreamily imagined him as my handsome prince. What a naïve fool I had been, but I was only twelve at the time.

He got out of the car, and I reluctantly followed him into his house. I immediately noticed the dust on the entryway table. He saw me looking at it. "My mother isn't much of a housekeeper," he remarked.

I rolled my eyes before I could stop myself.

"What?" he questioned.

"Nothing," I replied.

"Tell me," he demanded.

"It's just, your assumption that it's her job to clean the house just because she's a woman. You live here too," I added, gaining confidence in my argument.

"So, you're a feminist," he commented, surprising me with an amused expression. "This is going to be fun." His eyes took on a wicked gleam that unnerved me again. "I'll show you where the cleaning supplies are."

He led me to the laundry room where there were cabinets containing all the usual cleaning products. He pointed to a corner of the room where a mop rested inside an empty bucket. "Bring the bucket," he instructed.

I grabbed the mop in one hand and the bucket in the other, but he told me to leave the mop. So I brought the bucket, and he had me fill it halfway with water from the faucet over the laundry tub before pouring in some Pine Sol. He then had me carry the bucket to the kitchen as he walked empty-handed. I felt like Cinderella again, but he was no Prince Charming.

As I set the bucket down on the floor, Mason grabbed a brand-new pack of cleaning rags from the kitchen counter and ripped it open. "Here," he said as he handed me a rag.

I wet it at the sink and began to wipe the countertop.

"No," he snapped. "Mop the floor with it."

"But there's a mop," I protested.

"I told you what will happen if you argue with me. Do you want everyone to see that picture?"

His cruel expression left no doubt in my mind that he would do it, and I cringed at the thought of everyone seeing me naked, and in such a pornographic pose. Dropping the rag into the bucket, I began to crouch down.

"Take your shorts off first," he ordered.

Despite his threat, I opened my mouth to protest, but he cut me off before I could speak. "The shorts or the bra. It's your choice."

"Now!" he barked as I hesitated over what to do. "Or you'll take off everything."

I quickly pulled down my shorts and stepped out of them, feeling immediately exposed in the black lace panties covered only by the sheer, short skirt. They were so small that my ass cheeks were hanging out.

"Get down on your hands and knees and mop the floor," Mason commanded.

As I silently complied, I understood now what he was doing. Addison had been wrong. None of this was about sex. He wasn't making me expose myself to him because it aroused him to look at me. He just wanted to humiliate me.

And it was working. I had never felt so humiliated in my life as I did with him standing behind me as I wiped the floor in this demeaning position.

"Shit," he swore, "your body is fucking insane!"

His exclamation threw me. It sounded like he had uttered it spontaneously, and it was obvious that it wasn't part of his humiliation plan.

"Get up," he said gruffly. "Go get the fucking mop. It'll take you forever this way, and I've got a party to prepare for."

I hurried to comply before he changed his mind, but he didn't say another word as he watched me mop the floor. It was infinitely less degrading while standing on my feet, and there was actually something satisfying about removing the dirt to reveal a sparkling clean surface.

Mason appeared restless rather than satisfied though. "I've got to go get some supplies for the party. Finish cleaning the rest of the house. Mop the bathrooms too before you dump the water."

Without waiting for a reply, he left me alone in his house. I immediately put my shorts back on, so I wouldn't be caught in my underwear by his mom if she came home. I wondered how he would explain my presence, and my outfit, to her.

Wary of his threats, I got to work cleaning the rest of the house. I also wanted to get it done and get out of there. The only break I took was to drink a glass of water after the kitchen floor was dry. It helped alleviate the residual effects of my hangover, and I started to feel more like myself.

With a clearer mind, I assessed my predicament and decided that living with it was preferable to dealing with the consequences of that picture of me being circulated among my peers. Although Mason was picking on me in a more extreme way than before, he was still the same bully he had been for the past three years. He dealt in psychological warfare rather than physical, and as long as it stayed that way, I could deal with it until I could take my own revenge on him.

I had formulated my own plan while I scrubbed the bathtub. I knew that Mason's birthday was on November 17th, which was three months away from today. He would be eighteen years old, but I would still be seventeen until February. That meant that he would be an adult in possession of child pornography, since I was a minor. I had realized that I could go to the police now, but I wanted him to face the full extent of the law. The consequences would be a lot more severe if he was charged as an adult.

I just had to bide my time until then, and I would as long as he didn't take things too far. It would be worth it to see him pay for all the misery he had put me through. If I could make it through three more months, Mason would spend the rest of his life wishing that he had never taken that picture. He would regret the day he ever started messing with me in the first place.

When I happened upon his room as I vacuumed upstairs, I was surprised to discover that it was the cleanest room in the house. There was no dust on his dresser, and it had none of the clutter that was typical in a teenage boy's room. Nothing littered the floor to impede my way with the vacuum, and I was done quickly.

Yet I lingered to look around in his private space. There were a few bottles of men's cologne on his dresser along with his deodorant. Whenever I had gotten a whiff of him over the years, he always smelled good. The way he dressed in slacks and nice shirts was probably a remnant from his boarding school days. His appearance and his understated masculine scent left a more sophisticated impression than other guys his age.

Even his bedroom gave off that impression. There was nothing about it that indicated that it was a teenage guy's room. It looked like a man's bedroom with its elegant masculine look. The walls were painted a soft gray, and his bed was black and accented by a white bedspread and white pillows stacked by the black headboard. The refined look of this room matched the outward appearance of its owner.

The family photograph on his nightstand completed the effect. It showed Mason with his parents. They were all smiling and looking happy.

Yet looks could be deceiving. Mason's dad had been cheating on Mason's mom, so they hadn't been as happy together as they appeared. I didn't know what Mason had been like back then, but his bad behavior now ruined the good impression gleaned from his appearance.

"That was what your slut mother destroyed," he said, and I turned to see him standing in the doorway.

"Then why not go after her?" I asked. "Why are you taking it out on me? I was a kid, just like you were."

Surprise showed on his face. "You're not going to defend your mother? Try to tell me that it wasn't her fault?"

"It was just as much his fault as it was hers. Unless you think that she raped him."

"She knew that he was a married man," he argued, his voice rising in volume as he moved toward me. "She knew that he had a family."

"So did he," I retorted. "But that didn't stop him from cheating on his wife."

Mason went still, and his eyes took on that dangerous gleam. I froze at the realization that I had just poked at his wound. I had just called his dead father a cheater, which was true, but I was the last person he wanted to hear that from. Especially since his father had died while having sex with my mother.

Then I remembered the threat hanging over my head. "Mason," I began hesitantly.

"Did I say that you could address me by my first name?" he snapped at me. "Let me make something clear to you. You are my servant, and you will know your place. You will call me sir."

My temper flared instantly at that outrageous demand. "Sir?" I sneered. "Is that some bondage crap? Because if you think I'll ever let you touch me, you're out of your mind."

He smiled thinly. "Of course, your mind would go there. Look at who raised you. Well, let me set you straight. You're not going to get out of this by seducing me. I wouldn't touch trash like you, so you better remember your place and start showing me some fucking respect."

It hurt to be called trash, even by him. "You haven't done a damn thing to earn my respect," I lashed out at him. "Talk about trash! What kind of an asshole undresses an unconscious girl and takes pictures of her?"

He gave me a mocking smile. "You weren't unconscious. I was just going to take a video of you acting like a drunk fool, but you tried to seduce me. You were dancing suggestively and rubbing up against me, and then you took off your shirt."

I scoffed at his claim. "You're lying."

"I have the video to prove it," he replied. "I already had enough to make you squirm, but then you asked me if I wanted to see more. You took your clothes off for me."

As I watched him with a skeptical look, his gaze momentarily dropped from mine as he swallowed in what almost appeared to be a nervous gesture. His jaw hardened, and there was a steely look in his eyes when they met mine again. "You told me that you've had a crush on me since you were twelve years old."

I froze. "You're lying," I whispered.

He pulled his phone out of his pocket and swiped at the screen before coming to stand beside me as the video played. I saw myself dancing alone first, my body moving to the beat of the music. I stopped to take a swig of tequila straight from the bottle before resuming my dancing.

"Smile," a male voice said. "I'm taking your picture."

I halted and faced the camera directly, my face breaking out into a delighted smile the way it never would if I saw him when I was sober. "Mason! You're here! Dance with me!"

"Hold this," he said, presumably talking to Addison. "Keep filming."

He appeared in the camera frame, and I approached him with my arms raised, dancing seductively. "You're so hot," I told him. "I have sexy dreams about you."

"What happens in your dreams?" he asked in a low, seductive voice as he gazed at me.

I pressed my body up against his. "You touch me," I answered in a sultry tone.

"Where?"

I took a step back from him and pulled my shirt off, flinging it away. "Touch me," I urged, closing the space between us again.

The camera tilted crazily, and the floor and wall came into view at a sideways angle. "That's enough," Addison said.

"Keep filming!" Mason barked.

"You're not fucking screwing her, Mason. I won't—"

The camera view tilted again. "Get out of here," he growled.

"Are you kidding me?" she exclaimed. "You think you can screw her in my house?"

"Shut up!" he yelled. "I'm not screwing her. I fucking hate her."

"You hate me?" I heard myself wail. "But why?"

The camera view captured me again, and I was pouting. "Go," Mason commanded. "I want to get this damn video."

"I can—"

"Leave," he cut her off sharply.

"Promise you won't do anything with her."

"I fucking promise," he snapped. "Just let me get this done, and she'll be out of your hair."

I was drinking more tequila while they argued, but I set down the bottle as he approached me. "You're taking my picture?" I asked happily, apparently having forgotten the conversation we just had.

"Yes," he replied. "You've got a great body."

I smiled at him, pleased with the compliment. "Want to see more?"

"Yes," he said. "Show me more."

"Is this a dream?" I asked him. "You take off my clothes in my dreams."

"Yeah?" he responded, his voice sounding husky.

"You're so beautiful," I spoke dreamily. "I've had a crush on you since I was twelve. I want to marry you."

Mason moved the phone away from me and turned off the video. "Proof that you asked me to take off your clothes," he clipped out.

"How could you do that?" I demanded. "After I was all..." The word vulnerable came to mind, but I didn't voice it.

"Romantic?" he supplied derisively. "Yeah, I wasn't falling for that. I know your mother taught you to use whatever you can to get your claws into a man."

"I'm not like my mother!" I raged. "I don't use sex to get things. I've never even..." I trailed off in mortification. He was the last person I wanted to confess that to.

He snorted. "You've never had sex? Addison told me how you said you're a virgin, but I'm not buying that bullshit. Not with how you spread your legs for me last night."

I stared at him. "We didn't..."

His silver-gray eyes regarded me contemptuously. "I told you I wouldn't touch trash like you. You're my servant and nothing else. Is that clear?"

"Don't call me trash," I said as I glared at him.

"The only words that should come out of your mouth when you speak to me are yes sir. Say it," he ordered.

"I'm not calling you—"

"Say it, or I'll send that picture out to everyone on my contact list," he threatened as he raised his phone and held his thumb over the screen.

I lunged at him and tried to grab his phone, but he reacted with quick reflexes and twisted away from me in what looked like some kind of martial arts move. I skidded to a stop and turned to face him.

"Do you really think that I don't have that picture stored anywhere else?" he enquired coolly. "If you break my phone, you'll just have to buy me a new one. Now say the words."

Everything in me rebelled against it. Somehow it seemed worse than the indignity he had already put me through. "Yes sir," I said through gritted teeth.

His mocking smile made me want to slap him. "Now remember to address me that way at the party tonight."

Dread curled in my empty stomach. "The party?"

"You'll be serving drinks," he informed me. "Make sure you wear your uniform."

I blanched. "I can't wear this in front of everyone. That's almost as bad as having them see the picture."

His eyes traveled insolently over me before shifting to his phone. He didn't swipe at the screen, so he couldn't have pulled up my picture. His gaze was heated when he looked back at me though. "Not even close," he said, his voice pitched in a sexual tone that elicited a carnal response in my body.

Heat spread through me as our gazes locked. In that moment, I knew that he wanted me. I had fantasized about having him look at me that way, but I hadn't known how powerfully erotic it would be, how it would set my pulse pounding and shoot liquid fire straight down to my core. The intensity of his gaze made my knees weak as I stared back at him in a haze of lust.

His ringtone startled us out of it. Jerking his hand up, Mason scowled at the screen before answering his phone. "What?" he snapped.

"Yes," he answered in exasperation after listening for a beat. "I'm just about to drive her home."

He ended the call without waiting for a reply. "Let's go," he said to me and spun toward the doorway.

I followed his quick stride downstairs and out to his car. We remained awkwardly silent during the ride to my house as I became uncomfortably aware of the state my body was in after my intense surge of lust. I needed another shower to wash away the moisture between my legs. I couldn't wait to finally be alone, but Mason got out of the car too after parking it in my driveway.

"What are you doing?" I asked in alarm.

"I want what you're wearing back." He pulled a shopping bag out of the backseat. "This is your new uniform. Wear it tonight."

I eyed the bag warily, but I didn't have any fight left in me right now. I just wanted him to leave so I could get a break from everything. Walking up to the house, I unlocked the door. Fortunately, nobody was home, so I didn't have to explain why I was dressed like this. Mason surprised me by not following me to my room.

"Hurry up," he admonished me.

He didn't have to tell me twice. I was eager to get rid of him, so I dumped the new uniform he had bought me on my bed and quickly shoved everything I stripped off into the shopping bag. I kept my shorts, because they were mine. I hated to give Mason the panties I had worn, but I was afraid he'd come back for them if I didn't.

Putting on my regular cotton panties, I pulled my shorts back on and threw on a t-shirt before going downstairs and handing him the bag.

"Be at my house at eight," he said and left like he was just as eager to get away from me as I was to see him go.

Hope flared within me that he was already getting tired of having me around. If he hated me, it made sense that he wouldn't be able to stand to be around me very long. Maybe I wouldn't have to go to the police after all. Waiting for Mason's eighteenth birthday wasn't the only reason I was delaying reporting him to the police. I really didn't want anyone to see that picture, not even the authorities. I'd have to watch for an opportunity to get rid of it. Since Mason was giving me free reign of his house, I might be able to get to it and delete it from his devices.

Then I would be free of his threats and out of this bizarre predicament I was in.

Chapter 3

Mason had bought me a real maid's uniform. The straight skirt even came down to my knees. Nobody would mistake this plain style for a sexy costume, so it wouldn't be that embarrassing to be seen in it by my classmates at Mason's party. I could pass it off as a real job.

I gazed at my reflection in the mirror. With my curves covered up and my hair in a ponytail, I looked less like my blonde bombshell mother. Without any makeup, I was fresh-faced with only my baby blue eyes drawing attention with their vivid color.

My mother didn't even look up from her phone to notice that I was wearing a uniform as I walked past her. As usual, my dad was the only one who questioned where I was going. "When did you get a job?"

"I'm just starting today," I replied, inching toward the door.

"Where are you working?" he asked.

"It's a catering company," I lied. "They do parties, and I'll be serving appetizers."

"What's the name of the company?"

"I forgot. My friend's mom does it out of her house, and we're working for her. I've really gotta go. I don't want to be late on my first day. Thanks for letting me borrow your car," I said as I rushed out the door.

I mostly loved the fact that he took such an interest in my life. He had become the father I'd never had, and I adored him. Until now, I'd had no reason to keep secrets from him. I hated lying to him, but I couldn't tell him about Mason blackmailing me. The last person in the world I wanted to disappoint was my dad. I shouldn't have been drinking at all, let alone drinking enough to blackout.

I would never get drunk again. No alcohol would pass my lips tonight, that was for sure. The irony was that I had often wished that I could go to one of these parties. Unlike Addison, I had never desired popularity, but I didn't like being shunned either. Everyone had started ignoring me after Mason began bullying anyone who tried to be friends with me. Since he was popular, he got all his buddies to back him up. No one wanted to be targeted by them because of me, so I was left out of everything.

That was why I was so grateful to finally have a friend, and why I was so desperate to keep her that I had gone along with everything she suggested the previous evening. She had urged me to keep drinking, so I did. Since she hadn't been as smashed as I was, I could only assume that she had only pretended to keep drinking with me.

She was at Mason's house when I arrived, and she wasn't happy to see me. "What the hell, Mason? Why is she here?"

Addison apparently wasn't bothering to address me directly anymore, and it reinforced the realization that she had been faking her friendship with me. Being friendless again hurt worse than it had before. Mason had wounded me more by giving me a false friend than by denying me friends altogether. I felt the loss more acutely.

Blinking away the tears from my eyes, I reminded myself that she wasn't worth it. She was one of them now, the shallow people who only cared about themselves—the people Mason surrounded himself with. The people who were just like him.

"Because I told her to be here," he snapped at Addison. "She does what I tell her to do."

Her scowl turned into a deep frown. "She already cleaned your house. What are you going to have her do now?"

His eyes narrowed at her. "Are you going to nag me about everything? Because that's getting old fast."

Realizing her precarious position, she tread carefully. "It's just...I thought you got what you wanted. You made her miserable, and now—"

"I'm just supposed to let her walk away?" he cut in. "She's miserable for one day, and that's it?"

"But how is letting her come to your party making her life suck? This is what she's always wanted," she said, mistaking her own desires for mine.

He reprimanded her before I could. "Are you stupid? Do you really think she wants to be here? As a *maid*?"

"Guys think that's sexy. I bet she'll get hit on all night," she remarked flatly.

Mason eyed me with displeasure, seemingly disliking that prospect as much as she did. He had chased away all my potential boyfriends from the first day of high school, making sure that I had no social life. I should have realized that it was a trick when he allowed me to socialize with Addison.

"Don't talk to anyone," he told me. "You're not here to flirt. Just give them their drinks. Got it?"

I nodded, but that didn't satisfy him.

"Answer me," he demanded.

"Yes, I've got it," I said.

"What did I tell you were the only two words you are to say to me?"

"Yes sir," I huffed with an eye roll.

"With respect!" he snapped angrily. "If you don't show me respect, I'll make you the center of attention tonight. All my guests will see your picture."

"Yes sir," I repeated in a chastised tone with my eyes downcast.

"Sir?" Addison questioned, her voice rising in indignation. "You're having her call you sir? I knew this was some kinky sex thing. Otherwise you would have had her doing your homework and stuff like that instead of dressing up as your sex slave. I would have let you tie me up if I knew you were into that. You didn't need to blackmail *her* into doing it. I thought you hated her!"

He regarded her with disdain. "I don't need any help with my homework. And I sure as hell don't need to tie a girl down to make her my sex slave."

"So, you're admitting you had sex with her," she said, looking like she was either about to lose her shit or cry.

"I don't have sex with my maid!" he yelled, startling her out of her meltdown. "She's beneath me. Do you understand? That's what this whole thing is about. She is here as a servant, and she will know her place."

I wanted to tell him that he was full of shit and that he was born a few centuries too late to get away with that condescending crap, but I held my tongue.

Mollified at last, Addison directed a mocking smile at me. "You better remember your place, Ella."

"Yes ma'am," I retorted. "Serving your boyfriend. All day, and...all night." A small smirk played over my lips as I gazed at her with a wicked expression. "He likes when I'm beneath him."

Her smile withered, while cold fury emanated from Mason. I could sense it without looking at him, so strong was his effect on the atmosphere. It chilled me even as my pulse spiked with the fight or flight response to imminent danger. I did neither as I held the ground I had gained on Addison. Her jealousy had revealed her weakness to me, and I stomped on her with glee. My revenge was gratifying and sweet. *She* would not get the better of me at least.

"Get to your station."

Mason's tight, terse voice snapped me out of my gloating stare down with Addison. "Yes sir," I replied, injecting saucy, flirty enthusiasm into the words. "Where do you want me?" I asked, infusing the question with unmistakable sexual innuendo.

His glare hardened into the cold stare of a predator. "On your knees," he commanded with an icy calmness that conveyed complete control of the situation.

A moment ago, his voice had been stretched taut with barely contained anger, but the deliberate intimidation of it now was much more threatening. I didn't dare to defy him, but I hesitated in fear.

"Get on your knees," he said with that same frightening composure.

I obeyed, sinking down slowly with a feeling of inescapable dread. He stepped forward until he was standing directly in front of me. My face flooded with the shame of being in this subservient position with his crotch at my eye-level. My gaze lifted to his with the horrified realization that he would expose my naked picture to everyone.

Because I wouldn't do this. No way in hell.

"Respect," he warned. "The next time you start playing games with me, I'll call your bluff. Got it?"

"Yes sir," I answered, my voice tremulous with the relief of being spared exposure.

"Get up," he ordered.

I did, but that brought me up close to his face. I dropped my eyes from his intimidating stare as I took a step back away from him.

"I'll take care of you, Mason," Addison said.

My gaze turned toward her, and I watched her approach him. When she boldly placed her hand on his crotch, I looked away. More heat flooded my face as she offered to go up to his room with him and give him a blowjob.

"I have guests arriving soon," I heard him say, seemingly as unaffected by her offer as I was uncomfortable.

"I'll get you off fast," she promised.

"No," he stated flatly. "Come here maid," he called to me as I cringed in embarrassment for Addison over his rejection of her desperate attempt to please him. "Your station is in the kitchen."

He led me to where he had a keg of beer set up on the counter along with stacks of red solo cups. "You fill these for people."

I nodded in agreement, although I hadn't needed it explained to me.

"Answer me," he demanded.

"Yes sir," I responded.

"Look at me when I address you," he ordered.

My gaze shifted from the keg to him. "Yes sir," I remembered to say.

"Good, it seems like you know your place now," he remarked, but his tone was too neutral to be mocking me.

His gaze became cunning as he regarded me, and it made me nervous about what he was plotting.

"You told me you're not like your mother," he said.

"I'm not," I replied.

He gave me a warning look. "What are the only two words that should come out of your mouth when you speak to me?"

"Yes sir," I answered.

His features eased into an appeased expression. "So, you still think that you're not like your mother?"

I nodded in confirmation. "Yes sir."

"Yet you tried to seduce me."

I shook my head in denial. "No sir. I was just—"

He cut me off by moving into my personal space. "What are the words?"

"Yes sir," I supplied the correct answer as I instinctively put more distance between us, "but I wasn't—"

"I'm not interested in your excuses," he interrupted me again. "You tried to seduce me right in front of my girlfriend, which actually makes you worse than your slutty mother."

"I was just getting back at Addison for what she did to me. I wasn't trying to seduce you, and you don't care how you act in front of her anyway. You tried to make me…" I trailed off, my rant petering out with my reluctance to name the act.

"That's more than two words," he commented, "but I'll let it slide this time. Go ahead and finish your sentence."

I waved that offer aside. "I'm done."

"No," he insisted, "your sentence is incomplete. What did I try to make you do?"

My gaze shifted nervously away from him as I tried to think of a reply.

"Look at me when I speak to you," he commanded.

I complied. "Yes sir," I said in the hope that it would placate him.

"Speak," he ordered.

I shifted from one foot to the other under his unnerving gaze since I was forced to look at him. "You, uh, tried to make me give you…a, you know. What your girlfriend wanted to give you."

"What, exactly, did she want to give me?" he asked coolly.

The need to look away from him was too great, and I did as I spoke the words. "A blowjob."

"You act so innocent," he said before swooping in to whisper in my ear. "But your panties were soaked."

Before I could recover my wits, he was back out of my personal space. "Isn't that right?" he asked.

I flushed from head to toe as I recalled returning the previous "uniform" to him along with the black panties that came with it. Utter shame overwhelmed me, and I couldn't look at him.

"Answer me," he demanded. "Isn't that right?"

With my gaze fixed on the floor, I took a steadying breath.

"Eyes up here," he ordered.

My face burning, I forced myself to look at him. "Yes sir."

"They were soaked?" he pressed, drawing out my humiliation.

"Yes sir," I said.

"So that means you're like your mother."

I gritted my teeth, defiance rising within me despite everything. "I peed myself—sir."

He stared at me for a couple of seconds before barking out a laugh as his eyes lit up with comprehension. "Nice try," he said in actual amusement.

He took a step forward and leaned in toward me, his voice dropping in volume. "But I know the difference." He leaned in even closer to whisper in my ear. "You were soaking wet for me."

When he pulled back to look at me, his heated gaze changed what had been mortifying to something erotic. Once again, we stared at each other in a haze of lust until ringing snapped us out of it. This time it was the doorbell.

"Mason!" Addison yelled from the other room. "Someone's here!"

She sounded panicked, but I felt disoriented. What the hell was happening between Mason and me? How could he desire me if he hated me? And how could I possibly be attracted to him after how he had treated me? I had my mother's looks, so maybe that was all it took for a guy. Yet girls were supposed to need more than that. I was supposed to be attracted to the person rather than just his exterior.

Mason's physical beauty could make most girls jealous while simultaneously swooning over him. Just his lustrous dark locks alone were enough to inspire envy. The loose curls always looked perfectly tousled and touchable. He possessed those rare silver-gray eyes which were so arresting and unique. Their luminous color was strikingly set off by lush dark eyebrows and lashes. A straight patrician nose was another perfect feature on his handsome face. Then there were the kissable lips that had whispered in my ear.

Just the memory of that made me hot. Which was really twisted and wrong. I must seriously need a boyfriend if my tormentor could turn me on so easily. But he was the one who wouldn't let me have a boyfriend. Anger sparked within me again. I had to get out from under his thumb.

I longed to have the kind of experiences that most girls had. My first date, first kiss, first boyfriend. All of those had been denied to me by Mason. I'd gone to one school dance with a boy back in eighth grade, but I had turned my head away when he tried to kiss me. I hated to remember that now, because Mason had been the cause of that too.

Ever since I had become infatuated with him when I saw his picture, I'd had a stupid fantasy about him being my one true love. I'd imagined that he would fall in love with me too when he saw me, just like in a fairytale. I had put him up on a pedestal and cast him in the role of prince charming, and nobody else could measure up.

When I saw him on my first day of high school, I thought my dream was coming true. I was sure that destiny had brought us together, and my heart swelled with happiness and adoration. Mason's reaction was quite different however. There was a hard, cold glint in his beautiful eyes and his lips formed a cruel smile as he approached me.

"I've got you now, Ella," he said, but it didn't sound romantic at all.

The reality of meeting him was all wrong. I couldn't rejoice in the fact that he knew my name, because there was no warmth in his voice when he said it. His statement was a threat, and he carried through on it. He did nothing to me directly, but he bullied everyone who got close to me until I had no one.

I asked him why once. Back when I first found out that my friends were dropping me because of him, I approached him to ask why he was targeting me.

"I haven't done anything to you," he replied coolly.

He had spread rumors that my mom worked as an escort and got paid to have sex with rich men, but I didn't mention that to him. "You're making all my friends drop me. Why are you doing this to me? I've never done anything to you. You don't even know me!"

"You can't blame me for losing your friends," he stated. "It sounds like they just don't like you anymore."

"That's not true! They said that the mean girls are making their lives hell, and they said they'd only stop if they stopped being friends with me."

He smirked at me. "The mean girls? Am I supposed to understand your ridiculous references? What do these 'mean girls' have to do with me?"

I flushed, both in embarrassment at how immature he made me sound and with secret jealousy. "You're dating their leader," I said, and blushed furiously as I heard how silly that sounded phrased that way.

He regarded me silently with an unnervingly focused scrutiny that assessed all my responses. It was the first time I saw that predatory gaze, and his tone held a deadly calm when he spoke. "You've come to me, because you think my girlfriend is responsible for you having no friends."

He had thrown me off kilter, and my voice didn't convey as much conviction as I felt. "You put her up to it."

"Why would you think that? Who are you, by the way?"

Tears of frustration sprang to my eyes. "You know who I am. You talked to me on the first day of school, and you knew my name. Why are you being so mean to me? Please just leave my friends alone."

"The friends you don't have?" he enquired.

I saw that I wasn't going to get anywhere with him by pleading my case and that he apparently had no sympathy for me at all. There could only be one reason why he disliked me so much. "Is this because of your dad?"

If I thought that his gaze was intimidating before, it turned downright menacing now. I shrank back from him even though he hadn't moved from where he stood. "Don't ever say anything about him again," he warned.

I spoke timidly. "I just...it's not my fault."

His cold stare looked through me. "Get out of my face."

It was spoken so calmly but carried such an underlying threat that it intimidated me into hurrying away from him. I didn't try to talk to him again until my date for Homecoming canceled on me without explanation. He had a black eye though, and I suspected I knew who had given it to him.

This time I was so outraged that I didn't wait for an opportunity to catch Mason alone. His girlfriend was right beside him when I marched up to him. "You asshole! You beat up my date! What the hell?"

He looked down his nose at me. "Who the fuck are you, and what the hell are you screeching about?"

"I'm Ella Chase, and you can go fuck yourself, you fucking asshole!"

"Such language," he chided, infuriating me even more.

His pretty girlfriend confronted me. "What is your problem?"

I turned some of my ire on her. "What is *your* problem? Can't you think for yourself? He tells you to pick on my friends, and you just do it? Why? I've never done anything to you."

"He told me how obsessed you are with him, and I can see he wasn't exaggerating," she replied. "He tried to let you down nicely, but you didn't even care that he has a girlfriend. I guess it's no surprise with how you were raised. Still, I'm warning you, stay away from my boyfriend."

"I don't want your fucking boyfriend!" I exploded. "I just want him to leave me alone."

She wrinkled her pert little nose at me. "He wouldn't touch trash like you. Who knows what kind of diseases you have. I heard one of your mom's customers paid you to do a mother/daughter thing with him. That is so gross!"

Rage overcame me at hearing this, and I flew at Mason. "You lying asshole," I screamed as I pounded my fists against his chest. "It's not my fucking fault your dad died! He had a *heart attack*, you stupid—"

"Shut up," he roared, grabbing my wrists and silencing me with a look of such intense hate that I wilted under the force of it.

All the words dried up in my throat as he stared me down. His girlfriend was shouting for a teacher and yelling about how I had attacked him, but I stood trapped in Mason's grip and his vicious stare.

"I warned you," he said quietly before letting me go.

That ominous threat chilled me with dread about what he would do next, but it had been more of the same until he used Addison to get me to let my guard down. Now he had ensnared me in his twisted game of revenge, but his hate didn't seem to be as strong as before. It was all confusing as hell, and I just wanted it to end, but I could see no way out of it anytime soon.

Chapter 4

I heard them approaching the kitchen in boisterous conversation, and I braced myself to deal with them. Josh Meyers walked in first and stopped in surprise when he saw me. "Ella?" He glanced back at the doorway, probably looking for an explanation from Mason.

Tyler Hicks wasn't as hesitant. "Ella! Are you offering your services? You should have worn a sexier costume, but you're still hot. How much for an hour?"

"She's serving drinks," Mason said flatly. "Stop harassing my help."

"Your help?" Tyler questioned with a smirk. "What is she helping you with? Maybe she can help me too."

"She can get you a drink," Mason snapped at him and nodded curtly to me.

As I grabbed a cup and began to fill it with beer, Tyler wheedled Mason. "You're not gonna share? That's a little selfish. You've got two girls and—hey! Are you having a threesome? Awe man, that's hot!"

I scowled at Mason as I turned around, but he was too busy glaring at Tyler to notice. "I have one girl," he retorted, gesturing at Addison—who looked completely mortified. His sullen gaze fell on me. "This one is serving drinks. Give him his damn drink and do your fucking job," he commanded.

Tyler grabbed the cup from my hand. "Whatever man, just keep the beer coming."

"Could I have one too, please?" Josh asked me.

"Sure," I replied and filled a cup for him.

"Thank you, Ella," he said and smiled at me as I handed it to him.

I smiled back. "You're welcome."

The doorbell rang, and Mason told Addison to answer the door.

"Aren't you coming with me?" she asked. "It's your house."

"You get it," he said dismissively. "I want a drink."

I pulled another cup off the stack, but Mason snatched it from me. "Go home," he snapped as I turned my startled gaze on him. "I don't need you here to do this."

Thrilled to get this unexpected reprieve, I hurried to leave before he changed his mind. Tyler urged me to stay and party while Josh stated that he'd walk me to my car and followed me out of the room. Mason caught up to us and insisted on walking me out himself.

"She works for *me*. It's my responsibility to keep her safe," he claimed.

I almost asked him who would keep me safe from him, but I didn't want to push my luck.

"Uh, okay," Josh said reluctantly. "I guess I'll see you at school, Ella."

"Yeah," I agreed. "See you, Josh. Thanks for…uh, that was sweet of you to think of walking me to my car." I had almost thanked him for being nice to me, but saying that would have sounded really pathetic.

Having Mason walk me out felt very awkward, because it didn't fit my situation with him. There was nothing friendly between us, so concern for my wellbeing couldn't be the reason he was doing this. His abrupt dismissal of me gave me hope that he was already sick of having me around. Maybe he wanted to talk to me alone to give me some task that didn't involve being at his house. I didn't go as far as to succumb to my wishful thinking that he wanted to leave me alone completely. He was still radiating angry tension, so he hadn't let go of his misplaced wrath.

"What did I tell you?" he demanded when we reached my car and he spun to face me. "What were my instructions?"

I wasn't sure what he was talking about, and I stared blankly at him.

He didn't wait long enough for me to form a response anyway. "I told you not to talk to anyone. You were just supposed to serve them their drinks. I didn't bring you here to pick up guys."

"I wasn't," I protested. "It's not my fault that idiot, Tyler, believes all your stupid crap about me. You're the one who started all that shit about my mom being an escort," I added resentfully. As much as some of the things she had done upset me, nobody liked to have their mom's name dragged through the mud.

"I wasn't talking about Tyler," Mason said. "You were flirting with Josh. Did you think I'd let you use my party to hook up with him? You weren't a fucking *guest*. I didn't *invite* you."

"I wouldn't *want* to come to your party," I retorted. "You're the one who won't leave me alone. I don't want anything to do with you. And I wasn't flirting with Josh. He just happened to be the only person around who didn't treat me like shit. I wasn't going to be rude to him just because the rest of you are assholes."

His eyes glinted dangerously beneath the streetlight. "Don't think for one minute that I'll let you worm your way into my group. You're not one of us, and you never will be. FYI, fucking Josh won't get you in. His nice guy act stops after you give it up, so you can forget about him asking you to be his girlfriend, because that's not happening."

It hadn't occurred to me to think of Josh as a potential boyfriend after such a brief interaction with him, and I certainly wasn't looking for a way into the popular crowd. I didn't aspire to be part of the group who had ruined high school for me. I hadn't been able to beat them, but I sure didn't want to join them. Yet now that Mason was so opposed to it, the thought of pursuing it just to aggravate him was very appealing. The fact that he didn't want me to flirt with Josh suddenly made that something that I wanted to do.

I dismissed outright everything Mason had said about Josh, because I knew firsthand how he lied about people. I wasn't naïve enough to believe that Josh was a sweetheart either, but I would make my own assessments of his character. Trusting Addison had been a terrible misjudgment on my part, so I would be much more careful with Josh. I wasn't going to let down my guard with him, but I could still enjoy his gentlemanly treatment of me, even if it was just an act. I was long overdue for some normal attention from boys. Mason had interfered with all the other guys, but he wouldn't be able to thwart Josh. He couldn't bully one of his own friends.

I smiled at him with false sweetness. "It worked for Addison. She didn't have a prayer of being popular until she latched onto you. It's like a fairytale," I mocked. "You're her knight in shining armor."

"She's a bitch who's using me to get what she wants, but I got what I wanted too." He stepped closer to me and spoke with taunting satisfaction. "I own your ass now. You do what I say, or senior year will be hell for you. Even if you transfer to another school, that picture will never go away once it's online. Even if they take it down, people will already have it. It'll always be out there, and someone will find out about it eventually."

I feared that he was right, and I didn't want that picture to haunt me when I went away to college. I had been looking forward to being free of Mason after this last year of high school, but he now had something that he could use against me indefinitely. That thought made me sweat, but he had only mentioned senior year, so I hoped that he was planning to move on after that and leave behind his vendetta against me. It would be extremely immature to carry it on beyond high school, but then again, he had no reason to have a vendetta against me in the first place.

Feeling suddenly weary after the long, stressful day I'd had, all the fight drained out of me. "Yes, I know. Can I please leave now?" I pleaded.

He regarded me for a moment as I stood drooping on my feet. "I should make you do something else to pay for not following orders, but I'll let it slide this time since you seem to know your place now. Don't let it happen again though. From now on you do exactly as I say. Understand?"

"Yes," I answered tiredly.

"Good," he said, and pulled out his phone. "Give me your number. I'll text you when I want you to do something. You better not ignore my texts," he warned. "Don't give me any bullshit excuses about your phone not being charged. If you don't answer, you'll regret it."

"Okay," I said, just wanting the day to be over. I gave him my number and then saved his on my phone at his insistence.

"Go home now," he told me. "I'll see you tomorrow at dinner."

My gaze had drifted toward my car, but it flitted back to him. "Dinner?" I asked, thinking that he was going to have me come back tomorrow to cook for him.

"Yes," he replied. "I'm coming over your house for dinner. Six o'clock. Text me the address later. And make sure that your wonderful mother is there. I'm looking forward to meeting her."

"You want to meet my mother?" I asked in disbelief, my exhaustion forgotten.

"I imagine it will be a delightful evening," he remarked, somehow managing to set me on edge more by keeping the sarcasm out of his tone.

"What are you going to do?" I questioned suspiciously.

"I'm going to eat dinner with you and your lovely mother," he replied in that same light tone.

"My dad will be there too," I told him anxiously. "Please don't say anything in front of him."

"Your mother reconciled with your father?"

"No," I answered. "He's my stepfather."

"She's still with the same husband?" he asked in astonishment. "The one she married four years ago?"

"Yes, and he has nothing to do with this, so please don't do anything in front of him."

"Well, I never would have imagined your mother settling down into wedded bliss. I've got to see this for myself. Maybe she's changed." The sarcasm was clear in his voice this time.

"You won't say anything?" I prodded.

"If you don't give me any trouble, we'll just have a nice dinner with your family."

"Mason," Addison called, and I turned my head to see her approaching us. "What are you doing?" she demanded. "People were wondering where you were."

"I thought you'd be in your glory hosting one of these parties. This is the crowd you couldn't wait to be a part of," he said, sounding like he was taunting her.

"You're supposed to be with me," she complained as I opened the car door. "They expect to see you at—"

She cut off in midsentence as Mason grabbed my arm to stop me from getting into the car. "Did I give you permission to leave?" he demanded.

"You told me I could go home," I protested. "In the kitchen, you said—"

"I was speaking to you," he cut in sharply. "Regardless of whether someone interrupts me, you wait to be dismissed."

"Why are you touching her? You promised you wouldn't touch her!"

He disregarded his girlfriend's distress. "I promised I wouldn't have sex with her. I never said anything about touching her."

"Let go of me," I said.

"Ask me for permission to leave."

I hated his stupid games, but I acquiesced so I could leave and get this day over with. "Can I leave, please?"

"You know better than that," he chided. "Ask me properly."

I sighed in a long-suffering manner. "*May* I please leave?"

"Your grammar is correct," he commented mildly, but I could tell he was enjoying this. "However, you haven't addressed me properly. I told you would there would be consequences for not doing exactly what I say."

I couldn't overlook the threat in his words, no matter how harmless his tone sounded. I couldn't take the chance of him ruining my dad's opinion of me. So I swallowed what was left of my pride. "May I please leave, sir?"

He released a soft breath. "Yes," he said, his voice inflected with what sounded like sexual satisfaction to my ears.

Addison must have heard it too. "Mason," she protested but was unable to actually call him out on anything since he let go of my arm in that moment.

I was grateful for the cover of darkness to hide the blush creeping over my face. The sound of Mason's voice shouldn't have affected me this way. It seemed to have traveled straight down to my core. I quickly got in the car and shut the door. Fumbling to put the key in the ignition as my heart raced for no apparent reason, I finally succeeded and straightened up to see where I was going.

I jumped in my seat when Mason rapped on my window. "Put your seatbelt on," he commanded.

Too flustered to argue that I never wore my seatbelt, I put it on and shifted into drive. Glad that I had parked on the street, I pulled away and breathed a heavy sigh of relief. This long, strange day was over. Thinking back on it was surreal.

Had I really been at Mason's house this morning in lingerie? It seemed like it could be one of my sex dreams about him, albeit much kinkier than usual. My dreams centered more on kissing him as I felt his hands on my body. It never went very far before I woke up, which left me feeling aroused but unwilling to do anything about it. I was affronted by the fact that Mason was the one who had turned me on, even if it was only in a dream, and I refused to finish what he started. I had tried masturbation once while determinedly thinking about a hot rock star, but my mind had drifted back to my dream about Mason and expanded on it. Too far gone to stop, I imagined Mason's hand between my legs instead of my own, and my climax came upon me with blinding intensity. It was my first—and only—orgasm, and I was very ashamed of myself for it because it had involved thoughts of Mason.

Seeing him at school that day had been awful as I carried my secret shame. He had looked at me, and I had spun away as I blushed scarlet. He had pounced on me like a predator scenting blood. Catching up to me, he had blocked my escape in the crowded hallway.

"You're blushing!" he exclaimed before returning to his usual derogatory tone when speaking to me. "What makes a girl like you blush? Being your mother's daughter, you're surely long since past blushing. So, what nasty deed could possibly embarrass you?"

"Get out of my way," I said as I kept my gaze on the floor where I could see only his shoes in front of me.

"Why won't you look at me?" he asked suspiciously. "What could be so embarrassing for you?"

"I'm not embarrassed," I lied. "I just don't want to look at you, because I can't stand you." I darted a glance sideways in preparation for sidestepping him, but he stepped with me, even closer into my personal space.

My breath hitched at his proximity, and heat that had nothing to do with embarrassment flushed my skin. A soft gasp escaped me when he reached out and lifted my chin. His gaze captured mine, and the feel of his hand between my legs seemed like a real memory. That part of me ached for his touch, and his look became heated in response to whatever he saw in my eyes.

"Mason," a female voice called out, and he dropped his hand from my face like I had burned him.

I made my escape as his girlfriend at the time distracted him. That had been over a year ago, and he had stopped hassling me after that encounter. I had thought that the spark of sexual tension between us had disturbed him as much as it had me and that was the reason he backed off. Instead he had set me up and had been plotting for a year for a way to blackmail me into closer contact with him.

It was starting to seem like it was more about that than humiliating me, and Addison thought so too. She called me at two o' clock in the morning in a rage. "You're not going to steal him away from me. You hear me, Ella?"

"Are you seriously waking me up with your shit?" I demanded. "We're not friends anymore, and I don't give a crap about you."

"So now you think you can take Mason from me? Hell no! I'm not letting that happen, you fucking bitch. You're not going to get him with that submissive bullshit. Yes sir," she imitated derisively. "Whatever you want sir."

"You're the one who put me in this shit," I retorted angrily. "Why would you let your boyfriend take a naked picture of another girl? How stupid are you?"

"You weren't supposed to have your clothes off!" she complained, and I could hear the drunken whining in her voice. She had apparently partied harder than she had last night when she had only pretended to get drunk. "It was just supposed to be an embarrassing video of you being stupid drunk."

"You shouldn't have left him alone with me," I said, the fury against her rising up within me. "Forget about being my friend. What kind of girl leaves another girl alone and helpless with a guy who hates her?"

She snorted. "Hates you? I can't believe I fell for that bullshit. He's so hot for you, he doesn't even want anyone else."

"You had sex with him last night," I reminded her. "While I was passed out at your house," I added in disgust.

"Yeah, but not tonight," she said bitterly. "After he fucked you today, he didn't want me anymore."

"But he didn't," I protested in shock. "He never—"

"Why the fuck else wouldn't he want it?" she yelled, making me wince as I pulled the phone away from my ear to lessen the volume of her voice. "He's always loved getting blowjobs from me, even when he didn't want to fu—"

I cut her off by ending the call, because I sure as hell didn't want to hear about her sex life. Turning off my phone to make sure I wasn't disturbed by another call from her, I tried to go back to sleep. It wasn't easy though, because I kept thinking about what she'd said. Specifically, about Mason not wanting her because he was hot for me.

It couldn't be true. I mean, it wasn't that surprising that Mason would want someone else. Addison wasn't as attractive as his former girlfriends, who were all among the prettiest girls at school. She was more of the girl next door type of passably pretty rather than beautiful. I would have preferred her any day to the conceited girls he went with, until I found out she had been hiding just as bitchy of a personality as the mean girls.

What I couldn't believe was that Mason was forgoing sex because of me. While the spark of attraction I had felt between us last year had flared into lust a few times today, he still hated me. There was no way that I was the reason he had rejected Addison. He was probably just losing interest in her like he had with all his other girlfriends. He eventually broke up with all of them. At least that was the talk I had heard around school, that Mason was always the one initiating the breakup. Regardless of his reputation as a heartbreaker, he had no shortage of girls wanting to be with him.

It was really sad how fixated they all were on physical rather than inner beauty, but I couldn't exactly throw stones since I was still attracted to him myself. More than anyone else, I should have been repulsed by him—especially now. His actions were despicable even before he started blackmailing me. Yet that didn't stop me from having another sex dream about him after I finally fell asleep again.

I was laying completed naked in this one as he stood before me fully dressed, but I wasn't embarrassed. The way he was looking at me made me feel beautiful, and he said it aloud too. "You're so beautiful," he told me. "I wish…"

"Kiss me," I urged when he trailed off.

"I can't," he said. "I'll never want to stop."

"I don't want you to stop," I told him. "I want you to touch me." I spread my legs open in invitation.

"Fuck," he swore as his gaze became heated with desire.

"I want to feel your hand for real," I continued brazenly. "It felt so good when I pretended you were touching me."

His silver eyes were molten with lust when they met mine. "You were touching yourself?" he asked in a passion-roughened voice.

"Yes," I answered. "But I want you to do it."

His gaze burned so hot that it felt like a fever was raging through my body. "Close your eyes," he said.

Chapter 5

I woke up as intensely aroused as I had been in the dream, and I sprang out of bed to prevent myself from giving in to the temptation to relieve the ache between my legs. A cold shower did nothing but leave me chilled—and still aroused. Trying to distract myself, I browsed a recipe site for ideas about what to make for dinner.

I had received a text from Mason before I even arrived home last night. Address was the one-word prompt. I texted him the information immediately after parking in my driveway, not wanting to delay and be accused of ignoring his text. He replied with a reminder of the time he was coming over, six o'clock.

I decided on a chicken dish, figuring that everybody liked chicken. Unless he was a vegetarian, in which case he could stuff it for all I cared. It would be his fault for not informing me, and for inviting himself to dinner in the first place.

I mentioned it casually to Mom and Dad during breakfast. "A friend is coming over for dinner today."

"Addison?" Dad asked.

"No," I said. "Another friend."

"Oh?" he enquired, since I never had anyone but Addison come over. "What's her name?"

"Um," I began, already failing at saying it nonchalantly. "It's, um, Mason."

Mom perked up. "A boy? You've finally got a boyfriend?"

"No!" I quickly denied. "He's just a friend."

"Is he cute?" she asked, showing more enthusiasm for this than she ever had for anything else in my life.

I shrugged, not wanting to say anything to encourage her. If it were any other boy but Mason, it might have been fun to show him off to Mom and bask in her approval for once. She thought I was boring and took no interest in me.

Dad was frowning. "Why haven't you ever mentioned him before? How long have you been friends?"

"Not long," I replied, feeling the nervous tension start in my stomach at the thought of sitting through dinner with Mason while Dad scrutinized our supposed friendship. Would he pick up on anything wrong between us? At least Mom would be too thrilled that I had brought a cute boy home to notice anything.

"A new friend," he said. "What's his last name?"

As if that would give him any insight about Mason. "Sumner," I answered, my gazing sliding toward Mom to see if she reacted to the last name of the man who had died in bed with her.

Nothing. Maybe she didn't even remember his name. It would infuriate Mason if he knew that, and I sure hoped that he didn't mention his father to her. This dinner would be like walking through a minefield, and my anxiety spiked as the dreaded time approached.

Mason arrived five minutes early, and Dad beat me to the door. "Hello sir," Mason greeted him as he extended his hand toward him. "I'm Mason Sumner."

"Ella's friend," Dad noted as he shook his hand. "I'm her father, Charles Bradley."

Mason's gaze shifted to me, and I reacted nervously. "Let him in, Dad," I prompted.

"Sure, come in, Mason," he said as he stepped back and allowed him entrance.

Mason was still studying me as he stepped inside, so he saw me cringe at the sound of my mother's voice. "Ella! You didn't say a word about how handsome your boyfriend is. Hello there, I'm Ella's—"

"Sister?" Mason cut in smoothly.

Mom laughed in delight, so obviously flattered like she always was when people mistook her for my sister. Only I knew that Mason had done it deliberately to annoy me.

"I'm her mother," she told him.

"I told you that he's not my boyfriend," I huffed as I turned to confront her.

She was wearing a vibrant red dress that was an obvious attempt to show me up, since I was dressed casually in comfortable jeans and a t-shirt. My own mother was competing against me for looks, and she was the clear winner today.

"It's very nice to meet you ma'am. I'm Mason Sumner."

I whirled back toward him. "Dinner's ready!" I announced loudly, but his gaze was locked on my mother.

"It's a pleasure to meet you too," she replied. "Come and sit down. I know that Ella can't wait to impress you with her cooking."

"It smells delicious," he said, his eyes glinting dangerously as his gaze lingered on her.

With dread settling in the pit of my stomach, I went to the kitchen but Mason followed me, declaring lightly, "I'll help."

Once there, his expression became stone hard as it cut to me, but he didn't say anything. I glanced away and moved toward the stove. He grabbed the oven mitts before I could reach them and put them on. "I'll carry it," he said in a harsh tone. "You get the rest."

He picked the pan up off the stovetop where I had set it after taking it out of the oven, and I silently followed him out to the dining room with the grilled asparagus. Since the chicken breasts I'd made were stuffed with spinach and cheese and wrapped in phyllo, they needed no other side dishes.

After Mason sat down, I was left with the seat across from him. Dad waited until everyone had filled their plates before he started his interrogation. "So, you're a classmate of Ella's, Mason?"

"Yes sir," he answered as he cut into his chicken breast.

"And you just recently became friends?"

"Yes sir," Mason replied without missing a beat. "I got to know her because of Addison."

"She's—"

"She's my friend too," Mason talked over me, cutting off my explanation that Addison was his girlfriend. "We've been friends for a while."

I wondered why he would lie about that, but then I realized that it would seem strange if I had invited my best friend's boyfriend over without her. That had actually been a good save on his part, and I started to let go of my fear that he would say something awful in front of my parents.

"Oh," Dad responded, apparently happily surprised. "Addison is a nice girl."

Or a backstabbing bitch, I thought as I kept my expression neutral. Mason just mumbled, "Yeah."

"So, what do your parents do?"

"Dad," I protested, but Mason chose to answer him.

"Well, my father died, and my mother has been blowing through his fortune ever since."

All three of us stared at him while he took a bite of the chicken breast and chewed. "Mm, this is good. I *am* impressed."

Mom recovered first. "I'm sorry to hear that, Mason. When did he die?"

He looked directly at her. "Five years ago. It was a heart attack."

"Sad," she remarked, still oblivious to Mason's connection to the man who died while having sex with her.

His jaw clenched as he dropped his gaze down to his plate.

"I'm sorry for your loss," Dad said.

"Thanks," he muttered.

We ate in silence for a bit, using the food as a distraction. At least I was, because I barely tasted it. Dad ventured to speak to Mason again. "Regarding college, there are many options available, from scholarships to financial aid."

"Oh, she's far from out of money," Mason assured him. "There was quite a lot of it. We had an estate with a live-in housekeeping staff." His gaze slid toward Mom again, but she was listening with a pleasant expression on her face.

"Well, I'm glad to hear that paying for college won't be a concern," Dad said. "Do you know what you want to study?"

"I'm not sure yet," Mason replied. "Maybe photography." He looked directly at me then, and my heart seized.

"Photography?" Dad questioned, sounding unsure. "Is that your hobby?"

"Yes," Mason answered, still watching me. "It's true what they say about a picture being worth a thousand words."

"You should have Ella pose for you," Mom suggested excitedly. "I've been trying to talk her into getting into modeling, but she doesn't have any confidence. Maybe you could convince her. She might listen to you, since you're a photographer. Don't you think she's beautiful?"

He had been smirking at me while she spoke, but his expression altered with that question and made me uncomfortable in a different way. The look in his eyes momentarily made me believe that he meant the next words he spoke. "She's very beautiful."

Dad cleared his throat. "Yes. Uh, we'd like to see the pictures you take of her."

Mason's attention was on him now. "Of course," he said before sliding a sly look at me.

My stomach teetered back into anxiety. I wasn't sure if Mason was just toying with me, or if he planned to end this dinner by showing my parents that horrible picture. It would be an indirect way of taking revenge on my mom, but it would do much worse damage to me. I would never get over it if Dad saw that picture. He would be so ashamed of me, and he would regret adopting me.

I spent the entire meal on pins and needles as Mason ate. "Well, that was delicious," he remarked in satisfaction as he set down his fork. "I'll help clean up, and then we can go work on our assignment."

My gaze flew to his, wondering what he was up to now.

"I'll clear the table," Mom said. "You go ahead and work on your homework."

"What assignment?" Dad questioned. "School hasn't even started yet."

"It's for extra credit," Mason lied. "AP English gives us a list of novels we can read over the summer and do a creative project on. We're going to make a video for The Scarlett Letter."

He stood up, and I immediately followed his lead. He started toward the stairs and stood back at the base of them to let me pass and walk up ahead of him. I had no choice but to take him to my room. He glanced around as I shut the door and waited for him to tell me what was going on. His gaze was fixed on the letters I had attached to the wall above my bed spelling out a quote I liked: Turn your face to the sun and the shadows fall behind you.

He turned suddenly and stalked toward me. "What's my father's name?" he demanded with a fierce expression.

"Daniel Sumner," I answered instantly, and Mason halted in surprise.

"You know it," he said, "but your mother doesn't. She doesn't even remember the name of the man she killed."

"She didn't kill him," I protested. "She just happened to be with him when he had his heart attack, but it would have happened even if she wasn't there. He could have been doing anything else, and it still would have happened. Why can't you get that?"

He stepped away from me without replying and wandered around my room. I watched him peruse the books on my bookcase and even stood by as he opened my closet and peered inside. When he began rifling through my desk drawer, however, I moved to stop him. He had already snatched my journal out of it though, since it was right on top due to being used often. I hadn't ever had to hide it from anyone, and I hadn't expected Mason to be in my room today let alone be snooping through my stuff.

"Give me it," I demanded in outrage as I tried to grab it from him.

"Stop," he commanded, "or I'll show your stepfather that picture right now. I mean it, Ella!"

I halted, as much from the jolt of hearing him say my name as what he threatened to do. Mason never called me by my name. He rarely spoke to me at all, but when he did, he avoided addressing me at all, using only the pronoun you when he had to.

"Mason," I said, using his name as well in an attempt to be pleasant, "please give my journal."

"Is it your diary?" he questioned.

"No," I replied, exceedingly glad that I didn't have a diary for him to find. "It's just a journal I kept for English."

He regarded me speculatively. "Well, then you don't need it anymore," he declared.

"It's mine!" I exclaimed, losing my composure.

"Which makes it mine," he stated coolly before his gaze hardened. "I *own* you, and you better not forget it. I told you you'd pay for not following instructions, and I'm taking this as my payment. Do what I tell you from now on and you won't have a problem."

"This *is* my problem," I retorted. "How would you like it if I bossed you around and took your stuff? I bet you'd—"

"No arguing," he snapped. "I was just in the same room as your mother, and I'm not in the best mood. So, don't push me."

His warning stopped my protests. He was clearly on edge, and he wouldn't listen to me anyway. The journal wasn't as mortifying as the picture. In fact, it would be boring to anyone else but me since it only contained poetry that I had written. I had lied that it was for a school assignment, but he wouldn't know that.

He set it down on my desk and pulled a folded piece of paper out of his pocket. "We'll shoot this scene," he said as he handed it to me. "The first line is mine, and then yours."

I unfolded it and glanced at it before looking at him in bewilderment. "You really want to make a Scarlet Letter video?"

"In case your dad asks about it," he said as he pulled out his phone. "You film me first, then hit pause."

I stilled when he handed the phone to me, but he was quick to remind me that he had more copies of that picture. So I squashed my urge to smash his phone to bits and prepared to film him. Without any preparation himself, he stated, "Ready."

Starting the video, I watched him on the screen. "Come along, Madame Hester," he said, "and show your scarlet letter in the market-place."

When he didn't say anything else, I paused the video. He moved out of his stance and took the phone from me. "Your turn. Memorize your line, and then I'll film you."

I looked at the paper he had given me and silently read my line several times before setting the paper down and facing him. "Thou knowest that I was frank with thee. I felt no love, nor feigned any."

It felt odd to hear him speak his next line. "True. It was my folly. I drew thee into my heart."

Mine was simple and brief. "I have greatly wronged thee."

His gaze was hard as he spoke. "Think not that I shall interfere with Heaven's own method of retribution."

"Thy acts are like mercy, but thy words interpret thee as a terror."

His final line was spoken with a look of dark satisfaction. "Whether of right or wrong, thou and thine, Hester Payne, belong to me."

I stared at his face on the screen for a moment before his mocking smile made me realize that he was done. I hit pause, still unnerved by his delivery of that line.

He plucked the phone from my hand. "I'll send it to your phone. See me out now." He picked up my journal and started for the door.

I followed him downstairs, where he politely thanked my parents for dinner. Mom fawned over him and invited him to come back soon. It was awkward as hell for me to watch, and I couldn't wait for Mason to leave. Fortunately, she didn't follow him to the front door.

I opened it for him, and he made my pulse jump by suddenly leaning in to whisper in my ear. "Not a word to her about who I am."

My startled gaze met his. It was almost like he had read my mind, because I had been silently debating whether I should inform my mom about who Mason's dad was. Even if she knew, what could she say to him? There were no words to placate him. He refused to acknowledge that she wasn't to blame for his father's death.

"Okay," I agreed to his demand.

"Wear the hot pink dress tomorrow," he said.

"Oh, that's a bridesmaid dress," I explained, thinking that he had no clue that such a dress could only be for a wedding.

"I know," he replied.

I gaped at him. "I can't wear that to school! I'll look ridiculous."

"Are you arguing with me?" he demanded in a threatening tone. "I warned you about that. Now I'll have to add something as punishment," he continued in a deceptively milder voice. "What shall I do with you?"

"You can kiss my ass," I hissed.

His gaze honed in on me. "Only if you show it to me again."

I went hot with embarrassment.

"See you tomorrow," he taunted and left.

Chapter 6

I was grateful for two things the next morning. My parents weren't up yet when I left for school, and I didn't have to take the bus to school. Last night, I had talked Mom into letting me borrow her car with a story about a bunch of us kicking off our senior year with an after-school celebration at The Candy Shop. It was a local diner type restaurant run by a woman named Candy. Since Mom always wanted me to be a part of the social scene, it had been easy to convince her that I needed the car.

I had wavered over wearing the bridesmaid dress to school, but watching Mason say his last line in the video he had sent to my phone was intimidating enough to make me cautious about disobeying him. It was like he had been speaking directly to me with the words he had chosen from the book. I believed now that making that video hadn't been about corroborating the homework story to my dad. Mason had wanted to send me a message. Sending my nude picture to me would have been even more effective, but I was relieved that he hadn't. I didn't need that humiliating reminder of how I had exposed myself to Mason. It was bad enough to remember him showing it to me without having it displayed before my eyes again in vivid detail.

The embarrassment of being seen at school in a hot pink, mermaid style bridesmaid dress paled in comparison to the threat of being seen completely naked by everyone.

When I arrived at school, though, my cheeks burned as people laughed at me.

"I didn't know hookers were so classy," our current queen bee, Alicia, commented snidely.

"Your boyfriend wanted me to dress up," I retorted, the words leaving my mouth as a surge of resentment toward these people surfaced with my long-simmering desire to strike back at them.

An ugly expression momentarily diminished her beauty. "What'd you say to me bitch?"

Tyler blocked her from my view as he stepped in front of me with a grin on his face. "Good one, Ella! I'm glad to see you've decided not to hold back anymore and do whatever the hell you want. Who says you've gotta wait for prom to wear your prom dress? By the way, if you're looking for a date, I'm your man."

"What the hell, Tyler?" Alicia protested. "Are you trying to get a *disease*?"

"Don't worry about it," he replied dismissively without turning to look at her. "Ella's got somebody better than your boyfriend now."

"Yes, she does," a familiar voice said crisply.

"What the actual fuck?" Alicia swore angrily.

The murmurs got louder as Mason approached me, but I was speechless. He was wearing a freaking tuxedo. My former preteen self would have swooned at the sight of him looking like her fantasy groom, but I was stupefied. What was this? Alicia's crude question was justified.

His enigmatic expression gave me no answers about his intent. "Ella," he greeted me stiffly with a strangely formal demeanor.

"Oh my God!" a girl exclaimed loudly. "This is just like Pretty Woman!"

That ridiculous statement pulled me out of my stupor. "Why are you wearing that?" I asked.

"I put it on for you," he replied.

That didn't explain anything, and I didn't care to stand there and question him in front of everyone. I walked past him, but he followed and fell into step with me.

"Did you go out with Chase Sinclair?" he asked.

I stopped and turned to look at him in astonishment. How had he figured out that poem was about Chase?

"You did," he stated as he studied my expression. "So, he only kissed you?"

I shook my head. "It wasn't me."

"Then why'd you write that poem about him?" he questioned suspiciously.

"My friend—well, my former friend was secretly dating him. It was…the poem was…" I shut my mouth as embarrassment washed over me. Why was I telling him all this?

"It's good," he said and then stunned me again by quoting it word for word. "Frozen heart chills the summer sun. First kiss remembers drowning lips. Rose halted in mid-bloom. Petals falling like tears. Secret sinks in silent sorrow. No sweet smile tomorrow. Dream dies beneath murky depths. All tragedy by time is kept."

I hadn't read the poem since I wrote it, but it sounded like he had accurately quoted it. He seemed to have a knack for memorizing things, judging by this and the fact that he hadn't had to glance at his lines for the video yesterday. He was also astute enough to deduce from my vague references that my poem was about our classmate, Chase, who had killed himself two years ago by jumping off a bridge. It happened during summer vacation, and I had seen Alice sitting listlessly by herself on a bench in the park. She looked so depressed that I approached her to ask if she was okay.

"He's gone," she said, her eyes beginning to fill with tears. "I can't believe it, Ella. I can't believe he's really gone."

She started to sob, and I sat down beside her and tried to comfort her with a hug. Eventually, she confided the whole story to me. Chase had been popular and the life of the party, while Alice was the quiet girl who got good grades and kept mostly to herself. Nobody would have guessed that Chase would ever notice her, and he would have gotten flak from his buddies for dating a nerd.

"He didn't care about any of that," she told me. "But after what happened with Brooke...I didn't want..."

I understood that she didn't want to be on the radar of the popular crowd again. Brooke and her posse had been the ones to chase Alice away from me. With her shy nature, she couldn't deal with that kind of relentless public attention every day. She had withdrawn from me with a heartfelt apology and a suggestion that I should ask my parents to transfer me to another school. I had refused to let Mason run me out of school.

"I don't know how you can stand it," she had said. "The way everyone treats you, and all those awful rumors he's spread about you. I tried to tell people it's not true, but they won't listen."

Thinking about that now, I realized what was so different about Mason now—other than the tux. His gaze held no antagonism as he looked at me with a speculative expression. Just as I became aware of that, Addison's outraged voice hijacked my attention.

"Are you fucking kidding me?" she yelled as she stormed toward us. "What the hell is this, Mason?"

"It's the first day of school," he replied, pissing her off even more.

She trembled with fury as she spoke. "Why are dressed like that? With her."

"I don't have to explain myself to you," he stated.

She stilled, and her eyes narrowed at him. "No? You think you can use me to get her and dump me just like that? You get what you want, and I get nothing? Hell no! You're going down, Mason. Right now."

Her gaze shifted from him to scan the hallway. "Mr. Nichols!" she shouted to get the teacher's attention.

While she was causing a commotion, Mason pulled me aside. "I deleted it," he told me urgently. "They won't find anything. It's just her word, but she never saw it."

"You have to get him away from Ella," Addison exclaimed. "He's got a naked picture of her, and he's using it to blackmail her."

"She's lying," Mason declared as he strode toward her and Mr. Nichols while I stood frozen in horror.

Mr. Nichols eyed him with a grim expression. "Give me your phone."

Mason immediately pulled it out of his pocket and handed it over as my heart pounded in terror. "She's lying," he repeated. "She's mad that I broke up with her, and she's trying to get me in trouble."

"You never broke up with me, you cheating asshole!" Addison yelled furiously.

Mr. Nichols frowned at her, and I could tell that she had lost credibility with him. It helped me regain my composure enough to hold myself together when he called to me to come to the office with them. When he left us inside the main office to go talk to the principal, Addison took her anger out on me.

"You're such a stupid slut! Look at you in that—"

"Young lady!" the receptionist exclaimed sharply as she got to her feet. "That language will not be tolerated here."

"Whatever," Addison retorted and slunk down to sulk in her chair.

Mason gave me a pointed look before beginning to speak. "I guess coming out as a couple like this was a bad idea. We were kind of insensitive to Addison's feelings. I'm sorry, Addison."

"Fuck you," she said, earning another disapproving glare from the receptionist. "They're going to arrest you for that picture. They don't give a shit about you being Homecoming king."

"There is no picture," he said calmly while my stomach twisted up in knots. "There never was. I just told you that so I could spend time with Ella without you getting suspicious."

"They're going to find it," she said with great satisfaction. "Even if you took it off your phone, they'll search your computer and everywhere else you could have a copy."

He was unfazed. "Did you ever see this supposed picture?"

Her confidence faltered, and I glimpsed doubt in her expression. It gave credence to Mason's claim that she hadn't seen the picture.

His gaze shifted from her to me, and his eyes bore into mine. "*Nobody* has seen this picture, because it *doesn't exist*."

I received his message loud and clear. He was saying that nobody else had seen the picture. He and I were the only ones who had definite knowledge of its existence, and he wanted me to play along and feign ignorance. I wanted to question him about what he had done with it, but I couldn't in front of Addison.

"Mason Sumner," the principal called out as he exited his office.

Mason promptly stood. "Yes sir," he said as he walked toward him.

They went into his office while Mr. Nichols came over to us. "Mr. Delaney will talk to you soon." Looking relieved to be free of our drama, he walked out into the hallway just as the first bell rang.

I longed to escape too, but I also desperately wanted to know what was happening inside Mr. Delaney's office. Mason seemed so sure that the picture wouldn't be found. He claimed to have deleted it, but could I trust that he was telling me the truth? I was really grasping at straws to rely on his word, but I clung to the hope that he'd had a change of heart about me and decided to get rid of the picture and stop blackmailing me. The fact that he'd worn that tuxedo so that I wouldn't be in the spotlight by myself was a sign that this could be true.

"I knew you were a boyfriend stealer," Addison told me.

Aware that the receptionist was listening, I chose not to respond. That sent Addison off the deep end. Before I knew what was happening, she had slapped me. I put my arms up over my face and head to protect myself as she kept hitting me with her open hands. The receptionist was shouting, and then the blows stopped. I looked up from where I was hunched into myself and saw that Mr. Delaney had pulled Addison away from me. The security officer came sprinting into the office in the next instant as Mason crouched down in front of me with a concerned look on his face.

"Are you okay?" he asked.

"Yeah," I said as I lowered my arms.

The moment was surreal, and I wondered if I was having some kind of bizarre dream. I was sitting in the school office in a bridesmaid dress with Mason at my feet in a tux, and I had just been in a fight over him.

"Officer Collins," Mr. Delaney said, "please remain here with Addison while I talk to Miss Chase. Stay here, Mason," he added.

"Yes sir." Mason got to his feet and extended his hand to me in the classic gesture of a gentleman helping a lady out of her seat.

Still caught up in the unreality of the situation, I took his hand and let him tug me up. I looked down at his hand holding mine, and he let me go like I had chastised him. Still in a daze, I took steps toward the principal and ended up sitting in a chair in his office. When he closed the door, it shut out much of the weirdness and brought me back to reality.

"Ella," he began in a compassionate tone, "are you alright?"

"Yes, I'm fine," I replied.

"Addison will be dealt with," he said, "but first I need to know about the situation with Mason Sumner. Has he been blackmailing you?"

This was my chance to get back at Mason for everything he had done to me, but it would mean exposing all the sordid details. "No," I answered, following the script he had given me. "He's my boyfriend. Addison made that up because she's jealous."

Mr. Delaney continued without questioning that, since I was apparently corroborating the exact story Mason had told him. "And there was no nude photo of you?"

My heart lifted in relief. His question confirmed that he hadn't found a naked picture of me on Mason's phone. "No," I said. "She made that up too."

He nodded in agreement. "She had no right to hit you, and she will be disciplined for that. If you ever have any problems with her again, come to me right away."

"I will," I promised, eager to be done with my first ever visit to the principal's office.

"Uh, would you like to go home and change? Your dress isn't inappropriate, but—"

"Yes!" I exclaimed, jumping on the offer. "Oh, sorry," I apologized for interrupting him and hurried on, rambling in my haste. "We thought it would be fun to dress up as a couple, because people didn't know, but it's probably too much, and yeah I want to change."

"Alright. Which parent should I call to come get you?"

My face fell. "Can't I just drive home real quick? I drove my mom's car."

He shook his head. "I can't send you home during school hours without a guardian. I'm responsible for your safety."

"I'll stay here then," I decided. "My mom can't get me without her car, and I don't want to bother my dad at work with this."

"Okay. You may go to class now. Have the receptionist give you a pass."

"Okay, thanks," I said as I stood up.

"Tell me if anyone gives you any trouble," he said as he also stood up to walk me out.

"I will," I lied. He didn't know that people had been giving me trouble for years, and the worst culprit was the one I'd just passed off as my boyfriend instead of nailing him to the wall like he deserved. I realized that I had missed my only opportunity to get revenge on him, but I was too relieved about the disappearance of my picture to care.

"Give Mason and Ella return slips to class," Mr. Delaney instructed the receptionist. "I'll see Addison now."

"That's bullshit!" she exploded. "If it's not on his phone, then he's got it stored on his computer. Call the police! They'll find it."

My heart was back in my throat, but Mr. Delaney dismissed her ranting. "Settle down right now, Addison. Ella has refuted your accusations, and the police can't get a search warrant without proof or a victim. You, however, have violated school policy on fighting. Come into my office."

Addison scowled at me as the security officer escorted her toward the principal's office, but she seemed to have realized that even a verbal attack on me would get her in more trouble, so she pressed her mouth shut.

Mason walked out into the empty hallway with me after we got our passes. I led him out of view of the office before I spoke. "When did you delete it?"

"Right after I showed it to you," he said. "I had a feeling Addison might pull some shit like this, and…"

"And what?" I asked when he trailed off and shoved his hands into his pockets.

He rocked back on his heels before planting his feet on the floor and making direct eye contact with me. "I didn't want anyone else but me to see you like that."

His words shouldn't have affected me the way they did. They shouldn't have made heat rush through me, but the look in his eyes gave the words an intensely sexual possessiveness that was extremely hot. Nervously trying to break the suddenly overwhelming tension, I asked him where he got a tux so early in the morning.

The heat left his eyes. "It was my dad's."

"Oh," I responded awkwardly.

He pulled his hands out of his pockets. "We should get to class."

"Right," I agreed, glancing down to pull my schedule out of my purse.

"Since we're supposed to be a couple now, we should act the part."

My head snapped back up in surprise. "You want to pretend we're dating?"

His expression became unreadable. "Yeah, pretend. It'll look suspicious otherwise."

"Right. Um, so…"

"We'll act friendly when we meet in the hallways, sit together at lunch."

"Sit at the same table at lunch?" I questioned in alarm.

"It's what couples do," he noted. "I'll save you a seat."

"No." I shook my head. "No, I can't do that."

"Why not?" he asked.

"Because your friends are there. All the people who hate me."

"They don't hate you," he said. "They've just been following my lead, but they'll accept you once they see that I have. In fact, it's already happened. Since you were at my party, Josh and Tyler assumed that you're in with us now."

"Just like that?" I asked, starting to get irritated. "They've been treating me like shit for years, but now I'm in overnight? For that matter, what made you suddenly get a personality transplant? You've always been a complete asshole to me, so what happened this morning? Why'd you show up in a tux? Why weren't you in your regular clothes laughing at me with everyone else?"

"Because you might not have deserved any of the shit I've done to you," he said. "You're not anything like I thought you were. Your poems—"

"My poems?" I cut in incredulously. "You mean all I had to do was put together a few rhymes to stop you from being the dick of the century?"

His lips twitched like he was trying to hold back a smile. "The dick of the century?"

"Shut up," I retorted in annoyance. "It's not funny. You've been a total asshole to me from the first minute I met you."

"I have," he acknowledged. "but I'm giving you the benefit of the doubt now."

"Well that makes it better," I said sarcastically.

"Hey, you two better get to class," Officer Collins told us as he came walking down the hall toward us, having apparently just come out of the office.

"Right," I clipped out and began to walk away.

Now that I was free from the fear of exposure, I was starting to get pissed. If Mason thought that one nice gesture could make up for all the rotten crap he had done, he was very mistaken.

Chapter 7

I made an unavoidable entrance into my first class, what with being so late and appearing in my hot pink bridesmaid dress. Seeing what I was wearing made the teacher grin, but nobody laughed at me. Those who had seen me in the hallway earlier had apparently already told the others about it.

"You and Mason?" the girl next to me whispered shortly after I took my seat.

I was going to deny it, but then I remembered that it was the story we'd told the principal. I was still paranoid enough not to risk conflicting stories getting back to Mr. Delaney. If he became suspicious and decided to call my dad about this...

Putting on a fake smile, I nodded my head in answer to the girl's question. She immediately turned away from me to whisper to the girl on the other side of her. I sighed to myself, knowing that she was passing on my acknowledgement of Mason and I being a couple.

His friend, Josh, was in this class, and he walked out with me after the bell rang. "So, you and Mason, huh? Here I thought you dressed up to ask me to prom."

I laughed, my spirits lifting with his light banter. "I did, but Prince Charming showed up looking all desperate and pathetic."

"Prince Charming," Josh repeated with a rueful smile. "Wow."

I flushed in embarrassment, mentally kicking myself for letting my nickname for Mason slip out. It had become sarcastic rather than romantic after I actually met him and found out how lacking in charm he was, but Josh didn't know that.

"Well," he said, "it's a little hard to compete with that. I figured something was up when he wouldn't even let me walk you out to your car. I've never seen him so possessive over a girl."

"Yeah, well..." I trailed off, at a loss for words to respond to that.

"I get now why he's been keeping guys away from you all this time. It never made sense to me before. He acted like he hated you, but he obviously wanted you for himself."

I snorted out a laugh. "Yeah right. He said all those awful things about me because he wanted me."

Josh gave me a quizzical look. "You don't seem to like him too much." His expression changed to concern, and then turned fearful before he stepped closer and glanced around.

He leaned in and brought his mouth close to my ear. "Is he forcing you to go out with him?"

I froze in fear, wondering if Josh knew about the picture, if he had *seen* the picture. Had Mason showed it to his friends? The thought made me sick to my stomach.

"Oh my God, he is," Josh said in horror, and I realized that he had pulled back to look at me.

"Did you see it?" I asked him, the humiliation spreading through me and making my eyes prick with gathering tears.

"See what?" he questioned in hushed and fearful anticipation of my answer.

There was no indication in his eyes that he had any knowledge of what I was referring to. There was only fear and dread, like when you know something bad has happened but you don't know what it is.

"What did he do?" Josh asked anxiously before leaning in to whisper in my ear again. "Did he send you someone's ear?"

"What?" I exclaimed loudly, pulling back to look at him in bewilderment.

"Shh!" he hushed me with a paranoid glance around us. Leaning in again, he whispered, "The mafia thing. You know his family is in witness protection?"

I burst out laughing, and Josh took a startled step back from me. "Oh my God," I gasped as he watched me warily. "Witness protection. That is too funny!"

"Keep your voice down," he admonished me as people walking by gave us curious looks. "This is serious."

"Josh," I said as I composed myself, "Mason is not in witness protection. That's some bullshit story he made up."

Josh shook his head and stepped closer to me again, not leaning in to whisper in my ear this time but keeping his voice at a low volume as spoke with an urgent look on his face. "His mom doesn't work, but she bought him a new car when he turned sixteen. Mason doesn't have a job, but he always has money. Also, there were those 'accidents' that happened to the guys who didn't stay away from you."

My hackles rose at that statement. How many guys had Mason actually hurt? I only knew of the one he had given the black eye to, and I had thought that he mostly just verbally intimidated people. "What accidents?"

"Brent Celek freshman year. Someone broke both his legs. He said it happened skiing, but Mason told us that was the story they told him to tell, and that he was warned they'd killed him if he told anyone the truth. He even told us to go ahead and ask him and see if he would break, but Brent stuck to his story no matter what."

I rolled my eyes. "Probably because it was the truth," I remarked dryly.

"Jason Zucker broke his arm, supposedly falling on some ice. Tommy Drake said he broke his ankle skateboarding, but…"

"Yeah," I deadpanned, "because nobody ever gets hurt while skateboarding."

"Then there was Chase the next year," Josh said somberly. "Mason was even friends with him, but when he slept with you…"

"Mason said that he…that Chase was…he used that to…" I sputtered in outrage.

"They made it look like a suicide," Josh said in a hushed and sorrowful tone.

"I'm going to kill that lying asshole!" I exploded.

"No," Josh exclaimed in alarm. "Don't tell him I told you anything."

The bell rang just as I was yelling that Mason wasn't part of the fucking mafia, and I stormed off to my next class, arriving late again and breathing fire when I saw Mason. He quirked an eyebrow when he saw my expression, but I was forced to hold in my fury during class instead of gouging out his eyes like I wanted to.

The teacher made it especially hard when she commented on us. "Miss Chase, Mr. Sumner, that's very cute."

Taking that as a cue, the girl sitting beside Mason stood up. "You can sit here," she offered.

"No," I protested, but she was already moving to the only empty seat in the room.

"Sit down, please," the teacher told me. "I trust that you and your boyfriend will refrain from disrupting my class any further."

"We'll behave," Mason promised her.

Glaring at him, I swallowed down my retort that he wasn't my boyfriend and stiffly sat down next to him at the two-person table. Ignoring him and staring straight ahead at the teacher as she talked to the class, I didn't hear a word she said as I silently fumed. Of all the rotten things that Mason had done, this was the worst. Using the tragedy of Chase's death to enhance some stupid story of being connected to the mafia was a low that I hadn't expected even from him.

He nudged me, and I turned toward him with a snarl. "Fuck off!"

His brows drew together. "Class is over. You didn't hear the bell ring?"

Glancing around, I saw that the tables around us were empty, and our classmates were filing out the door. Scraping my chair against the floor, I sprang up and grabbed my purse. Mason was right behind me as I left the room, and I spun around to confront him in the hallway.

"What's your problem?" he demanded first.

"My problem? What the hell is your problem, Mason? How could you use someone's…" I shook my head. "You know what? You're not even worth me wasting my breath talking to you."

I started to turn on my heel, but he grabbed my arm and spun me in the other direction. Ignoring my protests, he pulled me around the corner and into the empty cafeteria. He finally let go of me but stood glowering in front of me. "Tell me what you're so pissed off about."

"Chase," I spat out angrily at him. "Your supposed friend? Great friend you turned out to be. Instead of mourning him, you told everybody some bullshit story about how you killed him."

Pain replaced the anger on his face. "All tragedy by time is kept."

"Don't do that shit!" I yelled. "Don't act like you give a shit when you used his death for your own—"

"I do care!" he yelled back. "Chase shouldn't have done that! Why did he do that? He had everything going for him. Football, popularity. Why would someone like that kill himself? Why?"

I shook my head. "I don't know."

"Was it because of that girl?"

I stiffened. "Don't you dare try to blame Alice."

"I can't see any other reason why he would do it," Mason argued.

"She loved him!" I shouted. "It broke her heart when he died. She mourned him, which is more than I can say for you. What kind of friend uses someone's death for his own personal benefit?"

"I did it for him too," he insisted. "What sounds cooler? Committing suicide or having a hit put on you by the mafia?"

I gaped at him speechlessly.

"Chase would have loved it," he said with a sad smile.

"You're demented," I told him, but my voice didn't have the same bite as before.

"Completely," he agreed. "That's why everyone is afraid of me."

"I'm not afraid of you."

His silver-gray eyes locked on me. "Prove it," he challenged in a seductive tone.

"Did you really delete my picture?" I asked as I gazed at him.

"Yes," he said, "but I didn't want to. I wanted to keep it and look at it every minute, because I've never seen anything so fucking hot in my life."

Heat engulfed my body like a fever. Those words spoken in that tone while he held my gaze with those incredible eyes.

"Do you know how hard it was not to touch you when you were begging me to?" he asked as he leaned in and brought his mouth a hairsbreadth from mine. "How hard it gets me just thinking about it even now?"

I was so caught up in him and so turned on by his dirty talk—something I never thought I'd like—that I couldn't wait for him to kiss me. So, I kissed him. He made a sound low in this throat and coaxed me past his lips into an exploration of his mouth that made me delirious with desire. The sensual feel of his tongue tangling with mine was beyond anything I had imagined kissing would be.

I very reluctantly pulled away from him when the bell rang, not caring that I was going to be late to yet another class. In the next instant, I stopped resisting the magnetic pull of his mouth and kissed him again.

He kissed me back hungrily before pulling away with a groan. "I told you I wouldn't be able to stop if I kissed you."

I was struck by the familiarity of those words, and then it dawned on me where I had heard them. "My dream. That really happened," I realized. "The night I got drunk. Begging you," I repeated, the words embarrassing me now.

"Oh God," I said, retreating from Mason as my cheeks flamed.

"No, Ella, that was hot," he assured me, but I wasn't comforted.

"I'm late," I threw out and sprinted around a table and out the door in my haste to escape my embarrassment.

It was only when I was sitting in class without Mason around that the realization that I had kissed him sank in. I had kissed him for real instead of only in my dreams, and I really couldn't believe my life right now.

Chapter 8

I decided to go to the library during lunch. It was what I used to do often before Addison befriended me, and I needed the time alone now after everything that had happened that morning. I felt like I hadn't really had time to catch my breath since Mason had hijacked my life with that picture. It was hard to believe that had been only two days ago. Things were changing so quickly that my emotions were in a constant state of flux. We had somehow gone from blackmail to kissing, and my brain was having trouble making sense of it all.

My long-awaited first kiss had finally happened—with Mason. That would have been a dream come true back when I was still under the delusion that he was the handsome prince of my girlish fantasies, but I didn't know how to feel about it now. It had been thrilling beyond even my imagination, but it had been with a guy who had treated me like dirt until today. How could I overlook all the crap he had put me through and kiss him like he was the only guy I wanted?

My phone rang, disturbing the silence and jolting me into answering it in a hurry. "Where are you?" Mason demanded. "We're going to be the last ones to get our food."

"I'm not hungry," I replied.

"Get over here," he ordered impatiently. "What do you want? I'll get it for you."

"I'm not coming," I told him. "Just be with your friends like always and forget about me."

"I never forget about you," he said. "So, get over here or I'll have to read them the love poem you wrote me to prove to them that you're my girlfriend."

My heart started beating faster in a prelude to panic. No, he couldn't have that poem. It wasn't in the journal he had taken. I had written it on a loose sheet of paper one morning and thrown it hastily into my desk drawer.

His next words confirmed that he did have it however. "Silver-eyed devil with a barbed tongue, from your phantom touch my moans are wrung. Your hands replace mine in a thicket of—"

"Stop!" I yelled as I knocked over my chair in my haste to get up. "I'm coming right now."

"Already?" he teased. "I haven't even told you what my tongue will do to your thicket of desire. By the way, leave it unshaved so I can see it glistening with—"

"Stop!" I shrieked and heard him laughing right as the librarian came running in apparent terror that I was being attacked.

Coming to a halt, she became extremely annoyed when she saw that I was unharmed and on the phone. "No talking on cell phones in here. Respect the rules or get out."

"Sorry," I replied. "I'm leaving right now."

"I liked it better when you were coming," Mason said in my ear, and I hung up on him.

Shoving my phone into my purse, I righted the chair I had knocked over and walked quickly toward the front of the library and out into the hallway. I saw Mason waiting for me as I came rushing toward the cafeteria. He looked so sharp in that tuxedo that it nearly took my breath away. There was an edge to his refinement, something that still wasn't quite tamed. Maybe it was the wolfish look in his eyes, or the coiled power in his lithe body beneath the sophisticated cut of the suit. Whatever it was, it was conveyed on a primal level without words.

That was probably why everyone believed that he was dangerous, because he exuded predatory cunning and confidence. Knowing better, I shouldn't have been fooled, but my body responded to him with a racing pulse and the simultaneous urges to flee and stand still in the mesmerizing power of his gaze.

I didn't realize that I had stopped until he started moving toward me with smooth, measured steps. He seemed to hold me there with the sheer force of his will as he approached me. My heart was pounding in anticipation of another kiss as he came to a standstill in front of me.

"You are so beautiful," he said, "the most beautiful girl I've ever seen."

I was amazed by how he delivered that line like he really meant it, like he really was my fairytale prince. Instead of kissing me like I expected him to, he moved to stand beside me and take my hand. Entering the cafeteria holding hands with Mason was a surreal experience. People stared at us as we walked through the room and up to the lunch counter.

Letting go of my hand, Mason got two chicken sandwiches and two bottles of water. He paid for them and started walking toward his usual table. My steps slowed, but he noticed immediately that I was falling behind. "C'mon," he urged. "We don't have much time to eat."

Balking at the thought of sitting with his friends, I protested that I already told him I wasn't hungry. "You should have just gotten your lunch like usual. We don't need to sit together."

"You're with me now," he said, "so we're sitting together."

"Don't you think you're taking this too far?" I asked. It had occurred to me that I'd allowed paranoia to get the best of me. The principal wouldn't be keeping up with our fake relationship. Without that picture there was nothing to investigate.

He stopped walking and turned his head to look at me. "How am I taking it too far?"

"Pretending to your friends. Enough people saw us together to keep the rumors going for a while. We don't need to—"

"Pretending," he cut in with a scowl. "Was it pretending when you kissed me?"

I blushed in response and shifted my gaze away from his.

"No," he answered for me. "So, we're going to show everyone that you're with me now. Let's go."

He stood there waiting, and it was drawing more attention to us. I realized that he wasn't going to move until I did, so I reluctantly started walking, and he went with me. "Hey guys," he said as we approached his table. "You all know my girlfriend, Ella."

"What?" Alicia exclaimed. "You're not seriously bringing your hooker here to sit with us!"

Mason set the tray down and fixed her with a hard stare. "Don't you ever call her that again." He swept a threatening look around at the others. "That goes for the rest of you too. Ella is with me now, and nobody is going to be spreading anymore vicious lies about her."

I marveled at the show he was putting on after being the main perpetrator of those lies.

"Yeah," Tyler agreed like he hadn't been trying to buy my "services" just a couple of days ago. "Welcome, Ella. Glad you're joining us."

I wasn't joining anything, but I sat down in the chair Mason pulled out for me as Josh echoed Tyler's sentiment. Mason sat down beside me and slid the tray toward me after taking a water bottle and one of the sandwiches. With everyone's eyes on me, I opened my water bottle for something to do and took nervous sips from it as Mason ate.

"So, you have to stay on a diet all the time?" Alicia questioned smugly. "I bet you gain weight real easy. That must be so hard. I'm lucky that I have a high metabolism and can eat anything I want."

"That must be why you're so pleasant all the time," I replied, my dislike of her overriding my nerves about being where I didn't belong.

Her eyes narrowed at me, but she couldn't call me out for my seemingly genial comment. "Tell us about your whirlwind romance with Mason," she urged slyly instead. "He told us that girl with him at his party was his girlfriend. I guess she didn't last long."

Her implication was that I wouldn't last long either, but I was unfazed since I wasn't really with Mason. "We bonded over cosplay. He was the red Power Ranger, and I was the pink one. It made me see him in a whole different light," I said with enthusiasm that secretly stemmed from my excitement over improvising a way to embarrass him.

There was total silence at the table as I smiled happily at Mason. His face gave nothing away as he chewed his food with his gaze locked on me.

"You're shitting me!" Tyler exclaimed.

Mason's stare was becoming unnerving, and I swallowed reflexively as he swallowed his food. "I was Deadpool," he said as his gaze shifted toward Tyler. "She just mistook me for the red Power Ranger." He shrugged, completely at ease. "I corrected her, but she's still confused."

He looked at me again. "Deadpool has swords. Remember I showed it to you."

"Them," Erin, the smartest of Alicia's minions, corrected, immediately looking uncomfortable about pointing out Mason's mistake. "Uh, plural swords," she explained, a slight flush appearing on her cheeks. "You said it, uh, you showed her it."

"Right," Mason responded with a smirk.

"That's kind of kinky," Alicia said, actually sounding envious.

Her boyfriend noticed that too. "Babe, I can dress up as a superhero if you want."

I looked resentfully at Mason. Not only had I failed to embarrass him, but he had twisted my attempt around into making it sound like it was some sexual thing we had done.

He deliberately said the wrong pronoun to turn it into sexual innuendo, and Erin had played right into his hands with her book smart but clueless emphasis on it.

It, I thought, inspiration striking again as I thought about it as the euphemism Mason intended. "It's not that impressive," I said. "That's why I keep forgetting about…the sword."

"Swords," Erin automatically corrected.

Tyler was laughing. "Burn," he exclaimed with glee. "Man, she got you good."

"Yes," Mason agreed, still exuding confidence and control. "I'll have to work hard—harder to impress her."

Tyler jumped right on that one. "Yeah man, put in some *hard* work."

Fortunately, the bell rang and put an end to that eyeroll-inducing conversation. I stood up to throw away my empty water bottle and uneaten sandwich, but Tyler asked if he could have it if I didn't want it. I handed him the sandwich, and Mason grabbed the tray from the table to throw away his trash and mine.

I took the opportunity to leave him behind, but he still found me in the crowd exiting the cafeteria and pulled me aside to press me up against an empty table. "How hard do you want it?" he asked low in my ear, his warm breath causing goosebumps to break out on my arms.

"I don't want it," I told him when he pulled back to look at me, although my uneven voice didn't sound very convincing.

"Really?" he challenged. "I burn for you in my dreams, and now I ignite for you in the shower. I imagine you—"

"Stop!" My face was burning as I looked around in mortification, but there was no one near us. Most of the crowd was already out in the hallway, and there were very few people left filing out of the room.

"I would love to join you in the shower by the way," he said.

"I bet you would," I retorted. "Now I know why you're suddenly acting like you like me. Because you found that stupid poem, and now you think I'll sleep with you."

"Sleep is optional," he quipped. "The poem isn't stupid, and it's not the reason I like you. Your other poems are more revealing about what kind of person you are."

"You seriously changed your mind about me because you read my poems?" I asked in disbelief.

He regarded me with a speculative look. "The fact that you write poems at all was surprising—and I know they're not for a school assignment. It's something that you do on your own. I didn't expect that from you."

"Because you know me so well," I stated bitterly. "You never even bothered to get to know me. You just went on the attack without giving me a chance."

"I'm giving you a chance now," he said. "I thought you were like your mother, but—"

"You don't know my mother!" I interrupted him in exasperation. "You just assume things about people without knowing anything about them. You were all hellbent on revenge and blaming her for your father's *medical condition*. And you *blackmailed* me. What kind of person does that make you?"

"I didn't do anything except trick you," he replied. "I never showed that picture to anyone else, and I deleted it right away."

"So that makes it okay?" I demanded. "You humiliated me."

He scoffed. "How did I humiliate you?"

"Seriously?" I asked. "You took my clothes off and took that awful picture of me."

"*You* took your clothes off," he emphasized, "and that picture was hot as fuck, and you know it."

I became aware of how close we were standing, and I knew that I should move, that I should leave, but I continued to stand there as he spoke. "You know you're hotter than any other girl. Don't you, Ella? You knew what seeing you like that would do to me."

He pressed himself against me. "You feel that? You feel what you do to me?"

Voices startled me away from him as the next batch of students entered the cafeteria for lunch. I bolted for the exit in embarrassment, feeling completely flustered and uncomfortably aroused, although probably not as uncomfortably aroused as Mason. At least nobody could look at me and tell what was going on between my legs. I wondered how long it would take for Mason's erection to subside. That was not where my mind needed to be, especially since I was late for yet another class. I was lucky the teachers were more lenient on the first day of school.

It was certainly a day of firsts for me. In the space of one morning, I'd had my first kiss and been exposed to a guy's erection for the first time. It had been so arousing to feel the hardness of it pressing against my body and to know how much he wanted me.

But it was Mason, and that was the problem. If it had been any other guy, I could have considered giving in to my desire and having sex with him. Not Mason though. Why should I give him what he wanted after how he had treated me? He had told lies about me and my mother and made everyone disrespect me. He had chased away all my friends and scared guys away from asking me out. In the meantime, he had enjoyed popularity and dated who he wanted.

Thinking about it pissed me off, and that was exactly what I needed to combat the lust I felt for him. By the time I saw him again after my last class of the day, my resentment was stronger than my attraction to him.

"Hey," he said, "let's go somewhere nice since we're all dressed up. I made us early dinner reservations at Morton's."

"No," I said. "I'm going home."

"I'll pay," he assured me. "I know you have to be hungry since you didn't eat anything for lunch."

"I'm not going anywhere with you," I explained haughtily. "Ever."

His eyebrows lifted in puzzlement. "What happened now?"

"You happened, Mason," I told him. "You treated me like crap for three years, and now you think you can just snap your fingers and make me forget about that. Well, that's not happening."

I walked past him out the door, but he followed me. "I'm sorry."

"I don't forgive you," I replied.

"I'll keep apologizing until you do. I'll start with dinner, and you can tell me what else I have to do to make it up to you."

"You can leave me alone, that's what you can do," I grumbled at him. "Why the hell are you going this way? Isn't your car in the school parking lot?"

"It is, but I'm walking you to yours. You don't have a parking spot?"

I had parked in the church parking lot next door to the school, which was where students who didn't have parking passes parked. "I usually take the bus. I just borrowed my mom's car today because you made me wear this." I gestured at my bridesmaid dress. "Another mean thing you did to me," I added.

"I wore the tux to make up for it," he said. "It wasn't easy to put it on, but I did it for you."

I refused to feel any sympathy for him for wearing his deceased father's tux, because he'd put himself in that situation. If he hadn't forced me to wear the dress, he wouldn't have been scrambling for a tux when he decided I didn't deserve his bullying. "It's too little too late," I told him. "You can't ever make up for all the things you did, so don't bother trying."

"Of course, I'll make it up to you now that you're mine," he declared.

I came to a dead stop and turned to look at him. "Who the hell said I'm yours?"

"You did," he replied.

"That was pretend," I reminded him, "just to cover our story with Mr. Delaney."

"I'm not talking about what we told other people. I'm talking about what you told me when you kissed me."

"When I kissed you?" I questioned, thinking back on it.

"You told me that you're mine."

"No, I didn't," I denied.

"Yes, Ella, you did. It was all in that kiss. Actions speak louder than words."

"I kissed you," I admitted, "but that doesn't give you any kind of claim on me. It was a moment of temporary insanity, and it won't happen again."

"No, Ella, the insanity is that we've denied ourselves for this long. That's completely my fault, and I'm very sorry that I wasted so much time fighting this when you could have been mine since I met you."

"I'm glad you're finally admitting it's your fault, but it's too late to change anything. You made your choices, and you'll have to live with them. I'll never be yours now."

"You're lying to yourself, Ella, but I did that for a long time too. If you won't admit you're mine, then I'll admit that I'm yours."

"That's too bad," I taunted, "because I don't want you."

"That's the biggest lie of all," he said. "You've told me that you want me with your body and your words. You've even written a poem about it."

"Which you stole from me," I huffed, ignoring the rest of what he'd said. "I'd like it back, and my journal."

"I'll give you the journal back after dinner."

I stared at him for a few seconds before my brain could comprehend his astounding audacity. "You're unbelievable!" I exclaimed. "Now you're going to blackmail me into going out to dinner with you? Seriously?"

"If that's what it takes to persuade you. I'd prefer it if you would accept my invitation without being unreasonable."

"And I'd prefer it if you dropped dead," I retorted.

His expression darkened, and I regretted saying those particular words when I realized that it had likely reminded him of what happened to his dad. "Fine, I'll go to dinner with you," I relented instead of apologizing, "but you better give me my journal back afterwards. Today," I emphasized.

"I will," he promised. "I'll drive you to Morton's and then bring you back here to get your car."

I sighed. "Okay. My mom's not expecting me home yet anyway. She thinks I have a social life," I added resentfully.

Mason turned in the opposite direction and started walking toward the school parking lot and waited until I was again walking beside him before he replied. "You didn't miss out on much."

"That's easy for you to say," I complained. "You have friends, and—"

"Do I?" he interjected.

"Uh, yeah, you're usually surrounded by them. Everybody wants to be your friend."

"I'm surrounded by people who like free booze and always having a place to party. They also like feeling badass because they associate with a criminal. Take all of that away, and how many friends would I have?"

I was taken aback by his perception of his social circle. "You don't feel like you have true friends?"

"I know I don't," he stated.

I didn't know what to say to that, so we walked in silence to his car. I had been too distraught previously to notice anything beyond it being a sports car, but I wasn't surprised to realize that it was a Mustang. It was exactly the kind of car I had imagined him driving. It was black with blue racing stripes on the hood and an image of a cobra poised to strike running up both sides of the car.

Mason observed my perusal and shrugged. "It's what everyone expects from me."

I smirked. "Yeah, tell me you don't like driving this car. It's a teenage boy's wet dream."

He fixed me with a steamy look. "I have better wet dreams than that, but some of them have involved you on this car."

I suddenly had a mental image of being on the hood of his car, and I chided myself for mentioning anything sexual. I had to steer clear of things like that with him. "I don't want to hear about your wet dreams," I snapped at him to cover how sexy I found the thought of him dreaming about me.

"I'd rather hear about yours," he said and unlocked the car.

I almost retorted with a hell no, but sudden inspiration to mess with him struck. "Sure," I replied as I got in the car. "Now don't interrupt me," I warned as I put on my seatbelt. "If you say one word, I'll lose my concentration, and you'll ruin it."

"I'll be quiet," he promised as he started the car and put on his seatbelt. "You can close your eyes too if it helps," he suggested.

I looked at him suspiciously. "No touching! Both hands on the wheel."

He smiled. "As much as I want to touch you, I don't want to crash the car. I won't touch you while I'm driving."

"Okay." I settled back in my seat as he pulled out of his parking spot. By now, the lot was mostly empty of student cars, so we shortly cruised out onto the street. I took Mason's advice to close my eyes, because I needed to concentrate to make up an erotic story.

"So…we're on the bed," I began haltingly, "and, um, we're naked. And…he's kissing me, and touching me. And I'm moaning. And then he penetrates me, and I'm saying yes. Oh yes, Josh."

My eyes flew open when Mason started laughing. I eyed him in consternation, peeved that he thought it was funny when I had expected him to be mad that I was calling out Josh's name instead of his. I had deliberately decided on Josh because Mason accused me of flirting with him at his party. He also hadn't allowed him to walk me to my car.

"Of course it would be Josh giving you mediocre sex," Mason said in amusement.

"Why would I be calling out his name if it was mediocre?" I challenged.

"You wouldn't," he replied. "But you're a virgin, so you have no idea how basic that is. A little bit of touching and then penetration? That's hardly any foreplay to speak of."

"I said kissing too," I reminded him. "And how do you know I'm a virgin?"

"I'd say the way you told that story was proof enough," he remarked dryly.

"What's wrong with the way I told the story?" I demanded.

"Nothing. It was completely adorable."

I huffed and faced forward in annoyance. He thought my sex story was adorable. Well, fuck me.

"Kissing is a good start to great sex," he said. "You just didn't take the kissing far enough. My mouth would be all over you, and you'd be calling out my name way before penetration."

His words created unbidden images in my mind of where his mouth would be. My nipples tightened in response. Just thinking about feeling his mouth on them got me hot. Starting on this topic of conversation had been a very bad idea.

"I'll lean close so you can feel my breath teasing you, building the anticipation for you. Then I'll sweep my tongue around very lightly, making you crave more contact."

My nipples were actually aching as I imagined his tongue teasing them the way he described. "I'll never let you do that," I said in a tight voice, "so stop talking about it."

"You've already let me do that. I just haven't used that particular technique."

I looked at him in alarm. "You took advantage of me while I was drunk? You said you didn't touch me!"

"You weren't drunk," he countered, "unless you got drunk this morning."

"This morning," I repeated in confusion.

"When we kissed," he explained. "I was talking about kissing you again."

"Oh," I responded, feeling my cheeks heat up.

"What did *you* think I was talking about?" he asked slyly.

"Nothing," I mumbled, turning my head away from him to look out the window.

"I think I know," he said. "I can see the thought of it turns you on. Either that, or it suddenly got very cold in here."

My entire face got hot as I crossed my arms over my breasts, but his low laugh sent heat that had nothing to do with embarrassment through my body. I shouldn't be reacting this way to him. He was an asshole, and I should hate him. It had been bad enough when my attraction to him had been my secret shame, but now he knew about it. He was too arrogant already, and I shouldn't be inflating his ego even more and giving him more reason to mock me.

He got quiet after that though. When he stabbed at the button to turn on the radio, I got the impression that he wanted a distraction. It was what I needed too, and it helped shift my focus to something safe. When one of my favorite songs came on, my distraction became enjoyment. I silently mouthed the words to Believer.

"I like this song too," Mason remarked, "and this band."

"You do?" I asked in surprise. I hadn't ever imagined him liking this kind of music. Maybe something with a pounding, sexually charged beat, but not the introspective, emotionally infused lyrics of Imagine Dragons. Also, he was so callous and quick to judge that I couldn't imagine him being any kind of a believer.

"Yeah," he said, "they're good."

"Have you ever seen them in concert?" I queried curiously, interested in this unforeseen side of him.
"No," he replied. "I had no one to go with. Have you been to their concerts?"

"No one to go with!" I exclaimed. "I'm the one who had no one to go with. You've got tons of friends, and all your girlfriends."

He grimaced. "My girlfriends wanted to see boy bands and Taylor Swift. As for my friends, I have no idea what their taste in music is, and I wasn't about to go to a concert with a guy anyway."

I rolled my eyes. "There's nothing wrong with going to a concert with your buddies. I didn't know you were so worried about your image. And you could think of someone besides yourself for a change and make your girlfriends happy."

"Oh, I made them happy," he said smugly.

I felt a stab of jealousy at his implied meaning, and it pissed me off that I envied them for getting to be with him in an intimate way. "I love Taylor Swift," I lashed out at him. "I bet Josh will take me to see her. He'll be the best boyfriend ever!"

 "You are not going out with Josh," he stated, his tone cold and hard rather than angry and provoked as I had anticipated. "You are *my* girlfriend, Ella. Only mine." He glanced at me then, and I saw the intensity in his eyes that was missing from his voice.

"Yours?" I sneered. "I don't think so. You can't treat me like crap for years and then expect me to be your girlfriend. Just because I was stupid enough to give you my first kiss doesn't mean that you own me. I'll go out with anyone I want, and you can't stop me."

There was silence for a moment, and I thought he was too frustrated by my rejection to speak. He had probably never been rejected before in his life, and I felt some measure of revenge at being the first one to do it.

"That was your first kiss?"

Oh shit. I shouldn't have told him that.

"You saved that for me?" he marveled, the tone of his voice matching the look in his eyes when he glanced at me again.

"I didn't *save* it for you," I retorted. "I didn't have a chance to kiss anyone else. You scared all the guys away from me, so don't act so damned surprised."

"There was middle school," he said, "before I convinced my mom to move here. A girl as beautiful as you. I know guys had to be tripping all over themselves to go out with you. And even since high school you could have met someone outside of school. I can't control everyone who comes into contact with you. So, the fact that you saved *everything* for me…"

I so didn't want him thinking that. "I didn't save crap for you," I snapped at him. "Don't think that you're getting anything else, because that's not happening. I'm just here to get my journal back, if you actually give it back to me like you said."

"Of course," he replied. "I promised I'd return it to you."

I had my doubts, but I waited to see if he would renege on that promise. When we arrived at the restaurant, he parked the car and pulled my journal out of his backpack in the backseat. When I excitedly tried to take it from him, he reminded me that he said he'd give it to me after dinner. Holding it in one hand, he took hold of my hand and proceeded to act like we were on a real date. He held my hand as we walked toward the entrance, and I realized why that seemed so different—besides the fact that he hated me. I had never seen him holding hands with any girl before, not with any of his girlfriends ever.

In fact, now that I thought about it, I had never seen him with an arm thrown over his girlfriend's shoulders or around her waist the way boyfriends usually touched their girlfriends in casually affectionate ways. Unless he was making out with one of his girlfriends in the hallway, he didn't show any interest in her. Maybe that was why his relationships always ended after a few months. I imagined that the girl would become frustrated with the lack of romance and affection.

Now here he was looking like we were going to prom together, escorting me into the restaurant in a tux and pulling out my chair for me like a gentleman. It irked me, and I glared at him after the waiter took our drink orders.

"What?" he asked in response.

"You kept me from this," I replied. "Going out on dates, dances, all of it."

"I did," he acknowledged. "But I kept you from a lot of crap too—drunk idiots, cheating boyfriends, players, and worse."

"Don't act like you did it for my benefit," I retorted. "You wanted to make me miserable."

"Maybe," he allowed, "but there was more to it. I didn't want you going out with those guys."

"Are you saying that you were jealous?" I demanded.

"Yeah," he admitted. "I couldn't have you, and I didn't want them to have you either."

His admission of selfishness should have increased my resentment toward him, but it had the opposite affect. His reluctance to give me up to another guy indicated that he felt possessiveness toward me and wanted me for himself. That meant that he didn't hate me, because he wouldn't have been able to stand me if he did. It was the same way I felt about him. I didn't hate him, even though logic dictated that I should.

Feeling suddenly shy, I looked down at my menu. Almost all the choices sounded appetizing, because I was getting hungry after skipping lunch. Since Mason had insisted on taking me out to dinner, I decided to make him regret it, so I got the expensive filet mignon. He didn't react to my choice, and he ordered a Porterhouse steak for himself.

When the waiter left, Mason opened my journal and read my poem, Elusive. "The perfect moment, happiness in a smile, heart lifting with joy. The weight of the world falling away. Childhood innocence regained. Simple, perfect, elusive."

He looked up at me. "Tell me about this one. What was this perfect moment that brought you joy?"

"It wasn't mine," I answered.

"Whose was it?" he prodded after I fell silent.

"Someone I know," I replied evasively.

"Who?" he demanded.

"No one you know," I told him.

"But who is this person to you?" he questioned insistently. "Friend? Family?"

"Friend," I said, reluctant to reveal too much.

"Guy or girl?"

"None of your business," I snapped in exasperation.

"Tell me or you won't get this back," he threatened, lifting my journal for emphasis.

"That wasn't the deal," I complained. "You said you'd give it back if I went to dinner with you."

"And if you tell me about these poems."

I wondered why he cared. It was odd that he wanted to know the inspiration for my poems. Except for the one about him, none of them were embarrassing subjects that he could use against me. I had just hedged on this one because it was something he wouldn't understand. Deciding that I didn't care if he belittled it, because he couldn't affect how special it was to me, I told him. "It's about the girl I mentor as a big sister."

He sat back in surprise. "You volunteer with kids?"

"Yeah," I threw out like it was no big deal. "I've got lots of free time since you sabotaged my social life."

He studied me with a contemplative look. "You could have spent that time doing anything else. Volunteering isn't usually the first thing to come to mind when people are bored."

I shrugged, feeling no compunction to explain to him something he could never understand. He was too self-centered to know how wonderful it felt to do something nice for someone else, how making someone else happy was its own reward. I wasn't actually a formal volunteer, but I had befriended a younger girl I saw often at the YMCA where I went swimming and played volleyball. Zoey seemed lonely as she watched other kids playing together in the pool, so I had approached her and asked her if she knew how to swim. We had spent an hour having fun together in the pool, and I had gotten to know her as we spent more time together over the past year and a half. Her mom had taken to referring to me as Zoey's big sister, and I liked feeling like I was. So much so that I took her out for ice cream and other places outside of hanging out with her at the Y.

"You said she's a kid?" Mason queried.

"Yeah," I replied. "She's fourteen."

"So, you feel like you've regained your childhood innocence with her?" he questioned.

I shrugged, not wanting to elaborate that I had been referring to Zoey's innocence in that poem. She had been through a lot and carried more concerns on her shoulders than most people her age. It was great to see those fleeting moments when she could let go of everything and just be a kid.

"Talk to me," he snapped in annoyance. "I want to know about these poems."

"Why?" I questioned. This whole thing was completely out of character for him, and I couldn't figure out his angle. What could he possibly get out of this?

"I have my reasons," he said, turning to another page in my journal. "Is this one about her too? In visions of imagining, she delights in everything she sees. Playfully, summer's breeze shifts her pretty frock around her knees. A cute boy gazes soulfully into her wide blue eyes, but vibrant butterflies are the recipients of her sighs. She walks in enchanted reverie through the beauty her mind has revealed, unaware in her innocent wonder that she is the loveliest flower in this field."

He glanced up from the journal and gazed at me with a look I had never seen on his face before. It held warmth, and I was able to bask in it for a brief moment before it waned. Mistrust replaced it as he waited for my answer. "Well? Who's it about?" he prompted.

"A video," I told him.

"A video?" he repeated in a tone that made it sound like it was something dirty.

I flushed in embarrassment, although it was as sweet and innocent as could be. "My favorite video. It's called Dream."

"Show me," he demanded.

I pulled up the clip on my phone and handed it to him. The lovely music played softly as he watched it, and I felt odd about sharing this with him. I hadn't even shown it to Addison when I had thought that she was my friend, because I had instinctively known that she wouldn't appreciate its enchanting charm. If it wasn't sexy or popular, she wasn't interested. So, what was I doing here showing it to Mason? None of this fit in with his callous and disdainful nature at all.

"Your poem matches it perfectly," he told me as his gaze lifted to fix an assessing look on me like he was reevaluating me.

His scrutiny unsettled me, because I couldn't pinpoint what it was about. I didn't know how to react to it, and I fidgeted nervously as my gaze shifted away from his.

"Are you really this sweet?" he asked, and my stomach dipped at the warmly sensual sound of his voice as it drew my attention back to him.

The potent look in his eyes took my breath away. It became heated as I stared at him. "I'm going to find out," he said, making it sound like a sexual promise.

Heat flared within me, flushing my cheeks again. Fire sparked in Mason's hot gaze as he watched my response, and he leaned forward as he held my phone out to me. "I can't wait to taste how sweet you are."

Blazing heat turned my face scarlet at the implied meaning of those words, and I hastily grabbed my phone and dropped my gaze in mortification. What he was hinting at seemed too perverted to even imagine in my fantasies, and the mere mention of it was beyond embarrassing. Unable to handle it, I scrambled out of my chair and rushed off in search of a restroom.

After locating it, I went in and was relieved to find it empty. Standing by the sinks, I looked at myself in the mirror and saw that my face was indeed as red as I thought. Out of all the embarrassment I had experienced because of Mason recently, this had flustered me the most. Maybe it was because I had been hungover and not able to muster the energy to be thoroughly embarrassed when he showed me my naked picture. During the humiliation while cleaning his house in lingerie, I had been plotting revenge against him. Now, however, there was nothing to distract me from my embarrassment—no misery nor antagonism.

My mind halted right there on that thought. No antagonism between Mason and me. That was why I had been thrown so off kilter and why I was losing my head. Now that I was away from him and could think clearly, I realized what he was doing. He had dropped the hostility immediately after discovering that I had written an erotic poem about him. It had nothing to do with the rest of my poems. He was just feigning interest in them in order to get me to drop my guard and sleep with him. It was all part of his seduction, and I was a fool for succumbing to it.

I needed to remember what kind of person Mason was and all the rotten things he had done. Just because he showed up in a tuxedo didn't mean that he had suddenly become a gentleman. I had learned long ago that he was no prince charming. He was cold, calculating, and ruthless, and I wouldn't allow myself to fall prey to his current scheme. How much more of a perfect plan for revenge could he come up with than to get me to have sex with him? Then he could prove once and for all that I was just like my mother.

I imagined him gloating, and it strengthened my resolve against him. I wouldn't allow him to shame me again. As humiliating as the picture had been, I had gotten off relatively unscathed. He had only deleted it to protect himself, and because he had come up with an even more devious plan. I could blame Addison for getting me drunk and Mason for taking that picture, but I would have no one but myself to blame if I gave up my virginity to him. It would be the ultimate revenge for him to actually make me feel like trash that he used and threw away. I wouldn't let that happen.

With my head held high and my eyes full of steely determination, I returned to the table just as the waiter was bringing our meals out. Taking my seat, I kept my focus on the appetizing food. Mason waited until we were alone again before making a sexual innuendo about dessert. I just gave him a haughty look of contempt and started cutting into my filet mignon.

"You're not blushing," he remarked. "You were so worked up earlier. Is that why you ran off to the bathroom, to relieve the pressure?"

I glared at him. "The only pressure I feel is to hold back from stabbing you with this knife. So, shut the hell up and eat your food so we can get out of here."

"So eager to be alone with me?" he queried.

"Eager to be rid of you," I retorted. "I just want my journal back, and then I want you out of my life. From now on I want you to leave me the hell alone. You got that?"

He responded with an amused smile. "Eat your food, Ella."

I wanted to shove the plate from me in defiance, but the delicious smell was making me too hungry. It tasted just as good as it looked and smelled, and I enjoyed every last bite of it. Sitting back after the satisfaction of a good meal, I saw that Mason was also done eating. He smirked when the waiter asked if we wanted dessert, but he politely declined. After he paid the check, he handed me my journal.

Feeling mollified, it didn't occur to me to ask for my poem back until we were driving away from the restaurant. "No," Mason said with his eyes on the road.

"You promised!" I protested.

"I promised to give you your journal back, and I have. That was the deal."

"That poem is part of it," I argued. "You took it with the journal. Give it back! It's mine!"

"Clearly," he acknowledged. "It's written on the back of your homework assignment with your name on it. You have such nice handwriting. I'm sure that everyone would agree."

My grip on my journal tightened. He had given me back my harmless personal poems and was threatening to expose the only one that would humiliate me. Unlike the picture, however, it wouldn't get him in trouble. He could just stand back and laugh while people made fun of me with my own words.

He began to quote them to me, and rage boiled up within me. "Bastard!" I yelled and flung my journal at him.

"Holy shit!" he shouted as he swerved into the curb before straightening the wheel. "Are you fucking crazy?"

"If I am, it's because you're making me crazy," I railed at him. "Stop with this blackmail bullshit!"

"Nobody said anything about blackmail," he replied, regaining his composure frustratingly fast. "I just think that people would enjoy your poetry. I know that I do."

"What do you want?" I snapped at him.

"You," he answered. "And I know that you want me too."

"You're not blackmailing me into having sex with you," I retorted. "I don't care what you show anyone. I'm not going to—"

"Did I blackmail you into kissing me?" he interjected. "No, Ella, you kissed me because you wanted to, and we'll have sex when you want to. I wouldn't try to coerce you into sex if you tell me no."

"Then why are you threatening to show everyone my poem?" I demanded.

"Because I won't let you break up with me," he said. "We won't do anything physical if you don't want to, but you're my girlfriend."

I regarded him suspiciously. "Nothing physical? I just pretend to be your girlfriend?"

"There's nothing pretend about it. You *are* my girlfriend, Ella. That means we go on dates, and you don't date anyone else. We'll just hold off on the physical stuff until you're ready."

"Then you'll be waiting a long time," I told him, "because I won't ever have sex with you. No kissing either," I added. "And if I'm not allowed to date anyone else, then neither are you."

He glanced over at me with a smirk. "Sure, Ella. I won't date anyone else. I know how jealous you get."

"I'm not jealous," I huffed. "I could care less who you date, but you're not putting your double standard on me. You're not getting away with screwing around and expecting me to be saving myself for you."

"But you have saved yourself for me," he said in a sexual tone that made my stomach dip again. "Haven't you, Ella?"

Denying it would be a lie, since I had never wanted anyone else. I resented him for that even as the way he spoke those words brought back the heat that had been simmering beneath the surface of my skin. It spread straight down to my core as he spoke.

"You've been waiting for me to claim what's mine."

His overly confident assertion should have infuriated me instead of increasing the ache between my legs. I wanted to feel his touch so badly, and my anticipation was almost painful as I waited for him to act on his statement. When he parked his car beside mine and looked at me with a smoldering gaze, I expected him to try to kiss me.

Feeling slightly dazed as I watched him get out of the car, I was slow to react and was still strapped in my seat when he opened my door and offered me his hand. Nervous excitement fluttered through me as I unbuckled my seatbelt and placed my hand in his to let him tug me toward him. He allowed the expectation of a kiss to build between us before beginning to lean forward with deliberate slowness. Closing my eyes in anticipation, the wait became excruciatingly intense for me when I felt his warm breath ghosting over my lips. After a prolonged moment during which the tingling sensation increased with the tantalizingly close proximity of his mouth to mine, he very lightly ran his tongue over my bottom lip. A moan escaped between my shallow breaths at the tortuously brief but exquisite contact.

"That's what I was talking about," Mason said.

I opened my eyes and saw that he had taken a step back out of my personal space and was watching me with a smug smirk on that mouth I craved to feel on mine. Realization seeped in through my haze of lust that I had allowed my hormones to take over again. A blush crept over my face at the knowledge that Mason was aware of his power over me and was laughing at me for it.

"I would have kissed you, but you insisted on no kissing. Have you changed your mind?" he asked slyly.

"Fuck you," I retorted.

"Whenever you're ready," he replied. "We should go somewhere private though."

I spun around and grabbed my car keys out of my purse so that I could get the hell out of there. He continued to talk as I yanked open the car door and quickly plopped down into the driver's seat.

"Aren't you coming to my house?" he taunted. "We'll be alone, and you can be as loud as you want. If you moan like that just from me licking your lip, just imagine how you'll moan when I lick your—"

I slammed the door to block out his voice and thrust the key into the ignition. Throwing it into drive immediately after starting the engine, I swerved recklessly out of the parking lot in front of a car that blared its horn at me. I was so pissed off at him and myself. Why couldn't he leave me alone, and why was I so damned attracted to him? It was all kinds of twisted and wrong, but I had never stopped wanting him. My resolve not to succumb to my desire hadn't lasted past the walk out to his car. I would have let him kiss me again, and it burned me that he had been the one to refrain. I had lost my head while he had been in complete control the entire time, and he had mocked me for it.

Never again, I swore to myself. Mason would never get another chance to shame me like that again. I might be forced to keep him close, but I wouldn't forget that he was my enemy.

Chapter 9

To my dismay, Mason followed me home. "What the hell are you doing here?" I demanded.

Ignoring me, he strode past me and started knocking on the front door. I had a key, but I didn't want to let him in. Mom, however, was thrilled to see him when she opened the door. "Mason! My goodness, you look so handsome in that tux. Is there a dance tonight?"

"No," he replied as I stood fuming in the driveway. "Ella and I dressed up for that photo shoot I told you about. My friend is a photographer also, and I thought we could get some pictures together too as well as the ones I'm going to take of Ella. Is it okay if we go do that now?"

"Of course," she told him as I came stomping up to the door.

"No," I protested. "I want to change out of this stupid dress right now! Leave me alone, Mason. I've had enough of you today."

"Ella!" Mom scolded me. "That is so rude! Mason is trying to help you. So, stop being a stick in the mud and go to the photo shoot with him."

"Help me?" I replied derisively. "You don't know what you're talking about. He wants to shame me and—"

"Give me a break," Mom interrupted in exasperation. "Honestly, Ella, sometimes you sound just like my mother. When are you going to act your age and have a little fun? You're not going to be able to keep your hot boyfriend by being such a prude."

"Mom!" I rebuked her. "That is so wrong! My mother isn't supposed to say things like that to me."

"You should be happy I'm letting you have fun," she insisted. "Am I right, Mason?" she asked him.

He looked at me with an inscrutable expression as he answered her. "Ella should have fun, but she'll keep me regardless. I'm not going anywhere."

"Sexy and sweet," Mom gushed embarrassingly. "The whole package! You are a lucky girl, Ella, so you better go with him."

"Seriously?" I complained. "That's all it takes? He tells you some bullshit line, and I'm supposed to go with him? I just told you he doesn't have good intentions. Doesn't that matter to you at all?"

"Oh, stop being such a goody-goody. You're going to have to get over your shyness if you want to be a model. You should probably get some shots of her in a bikini too, Mason. The agency will want to see as much of her as they can. I'll go get it for her."

She ran off just as I opened my mouth to protest, and Mason grabbed my arm as I tried to go in after her. "Let go," I demanded, shooting a threatening look at him.

"Just let her have her way," he said. "I won't make you wear the bikini, so it's not worth arguing with her about it."

"You won't make me do anything," I bristled at him, "so stop thinking that you can."

"I can make you moan," he said with a cocky smirk.

I rolled my eyes, but I could feel my fair skin flushing.

"We could test it out," he suggested, "and see how long you can hold out from moaning."

"Forever," I replied curtly. "Because you're not touching me again. So, let go."

He complied but continued to taunt me. "You know you wouldn't last long."

The idea excited me, but I wouldn't give him the satisfaction of knowing that. *He'll use it against you,* I reminded myself and scowled at him.

He gave me a knowing look like he could see right through me, and it flustered me and made me look away from him. When he suddenly leaned in and placed his mouth very close to my ear, every nerve ending in my body became hyperaware of him. Feeling his warm exhale raised goosebumps on my skin and sent a shiver down my spine. I gasped when his tongue grazed my earlobe before he lightly sucked it into his mouth. The sensation seemed to travel straight down to my core, bringing back the ache between my legs.

My ear had become an erogenous zone, and Mason was the devil whispering temptation into it with his hot breath. "I'll only touch you with my mouth and my tongue."

After wreaking havoc in my body with his wicked words, he moved back into his original position as my mom came rushing toward us with my bikini clutched in her hands. To my mortification, she thrust it at Mason, and he took it with a small smirk playing over his lips.

"Smile when he takes your picture," she admonished me. "A model needs to look like she's having a good time. You have to make people want to be you. That's what will get you jobs and make you popular."

"I don't want to be a model," I argued, "and I'm not having my picture taken." I still hadn't regained my composure after what had just transpired with Mason, and I felt even more uncomfortable with him standing beside me holding my bikini as my mom gave him free reign to take pictures of me "having a good time." I could just imagine what he was thinking.

"Don't be silly," she said. "Every girl wishes that she could be a model, and you've actually got the looks for it.

Why wouldn't you want to make lots of money getting your picture taken?"

"That's what *you* want, not me. I want to go to college and get my degree."

"I can't believe you want to throw away your chance. I would have loved to be a model, but I had to take care of you. I wouldn't have been able to afford living in New York with a baby. I sacrificed everything for you, but you can't do anything to make me happy."

Whose fault was it that you got pregnant at sixteen, I wanted to ask her, but I held my tongue like I always did when she started on one of her rants about how I had derailed her life. I couldn't argue with the fact that she had taken care of me and raised me rather than abandoning me like my biological father had. He had dumped her as soon as she told him she was pregnant, and I had never even met him. Mom had to drop out of school to take care of me after I was born, because her parents both worked during the day. They refused to help her with childcare anyway, telling her that she had to deal with the consequences of her actions.

Mom had told me that she spent a year stuck in the house being unable to go out and do anything, since my grandparents wouldn't babysit me even for a short time. As soon as she was eighteen, she moved out into an apartment paid for by her new boyfriend. She had once confessed to me that she had found him through a personal ad he had placed in search of a mistress. That was her first married man, but she had eventually left him for someone else after she got a job as a stripper and no longer needed her much older sugar daddy. She'd gone through many boyfriends before marrying my dad.

Her life was good now, but she still complained to me about her missed opportunities from her youth. I didn't need this today—especially not in front of Mason. "Okay," I grudgingly told her, "I'll go get my picture taken."

She smiled, and she looked so beautiful and happy that it momentarily seemed worth it to give her anything she wanted. Being back in Mason's car with him quickly had me regretting caving to my mom. I had already spent entirely too much time with him today, and I had discovered that even a minimal amount of contact with him was too much. I was like a moth drawn to the flame, even though I knew that Mason would burn me every time.

"You look like her clone," he commented. "It's like looking at younger and older versions of the same person. That's why I thought..."

He trailed off, and I wondered about his unfinished sentence. Who cares what he thought, I admonished myself. His opinion didn't matter to me. Yet I barely refrained from asking him about his next remark.

"It's amazing that you turned out the way you did."

How did he think I had turned out? No, I told myself firmly. The last thing I needed was to worry about what Mason Sumner thought about me. He was an asshole and a bully, even though he didn't look the part. Especially not in that tux.

That was why I had kissed him, I consoled myself. Wearing that tuxedo, he looked as close to my girlish prince charming version of him as I'd ever seen. My innocent twelve-year-old self couldn't have imagined the darker aspects lurking beneath the refined surface. Exuding raw animal magnetism, it was like the beast had been combined with the fairytale prince.

It was a disconcerting mix that had me dropping my guard and then feeling like prey whenever his silver gaze intensified into a predatory stare. How was I going to handle having my picture taken by him? What kind of expression would be on my face? I had been too preoccupied with seeing my nude body on display to notice my expression in the naked picture he had taken of me. Now that it had occurred to me to wonder about it, I felt even more embarrassed about the naked desire he might have seen on my face than about him seeing my naked body.

"What are you thinking about?" he asked. "You look so delicious when you blush like that, that I'm tempted to stop the car and have a taste right now."

"Stop talking like that," I demanded.

"Like what?" he asked.

I gave him a sideways glance. "Stop pretending to be obtuse. I know that you're not."

"Do you?" he queried. "What else do you know about me?"

"I know that you don't flirt, you don't hold hands, and you don't like me," I answered in irritation. "So, I don't know why you're suddenly acting like you're not you, but I'm not falling for it, so just stop."

"Like I'm not me," he repeated in amusement. "Well, Ella, I don't think that you know me anymore than I knew you."

"Oh, I know you," I retorted. "You're an asshole, a bully, and a manipulative liar."

"All true," he agreed to my surprise. "I play to win, and I use whatever advantages I have."

"That's nice," I said sarcastically.

"Nice guys finish last. It's a cutthroat world, and I strike first."

"There you are," I remarked drily.

"I thought my true whereabouts are unknown."

I froze before slowly turning my head to look at him. He glanced at me with an enigmatic smile and returned his eyes to the road as I reeled from the knowledge that he had somehow figured out that poem was about him.

"Here with you, I am alone. Your true whereabouts are unknown," he quoted. "Rather dark, but I like it just as much as much as the sexy one. Actually, I find the thought of you writing poems about me surprisingly sexy."

"Nobody said it was about you," I snapped.

"Now who's the liar? Who else are you obsessing about except me?"

"I am not obsessed with you," I replied in outrage.

"Of course you are. You told me so yourself, and you've written more poems about me than anyone else. I'm obsessed with you too, Ella. I have been since the first moment I saw you. I was supposed to be taking revenge on your mother, but as soon as the private investigator gave me that picture, I knew that I wanted to meet you. I talked my mom into moving here so that I could go to school with you."

I gaped at him. "You moved here because of me?"

"I told myself that it was because of your mother, that I could get to her through you, but I spent more time thinking about you than I ever did about her. You've gotten under my skin, Ella, and I'm glad to know I've gotten under yours."

More bullshit, I told myself, but it was impossible not to be affected by his words. He was playing me like he knew every note it would take to seduce my body and my mind.

"You'll never be alone when you're with me," he promised. "I take care of what's mine. Any problem or concern you have, you come to me and I'll take care of it."

I laughed derisively. "I wouldn't have any problems if it wasn't for you. You're the problem, Mason."

"Not anymore," he said. "Whatever you want, just tell me and I'll get it for you."

"I want you to leave me alone," I replied.

"Let me rephrase that. Whatever you *honestly* want, I'll do."

"You just can't believe that someone doesn't want you," I retorted. "Your ego can't handle it."

"You wrote an erotic poem about me and told me that you want to marry me. That doesn't sound like you don't want me."

I had forgotten about that video he had taken of me until he mentioned that ridiculous drunken declaration. Feeling my face flush again, I protested that I was drunk when I said that.

"What a sober person thinks, a drunk person says. Alcohol is like truth serum."

"That's not true!" I exclaimed. "People say all kinds of stupid things when they're drunk."

"What about when you wrote those poems about me? Were you drunk then too?"

"I never confirmed that they were about you," I said. "You just assumed that."

"Really? Who else do you know with silver eyes and a barbed tongue?"

"A character from a book," I lied desperately. "They always have spectacular eyes." I instantly regretted tacking that on.

"Well, thank you for the compliment. I think you have beautiful eyes too, perfect baby blues."

"I wasn't talking about your eyes," I insisted.

"Right. Which book was this?"

"Um, a romance novel. I forget the name of it."

"Okay, so what happened in the book?"

"What always happens in romance novels," I replied. "They fell in love and lived happily ever after."

"But what was it about this particular book that inspired you to write that poem? There had to be something memorable about it."

"The guy," I answered with a sinking feeling, realizing that Mason was making me dig myself into a hole.

He confirmed that with his unrelenting questions. "What about him?"

"Never mind," I belatedly tried to deflect him.

"What is it about this guy that turns you on? Besides his silver eyes and barbed tongue."

"A barbed tongue is not a turn on," I argued foolishly.

"It obviously is for you since you mentioned it in your sex poem. It gets you all riled up, and you want to put that tongue to other uses. Don't you, Ella?"

I tried not to think about those other uses and failed miserably. A telltale blush heated my cheeks, and Mason laughed quietly. Doing my best to ignore him for the rest of the ride, I started feeling nervous about what he would do once we arrived at his house. I was surprised when he took me to a park instead.

"It's a nice place for pictures," he said in response to my questioning look.

"Hey, Cassie," he called out when we got out of the car.

I was astonished to see her there and Mason approaching her with a greeting. "Thanks for meeting us here. Do you know my girlfriend, Ella?"

Cassie looked at me in bewilderment. "Uh, yeah. Hi."

"Hi, Cassie," I responded and glanced at Mason for an explanation.

"I asked Cassie to take the pictures, since she's the photography expert," he told me.

I knew that Cassie was on the yearbook staff, and that she also worked on the school paper. I had seen her taking pictures of people at school, and I had never been included in those photos. She wasn't part of Mason's crowd, but she had taken lots of pictures of them for the yearbook. I hadn't expected him to associate with her outside of school, but I hadn't expected him to associate with me either.

Under Cassie's direction, we proceeded down to the pond for picturesque photos that were bizarrely similar to wedding photography. She had us clasp hands while we gazed at each other.

"Beautiful," Cassie said.

It would have been if we were a real couple. I would have cherished these romantic pictures with my incredibly handsome boyfriend. Instead, I stiffened in his arms when Cassie instructed him to embrace me from behind. Being enfolded against the hard length of his body made me aware of his strength and size in comparison to mine. I felt overpowered by his masculine hold on me.

"Relax," he murmured quietly against my hair.

The seductive sound of his voice and the stirring of his breath over the fine hairs on my scalp made the sensation of being pressed against him feel good. It felt natural to yield to his superior strength and let him take care of me. I succumbed to languid desire and leaned back against him as I rested my head on his shoulder. He tilted his head down toward my exposed neck and grazed his lips over the sensitive skin in a tantalizing, featherlight trail. I threw my head back over his shoulder and whimpered out a moan.

"Um," Cassie's hesitant voice pulled me back to the realization that we weren't alone.

I stiffened again before tearing myself out of Mason's arms like he was on fire. Mortified heat consumed my entire body as I flushed from head to toe in shame. Cassie was speaking, but I had no idea what she was saying as I took off toward the parking lot.

"Take me home," I said when Mason caught up to me.

"Meet us at my house," he said, and I realized that he was talking to Cassie.

I reached for my purse, but it wasn't hanging by my side. "I've got it," Mason told me as I remembered that I had set it down at the base of a tree before posing for pictures.

I glanced toward him and saw it dangling from his hand. When I grabbed for it, he pulled it out of my reach and darted ahead of me to throw it into the trunk of his car and slam the lid closed. He clicked the lock as I lunged at it with the intent to open it.

"Give it back!" I demanded.

"Get in the car," he ordered.

"No," I retorted. "I'm calling my mom to come get me."

"Not without your phone," he replied. "Also, she wouldn't come. I'll call her right now if you insist, but she won't come if I tell her the photo shoot isn't done and that you're just being temperamental."

"I'm not being temperamental," I argued.

"Then what's the problem?" he queried.

I flushed again under his immutable gaze as he waited for my answer. His neutral expression gave no hint of his awareness of my embarrassment, but I knew that he had heard my humiliating moan and knew the effect he had on me. I wasn't about to admit any of that out loud, so I said nothing before trudging toward the passenger side of his car in defeat. He clicked the button to unlock the door for me, and he slid in beside me as I got in.

He drove to his house in silence, and I tried to use the reprieve to compose myself. I was still on edge when we arrived though, especially when he grabbed my bikini from the backseat and handed it to me. My gaze shot to Cassie, as if seeking her assistance. She seemed just as unnerved as I was, but she managed a weak smile.

"You can go change in my room," Mason said as he unlocked his front door. "We'll wait down here for you."

My embarrassment prevented me from voicing a protest that he had told me that I wouldn't have to put on the bikini. At least going up to his room afforded me a reprieve from him. My nervousness ratcheted up when I took my dress off and had to remove my bra. I had locked the bedroom door, but I didn't trust Mason not to somehow barge in. I hurried to put on the bikini top, but I felt the price tag in my hand when I grabbed it. Cursing, I ripped it off and dropped it on the floor in my rush to cover my bare breasts with the material. I tied it and tugged at it in a futile attempt at full coverage.

There was a reason that I had never worn this string bikini that my mother had picked out for me. The triangle cups left a lot of cleavage exposed. I debated whether to change back into my dress and refuse to pose in the bikini, but I knew that Mason was right about my mom being on his side about this. I decided to just get it over with so that I could go home.

Taking off my panties in Mason's room made me feel sinfully exposed—like I was undressing for him. It didn't help that putting on the bikini bottoms prolonged my partial nudity while I tied one side. Finally pulling the flap up to cover the apex between my legs so I could tie the other side, I was still exceedingly aware of how little of my body was actually covered. The sides of my ass cheeks hung out the back no matter how much I tried to pull the material over them.

I really didn't want to pose in this bikini like some Playboy centerfold. They're naked, I reminded myself. Girls wore bikinis like this on the beach. *My mother* wore bikinis like this on the beach. There was nothing shameful about me being seen in this bikini. Taking a deep breath, I forced myself to unlock the door and go downstairs.

Mason's eyes slowly raked over me. "A blonde in a white bikini. Classic," he commented. "Don't you think so, Cassie?"

She was slow to respond as she stared at me. "I didn't think people actually looked like that in real life," she said, sounding dazed. She glanced at Mason. "I mean you're already…"

She trailed off and shook her head. "Two of you. No wonder you're together. I bet your body is just as perfect under that tux."

Her gaze flew back to him and sharpened as she assessed him. "The tux. That'll be perfect," she declared excitedly. "It'll be such a cool contrast."

"I'm not sure what you're talking about," Mason said, "but I thought you could take pictures of her by the pool."

"You've got a pool?" I asked, hoping that he didn't mean the public pool.

"Yes," he replied. "It's this way."

He turned and led us toward the back of the house and out the patio door onto the deck. We passed a hot tub and went down the steps to the backyard. I was glad to be walking behind them where I wasn't on display to their gazes, and I was also happy to see that there was a privacy fence around the backyard to shield me from view of the neighbors.

The inground pool looked inviting under the heat of the sun, and I envied Mason for having his own pool. I went to the YMCA to avoid anyone from school who might frequent the local public pool. I sure didn't want to deal with them during my free time, but Mason was cutting into it more and more. Now he had dragged Cassie into this mess, but she seemed excited to be involved.

"Ella, come over here by Mason. You guys are going to look amazing," she said with enthusiasm.

"I just wanted a few pictures with her," he told her. "You can take the rest of her alone. This is supposed to be her photo shoot."

"I'll get some shots of her alone too," she replied, "but I have to get you two together like this. It's going to be the most amazing look."

I couldn't understand her thinking, since I thought it would look extremely odd for Mason to pose with me in his tux while I was in a bikini. Expecting him to refuse, I was surprised when he complied and beckoned me over. "Okay, Ella, let's do this."

Going reluctantly to him, I turned my attention toward Cassie. She had Mason face her with his hands in his pockets and posed me leaning sideways against him casually. The next pose was us facing each other while I grabbed his tie to pull him toward me—aggressively was how Cassie instructed me. She had us freeze with our faces close together, and I tried to keep a determined expression on my face as Mason's eyes smoldered at me. I felt like he would close the distance and kiss me in the next instant.

"That's hot," Cassie said. "Um, okay, uh—"

"Pull tighter," Mason told me, interrupting her.

I yanked, using the opportunity for retaliation, but Mason kept his balance and went with the momentum to bring his mouth a hairsbreadth from mine. My lips seemed to part of their own accord, and Mason's breath ghosted over them as his lips hovered in a near kiss.

"Hold! Just like that," Cassie said excitedly. "Perfect."

"Oh, I've got an idea. Do one of those tango poses where you bring your leg up and he holds it."

It involved me leaning into him with my arms around his shoulders and one leg bent across his waist while he held the bottom of my thigh with one hand and pulled me toward him with the other one splayed over my lower back. Both hands were touching my bare skin, and it felt extremely sexual, especially when he started stroking my thigh with his thumb.

For our final photo together, Cassie told Mason to take off his tux blazer and give it to me to put on. She also had him take off his tie and undo several buttons on his shirt before having him pose sprawled out on a chair with one leg thrown over the armrest. I was instructed to stand beside him with my wrists crossed up over my head in a stretch which pulled the blazer open to reveal my stomach and some of my cleavage.

"I want one of her like that alone," Mason said after Cassie took our picture.

I glanced at him. "These aren't for you."

"Of course I'll get copies," he replied. "I'm the one who's paying her."

I gaped at him. "You're paying her for this?"

"Why are you so surprised?" he retorted. "You'd need to pay any photographer you went to."

I had assumed that he had intimidated Cassie into doing his bidding, but I said nothing and turned my attention to her as Mason got out of the chair. I gasped when I suddenly felt his arms around my waist and his body pressed against my back and rear.

"You look so fucking sexy," he said into my ear, sending my temperature skyrocketing.

"Wow, that was the hottest one yet!" Cassie exclaimed. "I think you could get a lot of work modeling together."

"She doesn't need me to look hot," he replied before lowering his voice to whisper in my ear. "You're a fantasy come true."

He was playing havoc with my hormones, but his words also had the effect of making me feel sexy. I felt confident and sensual as I posed by myself while Mason watched me over Cassie's shoulder. My eyes were on him most of the time rather than looking into the camera, but Cassie was happy with the results. She took various poses of me around the pool and laying in a chair like I was tanning beneath the sun.

Mason disappeared part way through my solo photo shoot and returned at the end dressed in shorts and a t-shirt. "You can cool off in the pool before you change back into your clothes," he offered.

That was tempting, and I looked longingly at the water as I imagined indulging in having the entire pool to myself. It was Mason's though, and I couldn't let him seduce me in any way. Not with his looks, his words, or his possessions. I had to remember that he would use anything to breach my defenses and get his way. I had already softened toward him way too much and nearly forgotten that he was my enemy.

"No thanks," I said tersely. "I want to go home, like I told you hours ago."

"What's with the attitude?" he demanded. "I took you to a nice dinner, and I set up this photo shoot for you."

I snorted. "For me? Please spare me your bullshit. I liked it better when you didn't pull any punches."

"Um, I'm gonna go," Cassie said.

Mason had been scowling at me, but he put on a pleasant expression for her. "I'll walk you out."

Cassie glanced at me. "Bye, Ella. See you at school."

"Yeah, bye," I replied. "Thanks for taking the pictures."

"Yes, thank you," Mason said. "I lied to Ella's father about being a photographer, so I needed your help."

I followed them onto the deck and into the house before heading upstairs while they walked toward the front door. My aggravation only increased when I saw that my panties weren't with the rest of my clothes in Mason's room. I flung open the door and marched down the hall on a mission to confront him, but he was already coming fast up the stairs.

"Where are they?" I demanded as I strode toward him.

"Fucking finally," he said as he grabbed me and pulled me forward to crash his lips down on mine.

I struggled not to give in to the desire to kiss him back, and I managed to wrench free of him. "What the hell are you doing? Did I look like I wanted to kiss you? Can't you see that I'm pissed? Where the hell are my underwear?"

"You did look like you wanted me to kiss you. The looks you've been giving me all day have been driving me crazy. As for your underwear, when you take them off for me, don't expect to get them back."

"I didn't take them off for you," I retorted in outrage. "I couldn't wear them under this damn bikini. You have no right to keep my stuff anyway. Give them back!"

"No," he said.

I whirled around and stomped back into his room to begin tearing through his dresser in search of my panties. Deliberately throwing his stuff on the floor, I yelped when he grabbed me around the waist and pulled me away from the dresser. My protest died on my lips when I heard him groan.

"Fuck, you feel good," he spoke in a rough voice against my hair.

He did too. His hard body pressed against mine was a feeling that I wanted to sink back into. He lifted one hand to cup my breast, and I moaned when he brushed my nipple through the thin material with his thumb. His hand lowered to trail down my stomach, and I lurched out of his hold, spinning to face him.

"Don't touch me," I said breathlessly. "You promised you wouldn't."

"Right," he agreed. "With my hands. Let me correct my mistake."

He moved toward me, and I backed up. "I'm not letting you do anything. Get out so I can get dressed."

"Is that really what you want?" he asked, watching me with his smoldering silver gaze.

"Yes," I answered, my voice too weak to be firm.

He exhaled. "Alright, Ella. I know you'll be thinking of me when you make yourself come."

I blushed and glared at him. "I won't."

"Silver-eyed devil with a barbed tongue," he quoted, taunting me. "From your phantom hands—"

"Stop it!" I demanded.

"How was it feeling my hands for real? Did you moan like that when you were only imagining me touching you? I'm going to be thinking about hearing more of your sexy moans while you give me that fuck me look."

He laughed at my expression. "Not that one. That one looks like you want to stab me with something sharp."

"Good guess," I retorted. "Now get out before I do it."

He regarded me for a moment with an assessing look. "Seeing you all riled up is almost as sexy as seeing you turned on. That must be why I liked pissing you off so much."

I put my hands on my hips in consternation. "Well, it's nice to know that being mean to me turns you on. You're sick. Do you know that?"

"If I am, then you are too. You've wanted me this whole time just as much as I've wanted you."

It was the humiliating truth, and I knew that there was something very wrong with me if I could still be attracted to him after how he had treated me.

His gaze became heated as he stepped closer. "Nobody turns me on more than you, Ella."

My breath hitched, but I stepped back away from him. My butt hit an open dresser drawer, the resistance of it stopping my retreat. Mason moved into my personal space but didn't touch me. "Tell me what you want, Ella. I want to hear you say it."

I wanted him to touch me and kiss me, but I couldn't tell him that. All the pent-up passion that I had ever felt for him seemed to flare within me in that moment. I was so incredibly aroused that he had to see it in my eyes.

Holding on to my last shred of dignity, I refused to acknowledge the sexual heat emanating from my body. "Remember when you said that begging you on my knees was a good way to start? That's what I want you to do. Get on your knees and beg me for forgiveness for everything you've done."

"Fine, I will," he said to my surprise and actually kneeled down before me.

Gazing up at me for a beat first, he dropped his gaze to what was right in front of him. In that instant, I knew his intent. I bolted away with a shriek as his hands shot out to grab at the ties on my bikini bottom. "You asshole!" I yelled as I halted at the doorway and spun around to confront him. "You don't care about apologizing. You're just trying to get sex from me."

"I'm not trying to get anything," he replied, still on his knees. "I want to give you what you've fantasized about. I promised I'd only use my mouth, and that's what I'm going to do. Come here," he urged. "I've never done this for any other girl, but I want to do it for you. That should prove to you how much I want to make it up to you."

I recoiled from the very thought of what he was suggesting. It was too embarrassing and perverted for me to even consider, and I couldn't believe that he wasn't grossed out by the idea of putting his mouth there. While it seemed to me like it would be a worse punishment for him than anything he had put me through, the heat in his eyes conveyed that he actually found it arousing.

"Please leave," I pleaded desperately. "I just want to get dressed and go home."

An incredulous expression replaced his heated look. "You don't want me to lick your—"

"No!" I exclaimed loudly before he could finish that mortifyingly dirty sentence. "Just get out so I can get dressed. Please," I begged.

"Okay," he agreed as he rose to his feet. "If that's what you really want."

I backed away from him as he approached, not trusting him not to try to untie my bikini again. He smirked but didn't make a grab for me as he walked past and exited the room. He left the door open as he walked off down the hall, and I rushed to close and lock it behind him. Not daring to remove any clothing, I left my bikini top on instead of changing back into my bra. Quickly putting on my dress and shoes, I was ready to go but took a deep breath before I ventured out to face Mason again.

I was still flustered from his disconcerting behavior. He had gotten down on his knees before me, but he had given off no impression of groveling at all. Somehow, he had still managed to have the upper hand, and I now realized that he hadn't lowered himself one bit. There had been nothing remorseful about his actions, and he had only been trying to manipulate me into forgiving him. By choosing the naughtiest, most sinful thing, he had known that he would unnerve me and make me forget my resentment toward him.

Even now that I had figured out his game, I couldn't call forth the anger and outrage I should be feeling, and I could barely even look at him let alone scowl at him the way he deserved. It didn't help that I could feel his sultry stare as I concentrated on carefully descending the stairs. The atmosphere between us became as thick with sexual tension as it had been in his room, and I felt like he was still contemplating carrying through on his promise to use his mouth in that wicked way.

"When does your mom get home?" I asked nervously.

I felt the immediate change in the atmosphere even before he spoke. "She's not here," he answered flatly.

His tone prompted me to look at him. "What do you mean?" I queried. "Where is she?"

He shrugged. "Tahiti or Bora Bora maybe. I'm not exactly sure. She doesn't always keep me up to date with her travels."

I stared at him. "But...doesn't she...I mean...how long has she been gone?"

"Three, four months maybe," he replied, appearing to be thinking about it.

"She leaves you alone that long?" I exclaimed aghast.

He shrugged again. "I'm used to it. It's what every kid dreams about, right? Having free run of the house without parental supervision."

I frowned, imagining being left all alone for months at a time. Sure, Mason was almost eighteen, but...

"Is this some kind of dream vacation she's been wanting to do?" I asked, wondering why she hadn't waited another year until Mason was in college.

He snorted. "She's traveled all over the world several times since my dad died, and she went on lots of vacations before that too."

I gaped at him. "You mean she's been leaving you by yourself since you were twelve years old?"

He shook his head. "Fourteen. I was in boarding school before that until I convinced her to move here."

"Fourteen! That's not much better than twelve. I can't believe she would leave you alone at that age!"

"She certainly wasn't going to be stuck here in the suburbs," he remarked. "That was the deal we made—that she could trust me to stay here and not get in trouble while she traveled, or I would get sent back to boarding school. I had a live-in nanny at first, but I eventually convinced my mom that I could take care of myself."

I was stunned by his mother's lack of maternal affection, especially after his father died and she was all that Mason had left. That she couldn't be bothered to spend any time with him when he needed her most showed a level of selfishness that made my mom look like a doting mother in comparison. At least she hadn't abandoned me, despite her maternal shortcomings.

"I'm sorry, Mason," I told him with sympathy.

His expression suddenly became a smooth mask. "What for? I get to do what I want," he said flippantly. "Anyway, I should drive you back. Unless you want me to beg you on my knees again," he added with a smirk.

I didn't react in embarrassment that time, because I could tell that he had only thrown that comment in to change the subject. He apparently hadn't been comfortable with the conversation about his mother. I felt like I had gotten a glimpse beneath his perfect surface, and it gave me an equal footing with him that I hadn't had before. He wasn't impenetrable. Somewhere under there was vulnerability.

That knowledge gave me power, but I didn't realize that it could also be treacherous to my heart.

Chapter 10

I had expected the ride home to be awkward after what happened at Mason's house, but it wasn't. Mostly because he was distant and didn't give me any smug looks or smirks or taunt me about it. He seemed to have withdrawn from me completely and only spoke a perfunctory parting "bye" when he dropped me off.

He appeared to have completely lost interest in me now. It was a startling thought, because he had been relentless for so long that it was strange to imagine him ignoring me. It was disturbing to realize that the idea didn't fill me with relief. I couldn't possibly want his attention, could I? I didn't want to believe that I could be that twisted that I would rather have any kind of attention from him than none at all.

I had always hated how my mother sought male attention, and I had prided myself on being the opposite of her. Now I began to worry that I was more like her than I had ever thought. Mason had been my enemy, but I had let him kiss me twice today. I had succumbed to temptation just as easily as my mom had with all the men she had been with before she finally settled down with my dad.

I didn't want to follow in her footsteps and measure my self-worth by how desired I was. I had already allowed Mason to have too much power over me, and I needed to regain control of my life. Feeling too restless to stay home, I drove to the YMCA and indulged in the urge to cool off in the pool. Seeing the people in it, I momentarily wished that I had my own private pool like Mason. It would be amazing to have it all to myself and be in the privacy of my own backyard. I had changed into my one-piece bathing suit, but I still felt overly exposed when I noticed a middle-aged man ogling my body. I quickly got into the water and submerged myself up to my shoulders.

My mom would have loved knowing that he was looking at her, even if she had no interest in him. So, I wasn't like her in that regard. I didn't revel in having the attention of every guy around me. Yet when Mason looked at me that way…

I pushed that unwelcome thought from my mind and moved toward the swim lanes with determination. The steady, repetitive motions of swimming laps soothed my frazzled nerves. Everything else disappeared as I focused only on getting from one end of the pool to the other and back again. I kept going until my muscles were too fatigued to do another lap.

This was another thing that Mason had prevented me from having. I had been planning to try out for the swim team, but I had given up on that idea after he ruined my reputation with his humiliating lies. I knew that nobody would want me on the team, and it killed my enthusiasm for joining.

It was good to remember this and all the ways in which Mason had wronged me. He didn't deserve my sympathy, and he certainly wasn't deserving of anything else from me. I could only blame my behavior today on temporary insanity, but at least I'd had enough sense not to take it any further than kissing. It was bad enough that he would now always hold a place in my memories as my first kiss. And my second, I thought bitterly. No more, I vowed. My next kiss would be with someone else, and it barely even mattered who as long as it wasn't Mason.

My resolve for this to happen was reinforced that night when my mind kept drifting back to my kisses with him. First was the more romantic one with him looking so incredibly handsome in his tux and gazing at me like I had always imagined in my girlish fantasies. Kissing him that time had been a dream come true.

I at least tried to linger on that memory, but it led to another, sultrier one. Mason coming at me with smoldering heat in his eyes and pulling me into a hot, hungry kiss. If only it hadn't felt so good. Why couldn't he have been a bad kisser? Why did he have to be as sexy as he looked?

I needed to replace him with someone else, and sooner rather than later. He was holding that damn poem over my head though, and I really didn't want him showing it to anyone. It would be mild embarrassment compared to the naked picture he had threatened me with before, but the thought of having my private words exposed like that was cringeworthy and something I very much wanted to avoid. Yet I also wanted to defy him. The solution was to do it in secret, so that he wouldn't know about it.

That meant that I needed someone who wouldn't tell him. Remembering Josh's ridiculous fear of him, I decided that he was the perfect candidate. He was the only one of Mason's friends I would consider kissing anyway, since he was the only one of them who had been nice to me while I was still an outcast. I just had to convince him to go behind Mason's back with me.

Then Mason would no longer be the only guy I'd kissed, and I would have someone else to think about. I should have long since replaced him with another crush, but being ostracized had put a damper on everything. I hadn't exactly been in the mood to giggle over cute guys, and I knew that setting my sights on anyone would be a lost cause since Mason would ruin it for me.

Which was what he was still doing, I realized. He was still stopping me from dating, and I had been too distracted to be pissed off about it. Well, I wasn't going to play by his rules anymore, I thought as I went to change in the locker room. My vigorous swim had cleared my head and brought everything back into focus. Mason might not be acting like my enemy anymore, but he hadn't really changed. He was still an arrogant, selfish jerk who thought that he was entitled to have his way at all times. He never even considered other people's feelings.

I was ashamed of how easily he had manipulated me with only a small modicum of kindness after all the cruelty that had proceeded it. I had played right into to his hands and let him off the hook for that picture, which he could still have a copy of on his computer for all I knew. I had just taken his word for it because I wanted to believe him. I wanted to believe the guy who had been making my life hell up until the very day before he showed up to bail me out of the situation he had put me in. I had actually been grateful to him for sparing me more misery. How screwed up was that? Worst of all was that I had caved when he had shown me the slightest bit of interest that I had been craving from him. I had *kissed* him. That was something that I couldn't even blame on him, because I had done it myself. It was the very reason why he thought he had the right to kiss me whenever he pleased, but I was going to set him straight about that.

I went home that evening resolved to take back control of my life from Mason. I wasn't expecting him to call me, but I was ready with the right attitude when I saw his name on my screen. "What?" I snapped. "I'm not doing anymore crap for you. Clean your own damn house."

"That's not why I'm calling," he said. "I'm sorry I treated you that way, but I'm not sorry for making you wear that sexy maid costume. I'd like to see you in that again, but I wouldn't have you do any housework. You could just lay back and let me do all the work."

My body responded to the image his words made me picture. I knew that he wasn't talking about me watching him do housework, and the implications of what he would be doing while I lay back were sinfully hot in my mind. This was not what I needed to thinking about.

"You broke your promise," I exclaimed. "You said nothing physical, but you kissed me."

"You kissed me back," he countered.

"No, I didn't. I pushed you away, but regardless, you promised not to kiss me. Our deal is off if you can't keep your end of it. I'm not going to let you use me for sex like your dad used my mom. You said you wouldn't touch me," I ranted. "You said I was beneath you. But you're a liar, because—"

"Don't ever talk about my dad again," he cut in sharply. "You understand, Ella? Never again." His threatening tone chilled me, and his voice was ice cold when he spoke again after a short pause. "I'll keep my promise, but you better keep yours."

"I didn't make any promises to you," I began to argue despite how he had managed to intimidate me.

"You're my girlfriend," he retorted.

"Pretend girlfriend," I corrected him.

"Real girlfriend," he insisted. "Whether you kiss me or not, you're mine."

He might as well have called me his property, and it should have pissed me off more than it did. There should have been no part of me that was secretly reveling in hearing him call me his. "You're unbelievable," I said. "This is how you act when you're supposedly sorry for how you've treated me? What's different? Everything is still your way, so why should I forgive you?"

"What do you want me to do to make it up to you?" he asked. "I'll still beg you on my knees," he added in a darkly sensual tone.

I wasn't going there again with him, so I quickly blurted out the thing I wanted that he couldn't twist into something sexual. "Friends. I want you to let me have friends."

Hearing myself phrase that in that way reignited the fire of resentment within me.

"Sure," he agreed. "I'll get Erin to be friends with you. She's a nice girl, and she'll be a perfect friend for you."

Although I liked Erin, I rejected his offer. "I don't want you to *get* me friends. I want to make friends myself, without you having anything to do with it. You ruined everything the last time."

"That was different," he said. "Addison just wanted to be my girlfriend. Erin isn't like that. She's—"

"I don't care," I interrupted him, bristling at the mention of Addison's name. "I don't want you choosing my friends."

"Okay," he relented. "I'll stay out of it."

"Tell that bitch, Alicia, to stay out of it too," I demanded. "If she and her minions bully my friends like Brooke did, I'll—"

"They won't," he interjected. "Nobody is going to mess with you anymore now that you're my girlfriend."

"And when I'm not?" I asked him. "What happens then? Is it going to go back to how it was before? Are you going to do everything you can to make me miserable again?"

"Are you breaking up with me?" he demanded. "Because I told you what would happen if—"

"No," I cut in. "I'm talking about when you break up with me. Like you did with all your other girlfriends."

"That's not going to happen," he declared.

That wrested a laugh from me. "No? It's true love forever? Spare me the bullshit, Mason. Just promise me that you'll leave my friends alone. For whatever your promises are worth."

"I keep my promises," he insisted.

"Really?" I questioned sarcastically. "What about your promise not to kiss me? How long did that last?"

"Not long," he acknowledged. "That one is too hard to keep, especially with you hanging all over me in that bikini."

"That was your stupid fault," I retorted. "Kidnapping me for that damned, stupid photo shoot."

"It was a hell of a hot photo shoot," he said. "It almost makes up for me having to delete that picture of you."

"Did you really delete it?" I asked, my anxiety surfacing to push aside my other emotions. "You said it wasn't only on your phone. Do you have a copy on—"

"No," he cut in. "I lied that I had another copy. I deleted it right after I showed it to you, Ella. I swear."

"How do I know that you're not lying now?" I questioned him.

"Because I'm not. If I had it, I would still be holding it over you," he admitted.

"Nice," I remarked with sarcasm. "But you can't since I could call the police on you."

"Which was another reason that I deleted it right away. I knew you would go to them sooner or later."

I believed him then, because that fit him a lot better than his story about not wanting anyone else to see me that way. I knew that he would always think of himself first, and he had been smart enough not to keep evidence that could get him caught. How he must have enjoyed tricking me into doing those humiliating things by blackmailing me with a photo that didn't exist. The thought of it burned me anew.

"You asshole," I cursed angrily. "Don't you ever touch me again! Stay the hell out of my life."

I hung up on him and dropped the phone on my bed before stalking around my room in agitation. I'd gone through all of that shit for nothing. The fear and humiliation, wearing that skimpy maid costume for him, getting down on my hands and knees to scrub his kitchen floor, cleaning his whole damn house, cooking dinner for him—which had led to him finding my poems.

None of that would have happened if I had known that he'd deleted the picture. I should have called his bluff and threatened to call the police. Hell, I should have just called them period. But I had been so scared of people seeing that picture, and of my dad finding out about it. He would have, I realized now, regardless of whether it no longer existed. Since I was a minor, the police would have notified my parents if I accused Mason of taking a nude photo of me. I was screwed either way. Mason had the upper hand, as he always did.

I heard my phone go off with a notification of a text message. It was from him, of course. *Can't stay out of your life since you're my girlfriend. Can't promise not to touch you, but promise it won't be sexual until you consent.*

I shot him back a reply. *When hell freezes over*

Satan is in for one hell of a cold spell

I snorted at his reply and set my phone down on my nightstand. Mason thought it was a foregone conclusion that I would have sex with him, but I would show him how mistaken he was. When he got tired of waiting, he would end this ridiculous charade. In the meantime, I was going to start taking back everything that he had taken from me.

He foiled my plans to talk to Alice on the bus the following morning when he showed up at my house to drive me to school. "I didn't ask you for a ride," I complained in annoyance.

"You don't have to ask," he replied. "I know you don't have a car, so I'm driving you."

"I'm fine taking the bus. In fact, I prefer it to going with you, so just go on without me."

"Are you ready?" he asked, ignoring my protests like I'd never voiced them.

With a heavy sigh, I went and got my backpack, deciding to talk to Alice later. I was not a morning person at the best of times, and I couldn't muster the energy to argue with Mason now. Besides, the passenger seat in his car was much more comfortable than sitting on the bus, although I tended to space out on the way to school regardless.

The sudden appearance of Mason's face right in front of mine startled me and got my heart racing. "We're here," he announced softly, in contrast to his aggressive, in-your-face move.

I stared at him, feeling trapped motionless against my seat. His mesmerizing eyes were bright silver in the morning light and striking in their hypnotic beauty. A smile played over his lips. "You were completely zoned out. I could have driven anywhere, and you wouldn't have noticed."

The uneasy realization that he was right brought me back to complete alertness. I had let my guard down like I trusted him. How could I keep forgetting that he was my enemy?

Shoving him aside, I spoke forcefully in an attempt to assert control over the situation. "Don't touch me! You promised no more kissing."

"I was neither touching you nor kissing you," he answered coolly.

"You were in my face," I retorted. "Why else would you be so close if you weren't trying to kiss me?"

"I was trying to get your attention without touching you, because that's what you said you want. I'm just trying to be a good boyfriend and follow your rules," he said in a smooth tone.

I looked at him to see if he was serious, and I saw him watching me with a smirk on his face. "You could never be a good boyfriend," I told him, choosing to settle for the plain truth rather than firing off an insult at him.

He frowned at me. "I can be a good boyfriend."

I rolled my eyes. "Yeah right."

"I can," he insisted.

"That would require thinking of someone besides yourself," I stated. "Which you're incapable of doing."

His expression hardened. "Give me a list," he demanded.

"A list?" I questioned.

"Tell me all the things you think make someone a good boyfriend."

He appeared to be taking this seriously, and I didn't know what to make of it. "Um, well, no cheating."

"I've never cheated on my girlfriends," he stated. "What else?"

I regarded him dubiously, wondering if that was true. "And, um…being considerate of her feelings and listening."

"I can do that," he said. "What else?"

I snorted. "You're doomed to fail from that one alone."

"Give me your complete list," he demanded. "Everything that makes a good boyfriend."

I realized that I hadn't ever thought about it so specifically. I had a general sense of how a good boyfriend behaved, but now I tried to isolate particular things. "He, uh, doesn't pressure her for sex." I gave him a pointed look.

"That goes along with being considerate of her feelings," he noted, surprising me by making that connection. "Anything else?"

I took a minute to consider what would make a great relationship. "They have conversations. He talks to her, and they have a connection."

"Conversations about what?" Mason asked, bringing me back from imagining my fantasy relationship.

"About everything," I replied. "They know each other better than anyone else knows them."

He regarded me thoughtfully. "That's your list?"

I felt a bit awkward about getting caught up in it and revealing that last part, so I didn't reflect on it any further. "Yeah," I replied and glanced away from him.

"No cheating, being considerate, listening, and talking," he listed. "The same goes for you too though."

My gaze snapped back to his. "What's the matter?" he challenged. "You don't think you can be a good girlfriend?"

"I can be a better girlfriend than you can be a boyfriend," I retorted.

"Really? Want to bet on that?"

"Sure," I agreed. "That's a bet I'll win for sure."

"What will you give me if you lose?"

"What will *you* give *me*?" I countered. "You're the one who's going to lose."

"What do you want?"

"My poem," I answered decisively. "I want it back, and I want you to stop blackmailing me."

"Done," he said, as sure of himself in this as he was about anything else. "And if I win…" He trailed off before fixing me with a heated look. "I want to see you naked again."

"I'm not having sex with you," I immediately insisted.

"I didn't say anything about sex. I won't even touch you. I just want to see you naked."

"No way!" I exclaimed. "You're not getting another naked picture of me."

"I'll give you my phone, so you'll know I can't take your picture. And you can do it at your house, so you'll know I don't have a camera set up anywhere. I'll even get naked too if you want to make sure I don't have a camera on me."

The thought of seeing him naked sent an illicit thrill through me. I shook my head, trying to clear it of such wayward thoughts. "I'm not getting naked."

"Not if you win," he goaded me. "But I can't blame you for thinking that you'll lose. I know that I can beat you at this. You don't have any experience being someone's girlfriend, so you're guaranteed to screw this up."

That did it. "That's because you didn't give me a chance to be anyone's girlfriend! You beat up my date and scared everyone off like the animal you are, so there is no way you can act human enough to win this, so you're on!"

"I'm an animal?" he enquired. "Tell me more, because that sounds very sexual."

"It's not," I snapped, even as my face heated. "You just look like a predator sometimes when you get a certain look in your eyes. I guess that's how you scare people."

"But not you," he said. "You don't seem to get scared of me, but you do get turned on. Is that what makes you wet?"

I blushed furiously. "Shut up," I ordered.

"I'm just trying to be a good boyfriend and get to know you better than anyone else knows you," he replied.

I scowled at him but had to look away from his smoldering gaze. Happening to notice the time, I used it as an excuse although I was there earlier than I would have been if I'd taken the bus. "I have to get inside!" I declared and pushed open my door to scramble out of his car.

Mason caught up to me as I hurried toward the school building. "I'll walk you to class."

"No," I protested. "I want to make friends, and I can't do that when you're with me."

"I thought that would make it easier for you to make friends," he said.

"I just told you that you intimidate people," I retorted. "That's not going to make them friendly."

"Of course it is," he stated. "They'll be too scared to piss me off, so they'll be nice to you."

"That's not what I want," I complained. "I want real friends who like me for real."

"Good luck with that," he said.

I halted and turned to look at him full on. He took another step forward before reacting to me stopping and came back to face me. "You don't think that anyone could like me for real?" I asked when I had his complete attention.

He responded with a startled expression that became dismayed. "No," he denied. "Of course, I don't think that."

"But that's what you just said," I told him. "Good luck with that," I imitated him. "That means you don't think I can make friends."

"It's not you, Ella. It's other people. Most of them are just users who only like you when they can get something from you. That's what I meant by wishing you luck finding real friends."

"Oh," I responded, feeling somewhat mollified. "Well, I don't think that everyone is like that, but I'm not rich like you, so I don't have anything they can use me for anyway."

He gave me an enigmatic look. "Don't be so sure."

I didn't know what that look meant, but it made me nervous, so I turned away from him and began to stride through the parking lot. He kept pace with me until we reached the building and he hurried forward to open the door for me.

"So," he said, his gaze lingering on me. "Whoever breaks the rules first loses the bet."

I could feel my eyes go wide with my startled response, because I hadn't really taken this bet seriously. "You said it's on," Mason reminded me. "You could get your poem back," he continued, dangling the carrot in front of me.

"And you won't retaliate?" I demanded. "You won't spread anymore lies about me and my mom?"

"I won't," he agreed. "If I can't be the boyfriend you want, then I'll let you go."

It was an offer I couldn't refuse. I had no doubt that he would lose the bet, and I could now see freedom within my reach. "Okay," I said. "It's a deal."

"And you agree to what I want if I win?" he queried.

My stomach dipped at the thought of it, but I was confident that I wouldn't have to go through with it. "Yes, but no touching," I added just to be on the safe side.

"Not unless you ask me to," he said with a heated gaze. "I didn't last time, because you weren't sober. No drinking this time. I want you completely aware of what you're doing."

That same forbidden excitement rippled through me, and I hastily put an end to the conversation. "Okay, I've got to go. Bye."

"Wait!"

I stopped in the process of rushing off and impatiently turned back toward him. "What?"

He stepped up to me with a warm smile that I had never seen him direct at anyone. "I'll see you later, Ella. Are you sure you don't want me to walk you to class?"

"Uh, no thanks," I replied.

"Okay," he said and kept smiling at me in that disconcerting way.

I felt compelled to give him a quick wave goodbye before taking off. Puzzling over his behavior, I finally realized when I was out of sight of him that he was acting that way because of the bet. He was being "considerate" and pleasant, and it was very strange.

"Hey, Ella," a girl greeted me.

I focused and saw Erin approaching me. "Hey, Erin," I replied.

"So, um, I was wondering if you'll go to a concert with me," she said.

"A concert?" I queried in confusion.

"Taylor Swift," she told me. "This Friday. I've got an extra ticket, so..."

I looked at her suspiciously. "Did Mason put you up to this?"

"What?" she questioned, appearing bewildered.

"He suggested that I should be friends with you, and all of a sudden you're inviting me to a concert? That's an awful big coincidence," I remarked.

"It is!" she agreed excitedly. "I was hoping we could be friends, and I'm glad to know that he wants us to be friends too. I'm so glad he's finally dating someone nice, because he's such a nice guy."

I regarded her incredulously. "How much is he paying you to say that?"

"Nothing," she replied, looking utterly confused for a moment. "Oh," she said as she apparently had some kind of a realization. Moving closer to me, she spoke quietly. "He told me not to tell people about him being nice, so don't let him know I told you, but he helped me when my boyfriend broke up with me. He said it was okay to wait as long as I wanted to have sex, and that I should never let anyone pressure me into anything. And he said that I was still part of his group no matter what."

I stared at her as I tried to reconcile the Mason she was describing with the one I knew. She glanced around before leaning closer to me and dropping her voice to a near whisper. "I know that Alicia would have kicked me out if Mason hadn't stood up for me."

Alicia had certainly done it before, most notably when she had edged out Brooke as queen bee after Mason broke up with her. He hadn't done a thing to stop Alicia from ruthlessly usurping her power and kicking her out of his group. From what I had heard, nobody talked to her when she sat at their table, and she had left the cafeteria in tears. While I hadn't felt a bit of sympathy for her after how she had bullied my friends, it had been yet another example of Mason's cruelty. Unlike me, she hadn't withstood it for long, and she had transferred to another school.

"So anyway," Erin said as she moved back out of my personal space, "my boyfriend was supposed to go to the concert with me, but…" She trailed off with a sigh before pinning a hopeful gaze on me. "Will you go with me, Ella? I know it's short notice, but…I mean I'll understand if you can't."

I could see how desperately she wanted me to go with her, and I couldn't turn her down. "Okay, I'll go."

Happiness shone on her face. "Oh, thank you, Ella!"

"No problem," I told her. "I like Taylor Swift." What I didn't tell her is that I often listened to Shake It Off to psych myself up to face another day at this school.

"Oh, it's going to be so much fun!" she gushed. "Oh, I should get your number, and you should have mine."

We exchanged numbers, and I couldn't help getting excited about making a friend and having plans with her. We parted when the warning bell rang, and I drifted off to class on a cloud of contentment.

Until I received a text from Mason. *I miss you already. Can't wait to see you again*

I rolled my eyes, thinking that he was really overdoing it. Then I realized that I was doing nothing to win this bet. I racked my brain, trying to think of a response that would top him, but I couldn't come up with anything. My mind rebelled at the words I had settled on, but I sent them anyway. *Miss you too*

His response got an actual smile out of me. *Liar!*

Inspiration struck, and I typed with quick enthusiasm. *Yeah, but you started it!*

Not true. I really can't wait to see you. It's always the most exciting part of my day

I stared at the words, trying to tamp down on the feeling they gave me and convince myself that they were just part of this stupid bet. The truth came out in my response. *You've always been the most exciting part of my day too, even when I hated you*

I immediately regretted sending him that text, but I consoled myself that he would think it was just bullshit for the bet. His response came quickly. *You don't hate me anymore?*

I struggled over how to respond until I came up with what I thought was the perfect, sarcastic reply. *How can I when you're such a great boyfriend?*

There was no response from Mason, and I settled back in my seat in satisfaction as class began. All I had to do was wait for him to lose this bet, and I was sure that it wouldn't take long. Words were easy, but his actions would trip him up. He wouldn't be able to contain his true nature, and then I would finally be free of him.

My eyes zeroed in on Josh, and I caught him watching me. Speaking of being free, I thought, even though his gaze slid away from me. I knew that he was interested, and that many guys who saw me were attracted to me. I didn't often reflect on my looks, since it was a hated reminder of how much I looked like my mother. I hadn't ever wanted to use my beauty the way she did, but I knew that I turned male heads, and that the only thing holding them back from approaching me was Mason. Josh was no exception.

"Hey," I said to him as I hurried to catch him at his desk after class and slip him the piece of paper I had prepared for him. "Here's my number. You can text me anytime."

He looked at me in surprise but shoved the paper into his pocket. None too soon either, since Mason appeared in the doorway as we approached it. He was apparently continuing to play the caring boyfriend and had come to walk me to the class we had together. "So, did you get to talk to anyone you want to be friends with?" he asked.

"Only the person you want me to be friends with," I retorted, still a bit annoyed over his interruption of my planned talk with Josh.

"Erin? How did that go?" he enquired.

"We're going to a concert on Friday. Taylor Swift," I revealed with a short laugh, remembering how we had just mentioned her yesterday.

He responded with a laugh himself. "That's a funny coincidence. We were just talking about her concerts. I told you it's a girl thing."

"Hey!" I admonished him. "Stop being a sexist jerk."

Realization immediately dawned on his face. "You're right. I'm sorry."

I laughed at him. "You are trying so damn hard! It's hilarious. I should really torture you and make you do all kinds of things you hate to prove you're a good boyfriend. Too bad Erin doesn't have another ticket."

"If you want me to go to the concert, I will," he said.

"Yeah right," I replied. "It's probably sold out by now anyway."

"There are always scalpers selling tickets for double their worth," he told me. "All you have to do is say the word, and I'll go with you."

"I'm actually looking forward to some girl time," I told him, and then wondered why I felt the need to explain my rejection of his offer. I should have just said that I'd rather go with anyone else but him. Oh, but the bet, I remembered. I was supposed to be considerate of his feelings. As if he had any.

"What's that look for?" he questioned. "What'd I do?"

"Nothing, sweetheart," I said with false sweetness. "You're perfect."

"Hey," he said and gently took hold of my arm to steer me to the side and out of the way of all the students walking through the hallway. "What's wrong?"

"Nothing, honeybunch," I replied, laying it on thick. "You're the best boyfriend in the world."

"Okay, stop with that," he demanded. "Part of this is talking, so be honest."

"You want me to be honest?" I questioned rhetorically. "I don't think so. That wouldn't be very considerate of your feelings, *sweetheart*. You're not going to trick me into losing this bet," I added derisively.

"Forget about the damned bet," he retorted. "I won't hold it against you to be honest about your feelings. You probably need to vent at me before you can forgive me, so let it out."

"What if I can't forgive you?" I shot back. "Did you ever think of that, huh? No, of course you didn't, because it would never occur to you that you might not get your way."

He seemed completely taken aback by my rant, and his expression became troubled. "But there has to be something I can do to earn your forgiveness," he exclaimed. "I know it'll take time, and I'm not expecting it to happen overnight. I know I did a lot of shitty things, so I've got a lot to make up for, but it's not *impossible*."

I just regarded him with a flat expression and said nothing in response.

"Think up things for me to do to atone," he demanded in frustration. "I'll prove to you that I'm sorry."

The bell rang, and I huffed in annoyance. "Now I'm late again. I'm not going to have the teachers thinking bad of me too!" I rushed away from him and hurried down the hall to the classroom.

I was aware of him right behind me, but I ignored him as we quickly took our seats. Unfortunately, our classmates had saved us seats right next to each other again, and I could see Mason watching me out of my peripheral vision. I was therefore tense and distracted the entire time, and barely able to focus on the lecture. Although I would be able to make up for it by reading the textbook, it still irked me that Mason could affect my concentration.

I was glad to put him out of sight, since he wasn't in my next class. I smiled in triumph when I received a text from Josh. *Now you have my number too*

He was being cautious with what he wrote me, and I knew that he wouldn't dare make a move unless I did first. I was so unfamiliar with flirting though, so I just decided to be straightforward. *I'd like to see you outside of school*

Did Mason break up with you?

I thought for a minute about how to word my reply and just ended up going with honesty. *No. This has nothing to do with him. Can we have our own thing?*

It took him awhile to respond, but he agreed. *As long as we're VERY careful. He can't find out EVER!*

I smiled in amusement at his paranoia. *Our secret, I PROMISE. I'll let you know when I can see you*

Okay. Can't wait!

I was excited at the prospect of a clandestine rendezvous. My life was becoming more adventurous and busy. There were suddenly all these possibilities, and I resented Mason anew for denying me all of this for so long.

I walked into the cafeteria with fire in my blood this time and took my place beside him like it was my right. He owed me much more than a seat at his table, but he flabbergasted me when he stood up and shouted to get the attention of everyone in the vicinity.

"Hey! Everyone listen! I've got something to tell you."

He continued to speak loudly even as the room went silent. "I lied to everyone about Ella Chase. Her mother is not an escort. I made that up, because there is some bad blood between our families. Ella is a nice girl who didn't deserve any of the crap I threw at her, and I'm very sorry for the way I treated her."

His gaze swept over the people seated in the cafeteria before focusing on me. "I'm sorry I was an asshole to you, Ella. Please forgive me."

Heat flared in my cheeks from the embarrassment of being put on the spot like that, and I stared at him in dismay. His gaze lifted from mine, and his voice rang out again. "Okay, that's all I wanted to say. Go back to what you were doing."

He sat down, and conversation resumed, although a lot of it was about us judging by how many eyes I felt watching me. I still hadn't recovered enough to respond, and everyone else at our table remained silent too.

Alicia was the first one to open her mouth. "So now you're going to change her from a hooker into a good girl?" she sneered. "What is this? Pretty Woman? Are you *in love*?"

"Shut up, Alicia," Mason snapped. "I told you never to call her that again."

"Or what?" she challenged. "You'll break my leg? I thought you guys had some kind of honor code about not hurting women."

"Hey!" Josh exclaimed. "Is she in the family too? I mean like a rival family. You said there was bad blood between your families. Is that what you meant?"

"Like a Romeo and Juliet situation," Erin commented excitedly.

"Well," Mason said, "I can't talk about that kind of stuff, but…" He let the sentence hang as he fixed a hard gaze on Alicia. "You might not want to mess with Ella. Let's just say that the women in her family can be lethal, and they don't follow the same rules as my family."

I stared at him in shock over how easily he had been able to use the word lethal in relation to my mom, like it didn't bother him at all, when I knew how deep that wound still was. My reaction apparently helped to sell his story, because Alicia looked at me with a wary gaze.

"Sorry," she muttered.

"Don't let it happen again," Mason replied for me, and I felt like I was in some kind of an alternate reality where he was on my side and Alicia was afraid of me.

Josh added to the affect when he pulled me aside in the hallway later that day. "So, you're some kind of mafia princess?" he asked me secretively.

I shook my head at him. "I can't believe how you people buy into all of his bullshit."

"I know you can't talk about it," he continued as if I hadn't just refuted it all as bullshit. "I'm just glad to know that Mason isn't forcing you."

I practically melted at those words. What a sweetheart! Mason had told me that Josh was a selfish player, but Mason was a liar. I had witnessed it often enough myself, and I should know better than to trust anything he said. "Thanks," I told Josh sincerely. "I really appreciate that you care."

"A guy forcing himself on a girl is not a real man," he declared vehemently. "My dad told me how he beat the crap out of a guy who did that. The girl was too ashamed to press charges, but my dad and his buddies took care of him for her."

My eyes were wide with amazement. "Wow," I breathed, impressed and imagining his dad going after bad guys vigilante style. Josh had just become more interesting to me, and I was now hanging on his every word.

His fierce expression changed as he looked at me, and it was one I recognized as male interest in me. I found it flattering coming from a decent guy like him, and I suddenly felt shy about flirting my way into kissing him. "You're a great guy," I told him bashfully.

He looked away from me for a moment and then returned his gaze to me. "You're a special girl, Ella. I don't like going behind Mason's back. I wouldn't normally ever do that to a friend, but I can't stop thinking about you. I know it's wrong, but…"

"Mason and I aren't really," I began, wanting to put his mind at ease. "I can't go into the reasons why, but we're only pretending to date. Don't tell anyone that," I pleaded.

"Okay," he agreed uncertainly, looking confounded by my revelation. "So, he won't care if we're—"

"Oh, he'll care," I interjected and then scrambled for an explanation. "He doesn't want people to know we're faking, so he wouldn't want people to think I'm cheating with you."

AS soon as those words were out of my mouth, I suddenly realized the consequences for me. I hadn't even considered my defiance against Mason as cheating, but now it hit me that it would violate the terms of our bet. "He can't find out!" I said urgently.

"Then people shouldn't see us talking like this," Josh replied with a quick, nervous glance at the stream of students walking past us in the hallway.

"You're right," I agreed. "I'd better go."

I rushed off anxiously, worried now that someone would tell Mason about me and Josh. He couldn't get me for just talking to him though. That wasn't cheating. I hadn't actually done anything yet, and it wasn't too late to call the whole thing off.

Two things prevented me from doing that. One was that it bothered me that Mason held the distinction of being the only guy I had kissed, and I wanted to change that as soon as possible. The second thing was that I could actually see myself falling for Josh, and I didn't want to let go of him now that I had found a guy I liked—especially not because of

Mason. I wouldn't let him stand in my way yet again. I was going to have what I wanted for once.

I drifted into pleasant daydreams in class as I imagined going to Homecoming and prom with Josh and posing for pictures together at both dances. Which was why my reaction to Mason asking me to Homecoming was doubly disturbing. Excitement coursed through me as I immediately pictured myself dancing in his arms. I just barely suppressed the urge to exclaim yes, but I managed to regain my composure and answer him in what I hoped was cool detachment. "You're getting a little ahead of yourself. Homecoming is a ways away."

"Two months," he said. "I want to go to prom with you too, but I think it's too early to ask you to that."

I turned my head to stare at him and stumbled with my attention not on where I was going. Mason quickly took hold of me to steady me, and we came to a stop with one of his hands on my waist and the other on my arm. The contact felt good, and attraction sparked between us as our gazes locked. My breathing became uneven as he bent his head closer to mine, and I closed my eyes in anticipation.

"Ella," he said, the sound of his voice and the feel of his breath ghosting over my lips sending a thrill through me. "I want to kiss you."

My heartbeat kept pace with the frenzied fluttering in my stomach as my anticipation became nearly unbearable. "Please," I breathed.

"Do you want me to kiss you, Ella? I can't until you ask me to."

Even as feeling him speak the words made my lips tingle with desire, the reason he was saying them penetrated through my haze of lust. My rules. He had promised not to kiss me until I asked him to. I'd finally gotten Mason to follow one of my rules, and I had almost given up the little bit of power I had over him. My eyes snapped open, and I pushed him away.

Heat flared in my cheeks over how close I had come to succumbing to him again. Even worse was that desperate please I had voiced. I expected him to taunt me with that, and I turned face and fled toward where my bus was parked. Mason quickly caught up to me and got in my way.

"Where are you going?" he demanded. "I'm driving you home."

"No," I argued. "I'm taking the bus."

"Don't be difficult," he snapped. "I didn't break the rules, so you have no reason to—"

"I am difficult," I declared. "You should just break up with me right now if you want an easy girlfriend."

His lips twitched in amusement. "I know you're not easy."

"You know what I mean," I retorted, too annoyed to be embarrassed by the sexual implications of that word.

"I do know what you mean," he said and fixed an intense gaze on me. "Either way, I don't care if you're not easy. You're mine, and I'm not breaking up with you."

My heartbeat accelerated again, and I had to look away from him to be able to think. "You said you'd be considerate of my feelings," I finally said, "and I feel like taking the bus home."

"Fine," he relented in frustration. "Go on the damn bus."

I needed no further encouragement and bolted around him. He scowled but made no move to stop me this time. Distance from him was exactly what I needed to stop craving that kiss we almost had. Why was I so incredibly attracted to him?

It didn't help that he started sending me text messages as soon as I got on the bus, and I wasn't strong enough to resist reading them. *I want to kiss you so bad I can't stand it*

Your lips were so close I could almost taste them. I wanted to lick them and suck them, and slide my tongue into your mouth

I want to kiss you deep and long

It hardly seemed like he was referring to kissing anymore, and my body was responding to his deliberately sexual choice of words, which was probably his intention. Vowing to ignore his texts, I nevertheless immediately read the next one he sent.

You were so sexy. All breathless and ready for me

I finally replied to him. *Stop texting and driving!*

Do you care if something happens to me? Would you miss me?

I was taken aback by those questions and was at a loss at how to respond. No seemed like too harsh of an answer. I thought about being free of him that way but felt no satisfaction imagining it. *I don't want anything to happen to you*

 But would you miss me?

I didn't want to deal with that question. *Don't make me find out. Stop texting and driving!*

I'm still in the school parking lot. Wishing you were here with me. So I could kiss you

I smiled at his reply. *Go home*

Come over. PLEASE

I was sorely tempted to do just that and indulge in the kissing he was offering me. I just barely restrained myself by thinking about how much he would gloat if I gave in. Getting a text from Josh also helped.

Hi Ella. How are you?

Good. How are you?

I have ice cream. That one was from Mason, and the rest of it was more temptation. *I want to kiss you after you eat it. Your mouth will be cold and sweet, and mine will be hot and hungry after watching you take delicious spoonfuls*

Good. Was wondering when we can get together to work on that class project

That one was from Josh, and I appreciated how cautious and careful he was being about texting me. I was careful in my response only in making sure that I was sending it to him and not Mason. Damn him! I was now craving not only him but ice cream as well. I was glad to have Josh for a distraction.

How about now? I'm almost home. Do you have a way to get here? I texted him my address too.

I have a car. Not as nice as some people's cars, but it runs. Will be there soon

That was clearly a reference to Mason's nice car, and I wondered if Josh was jealous over it. I wondered if he would still be jealous if he knew that Mason lived alone. Maybe he did know, since they were friends.

Why was I still thinking about Mason? I should be excited about seeing Josh. And thinking about kissing Josh. So that I could stop thinking about kissing Mason. I could so clearly imagine it that I could almost taste the cold ice cream in my mouth and how it would feel to have Mason's hot mouth mingle with that coldness.

Guess I'll have to go home and eat that ice cream by myself

I knew that was meant to entice me, but it actually seemed like a forlorn statement about how alone he was living there by himself. He didn't deserve my sympathy though, since he'd never had any for me. He had been mean and ruthless and done everything in his power to make me miserable. I wasn't going to allow myself to soften towards him now that he'd supposedly given up on his vendetta against me. I didn't want to be with him. It was much too late for that.

I was going to start fresh with a new guy. A guy who truly was considerate and deserving of my attention. Josh had all the attributes of a great boyfriend, and he was attractive. Not as attractive as Mason, but still much better than average. He was the one I would kiss. Then I would forget all about kissing Mason. Damn it, I had to stop thinking about Mason!

Once I saw Josh, it was a little easier to focus entirely on him. His timing was perfect, because he pulled into my driveway just as I reached my front door. I went to meet him as he exited his car, and I took a better look at him than I had before. He really was handsome with his dark good looks. His eyes were a deep brown that I noticed could really draw you in when they were focused on you with that sensual look he was giving me now.

"Hey," I greeted him flirtatiously, finding it surprisingly easy to flirt with him.

"Hey," he responded and wasted no time closing the distance between us.

He leaned in and pressed his lips to mine in a brief, tentative kiss. Pulling back, he smiled at me. "Hey," he repeated.

"Hey," I responded as I smiled back at him.

It was a sweet and cute real boyfriend kind of thing to do, and it would have been the perfect, innocent first kiss if Mason hadn't gotten there first and ruined it for me. My first kiss with him had been so hot and exciting that it completely overshadowed this tame kiss with Josh.

That was because I hadn't gotten to that point with Josh yet though. He was pacing himself and doing things the right way, while nothing with Mason was the way it was supposed to be. He had skipped right over a proper first kiss and seduced me into French kissing him.

No, I chided myself. I wasn't going to think about Mason while I was with Josh. I could finally let things happen naturally with a guy I liked, without Mason's interference. So, I just had to be patient and let Josh sweep me off my feet.

"Do you want to come in?" I invited him, and it all felt so proper and stilted.

This is what you want, I admonished myself. A nice guy who respects you. This was the way it was supposed to be. It would take time to form a connection and lose our inhibitions with each other. We weren't supposed to feel wild passion for each other immediately. My messed-up experiences with Mason had skewed my expectations.

Ugh, I felt like screaming in frustration at myself for letting my thoughts constantly circle back to the last guy I should ever be thinking about. "Josh," I said to reinforce my focus on him. "I'm glad you're here. I've always liked you."

"Yeah?" he questioned, looking pleased.

"Yes," I lied, although it was partially true. I had liked him since I started paying attention to him at Mason's party, but I had barely noticed him before that. I could have had a crush on him for all he knew, so there was no harm in letting him think that.

"I like you too, Ella," he told me. "You're—"

"Well, hi there," Mom interrupted him and threw an impressed look at me. "Who is this fine young man, Ella?"

"This is Josh," I replied. "Josh, this is my mom," I introduced her reluctantly, hoping that she wouldn't say anything embarrassing.

Her gaze was already on him again as I spoke, and she was blatantly ogling him. That was sadly not that surprising to me considering how she had checked out Mason, albeit with a bit more subtleness since my dad had been home then. What was more unexpected was how Josh was staring at her.

Yeah, she was flaunting her body in her short shorts and midriff-baring tank top, but he wasn't even trying to look away. Her ego inflated like a hot air balloon, and her smile grew even more vain and self-satisfied. "Hello, Josh, it's *so* nice to meet you," she flirted.

He seemed momentarily speechless before responding in an apparent daze. "Yes."

Having had enough, I took action to remove him from her presence. "We're going to my room," I announced and took hold of his hand to lead him away.

He went with me but turned his head to look back at her. It was disappointing to see this weakness in him, and disturbing to realize that Mason had withstood her sexual allure better than Josh. Then again, Mason hated my mother.

But he had hated me too, and that hadn't stopped him from being attracted to me. The realization that I was thinking about Mason again prompted me to aggressively kiss

Josh as soon as we entered my room. I wanted to drive all thoughts of Mason out of my head and replace him with Josh.

He was startled at first, but he was soon kissing me back. I tried to replicate the passion I had experienced with Mason, and I threw myself into the kiss with determination. I pulled him into me and plunged my tongue into his mouth in search of the spark that would inflame me, but I couldn't find it. I was too aware of myself and what I was doing and too able to evaluate how he was kissing me instead of becoming lost in the sensations I was feeling. There was nothing wrong with his technique, but he was lacking the hot, hungry urgency that Mason had when he kissed me—like he couldn't get enough of me.

His kiss didn't thrill me, even when he got more into it and started running his hands down my back and slipped them under my shirt to touch my skin. I pulled away from him and took a step back. He looked at me with a heated gaze, and I wondered why I wasn't as attracted to him as I was to Mason.

It didn't matter though, because Josh was the kind of guy I should be with. He wasn't antagonistic or cruel, and I could have a normal relationship with him. That was more important than lust. In fact, I should be glad that I didn't have to worry about succumbing to temptation and going too far with him. He would be the perfect first boyfriend for me.

"So," he said and just let the word hang between us.

"So…" I trailed off too as I sought the words to establish the relationship we had begun. "Um, do you want to be…uh, do you want to go out with me?" I asked awkwardly.

"You mean date?" he questioned.

"Yes," I answered. "It would have to be a secret for now. Just until I break up with Mason. Not that we're really dating, but he can't know about us yet."

Josh ran a hand through his hair and expelled a breath forcefully. "Are you sure that you can keep this a secret? I mean you can't tell anyone, not even your best friend."

"I don't have a best friend anymore," I told him. "She turned out to be a backstabbing bitch."

"Good," he responded before realizing what he'd said. "I mean good that you won't be telling her. But I know that you wouldn't anyway, since you know how dangerous he is."

I snorted. "Mason is not dangerous. That mafia story he told you is all bullshit. Seriously, Josh, he's just a liar."

"Then why are you afraid of him finding out about us?" he challenged.

"I'm not afraid," I insisted. "Well," I hedged, "I'm not afraid of Mason. It's just that we made this bet, and I don't want to lose."

Josh's expression became bewildered. "A bet? About what?"

"I can't tell you," I replied. "But I have to wait until he loses it to break up with him. If he finds out about this before then, I'll lose."

"Um, okay," he said uncertainly, obviously not sure what to believe.

"So," I began in a tentative tone, "we can go out? As long as we keep it a secret?"

His expression smoothed out as he studied me, and his voice sounded more confident when he spoke. "We probably can't go out on dates if we want to keep this a secret, Ella. If someone sees us out together, it'll get back to Mason. It's best to meet in private like this, don't you think?"

Disappointment deflated my hopeful mood. Mason was still ruining things for me even unknowingly. I'd managed to defy him, but it wasn't the satisfying victory I had expected. I had wanted to go out on real dates with Josh and get the full boyfriend experience that I had missed out on, but Mason was still preventing me from having that.

"You're right," I acknowledged, and Josh smiled at me.

He seemed okay with this situation at least. He could have just decided that it wasn't worth the trouble of sneaking around and being so limited about where we could go, but he was willing to do this for me. He must really like me if he was willing to wait for me to be free. That thought buoyed my spirits, and I smiled back at him.

"So," he said as he stepped closer to me, "where were we?"

I backed away as he leaned in for a kiss, and I didn't think to question that instinct until later. The notification of a text message on my phone saved me from having to come up with an excuse for dodging his kiss. I snapped to attention when I saw it was from Mason.

I'm eating that ice cream and thinking of you as I lick it off the spoon. Come over and get some Ella

The heat that had been absent from my interactions with Josh flared within me as I read Mason's message. "He's coming over," I lied. "You have to go."

Josh reacted in panic, and I felt bad. "He's just leaving his house now. It'll take him some time to get here," I assured him as I followed him in his rush out of my room.

He didn't answer as he hurried down the stairs and yanked open the front door to dash out to his car. I ran outside after him, but he didn't spare me a look as he got in his car and peeled out of my driveway. Despite everything I'd said, his fear of Mason apparently hadn't lessened one bit.

He believed Mason over me, but I tried not to hold that against him. After all, he had known Mason much longer than he had known me. And hadn't I just lied to him myself?

The question was why. Why had I wanted Josh to leave? Why hadn't I wanted him to kiss me again? And why was I still tempted to go see Mason?

Ice cream, I decided. I wanted ice cream. That was the only reason.

My first instinct was to call Zoey, but then I remembered that she was still in school since the middle school got out later than the high school. Recalling my desire to make friends, I thought of Erin first, but I had already connected with her today, and she also had an unfortunate association with Mason. I was suddenly desperate for someone who could make me forget about him, and I knew just the person. She was from the time before Mason had wreaked havoc with my life, and I was nostalgic for those simple, uncomplicated times.

I wasn't sure if she still had the same phone number, so I just went to her house and rang the doorbell. Alice stood there staring at me when she answered the door.

"Hi," I said. "Want to go get ice cream? My treat."

She glanced around warily, like someone might be lying in wait off to the side of me beyond her sight. "I wish I could, Ella, but—"

"It's okay," I assured her. "Mason is not going to retaliate against you. He said I can be friends with whoever I want."

Her gaze sharpened, and her mouth compressed in disapproval before she spoke. "That's it, Ella, you need to go to the police. It was bad enough when he was bullying you, but you can't let him abuse you like this."

"What?" I exclaimed. "Why would you think he's abusing me? He's never hit me or anything. All he did was tell people lies about me. That's all. He's an asshole, but he's not abusive."

"You have to have his permission to have friends," she countered. "That's one of the signs of an abusive boyfriend. He isolates you from people so that you have nobody but him."

"But he's doing the opposite," I argued. "He's stopped doing all that, and now he's letting me make friends."

"Letting you," Alice repeated scornfully. "What a great boyfriend. He's letting you do something that you have every right to do. Open your eyes, Ella. You have to see how screwed up that is."

I sighed heavily. "I do know how screwed up it is, and you don't even know the half of it."

Her righteous anger was replaced with a troubled expression, and she pulled the door open wider. "Come in," she invited me solemnly.

I stepped inside hesitantly, glancing around at the familiar surroundings where I'd once felt so comfortable and welcome. Alice had been my best friend in middle school, and we had spent lots of time over each other's houses. She had tried to secretly continue our friendship outside of school after Mason started targeting my friends, but I had been too paranoid about him finding out and causing more trouble for her. I wouldn't even let her text me or call me for fear that he was somehow keeping tabs on my phone. I had severed all ties with her in order to protect her, and being back here was a bittersweet reminder of the time I had lost with her. We had only just started high school the last time I was here, and we were seniors now. We had once known everything about each other, but things had changed for both of us since that innocent, carefree time in our lives when neither of us had yet been kissed. I wasn't sure where to start to bridge the gap of those years.

"Nobody else is home," Alice told me. "So we can talk without worrying about anyone overhearing us."

I smiled faintly, because we were the ones who were always eavesdropping on the conversations of her older sister and her friends. "How is Madison?" I enquired.

"Good," Alice replied. "She's a sophomore at UCF, so she actually did more than work on her tan last year. I thought for sure she just had her sights set on the beaches when she picked a college in Florida, but she's doing really well. I guess she really did find her passion."

"Oh?" I responded in surprise. "What's she taking?"

"Theme Park Management," Alice answered. "I didn't even know that major existed, but leave it to Madison to find the only college in the country that has it."

"That's actually perfect for her," I said, marveling over it. "She always loved working at Six Flags."

"I know," Alice agreed, "but I didn't know she could make a career out of that. I expected her to try to become a professional cheerleader for one of those NFL teams."

That wasn't a farfetched assumption, since Madison had been into cheerleading from a young age and had ended up being captain of the cheerleading squad in high school. She was as popular and outgoing as Alice was shy and introverted. They were polar opposites, but they got along alright despite the typical sibling squabbling. I had often wished that I had a sister too, and I wondered if Mason wished that he had a brother or sister. Then he wouldn't be living in that house alone, and he would have family by his side. Even if they argued and got on each other's nerves, he would still...

Shit, I was thinking about Mason again. I had to stop that. I didn't care about him or his troubles. Poor little rich boy. Who cared if he was lonely or abandoned? That was his bullshit excuse to act like an asshole. If he was a decent person, then he would have had real friends to fill the void of his absent mother and deceased father. His dad was a selfish bastard anyway. And Mason had been away at boarding school, so it wasn't like he wasn't used to being away from his parents.

I started to imagine him in a Harry Potter situation, unwanted by his family and being taken to an enormous school where he didn't know anyone. Had he made any real friends there? I remembered then that it had been his choice to leave that place and move here, so he must not have been attached to it if he could leave it behind so easily—for me. My heart skipped a beat at the thought of him coming for me. But it wasn't like that. He had been hellbent on revenge rather than prompted by passion and desire. I was romanticizing him again and I had to stop before I lost my resolve. I couldn't let him win.

"So, you and Mason," Alice said, making me snap guiltily back to attention with the uneasy feeling that she had guessed that I was thinking about him. "How did that happen?"

My skin flushed with embarrassment, and I tried to make up a story she might believe. I couldn't do it though, because she was my best friend, and I had never lied to her before. "I've got a lot to tell you," I said.

She nodded. "Yeah, I would guess so. Let's sit down," she suggested. "Do you want something to drink?"

"That's what got me in trouble in the first place," I muttered, flashing back in disgust on Addison urging me to drink.

Alice raised an eyebrow as she regarded me, and heat crept over my face again. "Uh, just water please," I told her.

"Have a seat," she replied and gestured toward the living room before walking off to the kitchen.

I used the short time she was gone to compose myself and attempt to plan out what I was going to say. I was standing nervously beside the couch when she returned with two bottles of water.

"It's okay, Ella," she said. "You know you can tell me anything, so relax and stop wringing your hands like I'm going to punish you. This isn't the principal's office. Yeah, I heard about that," she added when I looked at her sheepishly. "You must have been a nervous wreck, knowing you."

"I was," I confirmed, relaxing a bit with the realization of how well she knew me, and that she wouldn't judge me as harshly as people who didn't and make assumptions about my character.

She handed me one of the water bottles, and I sat down on the couch as she sat down on the coffee table in front of me. I smiled at this little quirk of hers that her mother always yelled at her for. It was such a familiar memory. Alice always liked to sit on the coffee table. When we were talking, she would face me like she was now. When we were watching TV, she would sit on the other side closer to the TV and lean forward as she gazed at the screen.

"I've missed you so much," I said, my voice suddenly heavy with emotion.

"Me too," she responded with the same emotion in her words and her expression. "I missed you, Ella. It hasn't been the same without you, and I hated him for doing this to us, and I know that you hate him too. So how has he forced you to be with him?" she demanded. "I know that you wouldn't be if he wasn't forcing you."

I hoped that she would attribute the deep blush staining my cheeks red to what I was about to tell her, because I would be ashamed for her to know that I was still attracted to him after everything that he had done. "Addison tricked me into getting drunk, and he took a naked picture of me."

Alice gaped at me in shock before regaining the ability to speak. "That's blackmail! You have to go to the police," she exclaimed in outrage.

"He deleted it," I told her quickly, "but, um, he's got something else. A poem I wrote, about him," I admitted reluctantly.

She blinked as she absorbed that and tried to make sense of it. "A poem? Who cares?"

Heat suffused my face. "It's a sexual poem. I wrote it before I knew how he was," I lied, my shame greater than my hatred of lying to her. "It's on the back of an old homework paper, and it's got my name on it."

"He could have written it himself for all anybody knows," she declared. "He's got nothing."

"You know how people always believe him," I said. "They believed that he was in the freaking mafia for goodness sake."

"What?" she asked in dismay.

I filled her in on his story of being in witness protection and alluding to ties to the mafia, and we both laughed at the utter ridiculousness of it. "Did you tell them where he really got his money from?" she questioned.

I sobered. "No. I didn't want to get into that."

Alice was the only person I had told about my mom's connection to Mason's dad. I knew that she wasn't responsible for his death, but him dying in bed with her wasn't something I wanted to advertise. Alice understood that. "You could have just told them that your mom worked as a maid in his house," she suggested.

I waved that off. "It doesn't matter what they believe about him."

"It would prove that he's been lying to them," she argued.

"It's still his word against mine," I retorted, "and they always believe him."

"So what?" she said. "Even if they believe you wrote that poem, so what? They believed much worse things about you, and you got through it. This is nothing compared to that."

I averted my gaze from hers, unable to look her in the eye with the shameful answer floating around in my head. Because those things weren't true, and this was. That was why I couldn't just shrug it off. That was why I didn't want anyone to know.

"Ella," she began, and the suspicion in her voice made my heart pound that she had figured it out and was about to call me on it. "Did he really delete that picture or is he still blackmailing you with it?"

I breathed in relief. "He deleted it. Mr. Delaney even looked through his phone after Addison accused him of having it, and it was gone."

"So, Addison told on him?" Alice asked. "She felt guilty for getting you drunk? But wait, how did he get a picture of you? Were you at a party?"

"We were at her house," I explained bitterly. "She set me up." I went on to elaborate on Addison's betrayal and how she had only been pretending to be my friend.

"That's awful," Alice said, seeming to momentarily lose herself in somber contemplation of it. When her gaze refocused on me, a look of reproach entered her eyes. "Why'd you decide to be friends with her?"

I heard the note of hurt in her voice, and I realized that she thought I had chosen Addison over her. "Because she was the only one he would let me be friends with," I explained. "She wasn't important to me, so I took a chance when she started talking to me. I kept thinking that he was going to do something to stop her, but he didn't. Now I know why. He was using her to get to me."

"And this is the guy you're dating," she remarked. "I think I'd rather be embarrassed in front of everyone than go out with him."

"We're not really dating," I said. "We're just pretending to, because..." I trailed off, since I didn't have a good reason for that besides Mason demanding that I do it. "Well, anyway, he's not really my boyfriend."

"So, how long are you going to pretend that he is?" she questioned. "And why would he need to pretend to have a girlfriend when he can easily get a real one? Girls are constantly flirting with him."

I felt a stab of jealousy at the reminder, and I chose to focus solely on her first question. "Until he loses our bet," I replied. "He bet me that he could be a good boyfriend, and he'll give me back my poem when he loses."

Alice regarded me with a perplexed expression. "What are the criteria of him being a good boyfriend? What does he have to do to lose the bet?"

"Cheat, be inconsiderate of my feelings, basically be himself," I stated. "There is no way he can win this bet."

"What does he get if he wins?"

My gaze slid away from hers as I shifted my legs nervously. "It's impossible for him to win. This is Mason we're talking about. He could never be a good boyfriend. You should have seen the way he treated Addison. I would have felt sorry for her if she wasn't such a backstabbing bitch."

"He was her boyfriend?" Alice asked in surprise. "When? I never heard anything about that."

"That's because he dumped her the same day he went public with her, but he was secretly her boyfriend the whole time she was pretending to be my friend. That's why she helped him set me up."

"Wow, that is messed up," Alice said. "I guess it really backfired on her when he dumped her for you."

"What? He didn't," I denied.

She gave me a pointed look. "Come on, Ella. He broke up with his girlfriend so that you could pretend to be his girlfriend? That doesn't make any sense. He obviously wants to be with you."

"Well I don't want to be with him," I retorted.

"You did once," she reminded me. "This would have been your dream come true back then. Are you really doing this because of some silly poem, or are you living out your fantasy from middle school?"

She knew me so well, and she had hit right at the heart of my conflicted feelings for Mason. She was the only one I had told about him, and she had witnessed some of my heartbreak over him before he severed our friendship.

"I'm not sure," I admitted, deciding to share some of the truth with her. "Sometimes it feels like that. Like when he wore the tux and acted like my boyfriend. It was how I used to imagine him before I knew what he was really like."

"I heard that he apologized to you in the cafeteria today in front of all of his friends," she said.

"He did," I confirmed. "He told them he's been lying about me and my mom."

"So, you forgave him?" she asked.

"No," I declared. "He doesn't get to just say he's sorry after all of that."

"Did you tell him that?" she questioned.

"Yeah," I replied. "He says he's going to make it up to me, but I don't see how he can. I'm just going to get my poem back and be done with him."

She regarded me with a troubled expression. "Do you really think he'll let you? He hasn't left you alone the whole time he's been here. What makes you think it'll be different now?"

"Because it will be," I stated.

I couldn't explain it to her, but somehow I just felt it in my gut. Of course, the last time I'd had such a strong, intuitive feeling was when I saw Mason's picture and knew with my whole being that he was my one true love, and my instincts had been so completely wrong about that.

Chapter 11

Reviving my friendship with Alice made me feel like something was right with my life though. It gave me the boost I needed, the one that starting a relationship with Josh had failed to provide. I guessed that romance couldn't compare to the comfort of a true friend. She was someone I could trust and be myself with, and she accepted me the way I was. Within a short time, I felt as comfortable with her as if we had never been apart. I had already confided my secret rendezvous with Josh to her. The only thing I was holding back on was my shameful attraction to Mason, but I hardly even wanted to admit that to myself.

She had given me a skeptical look when I told her about Josh. "Isn't he one of them?"

I knew that "them" referred to Mason's crowd. "Yeah, but he's never been mean to me. He's actually a nice guy."

"How nice can he be if he's going behind Mason's back with you? Did you tell him that you're not really dating Mason?"

"Yes," I replied.

"Oh," she responded. "That's different I guess. But I still don't like it. What if Mason finds out? What do you think he'll do? He might show everyone your poem for spite. Isn't that what you're trying to avoid?"

A strange thrill of fear and excitement shot through me at the thought of what he would do, and I took a shaky breath before speaking. "He won't find out. Josh knows to keep it a secret, and we're being careful. I'm not going to let Mason keep me from having this. He's not going to keep me from anything I want anymore. Not friends or dating or anything. Once he loses this bet, I'm done with him for good."

"I hope so," she said with a sigh. "This whole situation is so messed up. How did he go from hating you to wanting you to be his girlfriend?"

"He said it was reading my poems," I told her with an embarrassed laugh. "He took my notebook from my room, and—"

"He was in your room?" Alice exclaimed. "He was in your *house*? Was your mom there?"

"Uh, yeah," I answered uneasily. "He invited himself to dinner, and—"

"What did he say to her?" she questioned urgently, interrupting me again.

"Nothing," I replied. "He just introduced himself, but she didn't know who he was."

"And he didn't tell her?" Alice asked in disbelief.

I shook my head. "No. My stomach was in knots the whole time waiting for him to confront her or say something about that picture, but he didn't. He was really pissed off though, even though he didn't show it in front of them."

"I thought you said he deleted the picture?" she questioned me suspiciously.

"He did, but I didn't know it. He was still using it to blackmail me. That's why I had to let him come over for dinner."

The suspicion in her eyes deepened. "What else did he make you do?"

I could see where her mind was at, and I shook my head emphatically. "Not that. He just made me wear a maid uniform and clean his house."

Surprise flitted across her face, but she still looked like she didn't trust my answer. "You know it's not your fault if he blackmailed you into anything, so—"

"He didn't," I interrupted her quickly as my face flushed with the knowledge that it had been entirely my fault, because I had kissed him first.

Her eyes widened in horror as she stared at me. "Ella," she whispered.

"No, it was just a kiss," I assured her. "That's all that happened, I swear!"

Relief broke through her horrified expression but then was chased away by outrage. "He forced a kiss on you?"

My gaze flitted away from hers as my blush deepened.

"Oh," she responded with the realization clear in her voice. "Not forced."

After a moment's hesitation during which I hoped she would just decide to drop the subject, she continued the conversation. "So, you still have a crush on him?"

"No," I replied. "I was just caught up in the moment. He was wearing the tux, and it almost felt like we were at prom, and I forgot for a minute that he was Mason."

That last part was an outright lie, because I hadn't for one instant forgotten that he was Mason. I couldn't admit that to her though, because she would never understand how I could still be attracted to him. I couldn't even explain it to myself.

"Oh," she said. "Yeah, I can see how that could happen. He is very good-looking, and if you just imagined him as some other gorgeous guy…"

"Exactly," I agreed enthusiastically, eager to lay this subject to rest with a reasonable-sounding explanation. "So, anyway, I'm so glad that we can be friends again! We should make plans to do something soon. I'm free any day except this Friday."

Her face fell. "Oh! Was that your first kiss? Did he steal that from you?"

Heat suffused my face, ruining my attempt to act nonchalant about it as I told her that it didn't matter.

"Of course it matters," she insisted. "Oh, Ella," she sympathized with feeling.

"I'm considering Josh my first kiss," I lied. "That's the one that counts."

The truth was that it had already faded from my mind, and I couldn't recall it in the same detail as my kisses with Mason. That was because I'd only had one kiss with Josh, I assured myself. Once I surpassed the number of kisses I'd had with Mason, kissing Josh would be foremost in my mind.

"Right," she agreed. "You take back control of your life and be with the guy you like."

"Right," I echoed and tried to ignore the nagging sense of disappointment I felt.

It was the clothes, I told myself. That's what had made my kiss with Mason so memorable and special. And also the fact that it was my first kiss. I couldn't rewrite history, as much as I might want to. The thought that I wouldn't trade that amazing first kiss for the one with Josh flitted through my mind, but that was something that I didn't want to acknowledge. Josh is the right guy for me, I reaffirmed to myself. He's the one I want—not Mason.

Yet my pulse automatically sped up when I got a text from him. *Where are you? I brought you ice cream*

My excitement turned to alarm. *You're at my house?*

Yes. I had to give your ice cream to your mom. It was starting to melt. Where are you?

I couldn't imagine him there alone with my mom. What had that been like? *Are you still there?*

My phone rang after I sent him that text, and I saw that he was calling me. "Where are you?" he demanded as soon as I answered.

"A friend's house," I replied as Alice watched me with interest.

"Is that him?" she asked quietly.

"Yeah," I answered her.

"Which friend?" Mason questioned.

"*My* friend," I retorted. "Which means it's my business and not yours."

Alice nodded at my assertion and gave me a thumbs up.

There was a pause, during which I anticipated an angry reaction from him. Instead, he spoke in a silky tone that put me on edge. "You're not being very considerate of my feelings, Ella. I introduced you to my friends, but you don't want me to know yours? Do you think that's fair? Is that something that a good girlfriend does?"

"Fine," I relented, realizing that I had made the criteria of what constituted a good girlfriend or boyfriend too broad. I knew that he wouldn't hesitate to exploit that blunder on my part in order to win the bet. "It's Alice. She was my best friend before you ruined that for me," I added, letting the resentment be heard in my voice.

There was another pause. "I'm sorry," he said.

"You should be," I stated.

"I am," he confirmed and expelled a breath. "I really am, Ella. Even spending just five minutes with your mom, it's so obvious that you're nothing like her. I shouldn't have assumed that you were, because I'm nothing like..."

He cut off abruptly, but I could guess what he was going to say—that he was nothing like his dad. I held a different opinion on that, but it wasn't as firmly entrenched in my mind as before, and that worried me even more than my attraction to him. I was starting to think that he really wasn't such a bad guy, and that was dangerous thinking. I would have to be a complete fool to ever trust him.

"So, that's the girl that was Chase's secret girlfriend," he said. "Alice."

I mentally cursed his ability to remember things so well and chided myself for letting her name slip out during that conversation. I would have to watch what I said around him from now on. "Yeah," I acknowledged and hurried on. "So I'm here to see her, not talk on the phone with you. So, bye."

I hung up before he could respond. "Sorry," I said to Alice.

"What'd he say?" she asked. "He wanted to know who you were with?"

"Yeah, but I promise he won't bother you again," I told her. "It won't be like last time."

"I think you're right," she said, surprising me.

"Oh," I responded in relief, glad that she was no longer wary about continuing our friendship.

"I think he would only have a problem with me if I was a guy," she remarked. "He sounds possessive and jealous, Ella. You better believe he thinks you're really his girlfriend. You better break up with him before you start dating Josh."

"I can't," I replied. "I have to get my poem back first."

"What did you write in this poem?" she questioned in bewilderment. "How bad could it be?"

I looked away from her as I blushed in embarrassment.

"Okay," she sighed. "Just promise me that you'll call the police if he threatens you. Or call me if you're afraid, and I'll call them for you. We can have a code word if you want, something that he wouldn't suspect."

I had returned my gaze to her as she spoke, and I emphatically shook my head. "He's not abusive. I know that much about him."

"He might be when he loses his temper," she argued.

"No," I stated. "He gets cold and distant. The more pissed off he gets, the more he pulls back."

She studied me intently. "So, you're hoping to make him mad enough to break up with you?"

I hadn't considered that possibility, but he certainly did have a tendency to freeze girls out when he was done with them. He hadn't spared Addison another glance after he dropped her, and Brooke had transferred to another school after he gave her the cold shoulder. If wondered if I should try annoying him and getting on his nerves.

"That's brilliant!" I exclaimed. "I can overdo the enthusiastic girlfriend thing and annoy the crap out of him. What should I call him? Honey? Sweetie pie? Pookie bear? Yes, that's it! He'll hate that."

Alice giggled, and the sound gave me the warm fuzzies. I hadn't giggled over silly stuff with anyone in ages. "I would love to see the look on his face if you called him that," she said.

"Oh, I will," I proclaimed. "And I've got to think of more things to do to annoy him, but it has to be stuff that a girlfriend would do, maybe like nag him or something."

"You could do the whiny voice," Alice suggested. "But pookie bear," she whined in example.

I giggled in response. "That's perfect! Too bad I'm going to the Taylor Swift concert with Erin, or I could have whined for him to take me."

The smile slid off Alice's face. "You're going to a concert with Erin Michaels?"

"Yeah," I confirmed awkwardly. "She had an extra ticket, and she asked me to go. It's really last minute, so I didn't have a chance to ask you. It's probably sold out, since it's this Friday."

"No, I wasn't...no, that's fine. Erin's nice."

"Yeah," I agreed. "But I'd rather be going with you. We should make plans to do something. We need to make up for lost time."

"We will," she told me, "but we don't need to make any special plans to do that. We can talk every day again, even at school, and sit together at lunch."

"Yes," I agreed with growing excitement, "and you can come over my house, and we can even sit together on the bus now!"

We beamed at each other, and just like that it felt like we were back to what we had before. "Senior year!" we exclaimed simultaneously, both of us apparently having the giddy realization that we would be able to spend it together.

Addison had made the last school year more tolerable than the previous two, but I hadn't felt this sense of connection to her and the surety that I had a real friend who I could be myself with and bask in her total acceptance. It occurred to me that this was what Mason was lacking in his friendships, and that was why he felt like he didn't have any real friends.

Alice threw her arms around me in a spontaneous hug, and I pushed Mason out of my thoughts as I hugged her back. "You're the best," I gushed. "You'll always be my best friend."

"You'll always be my best friend too, Ella," she said as she pulled back to look at me. "It's just not the same with my other friends. Nobody else knows me as well as you do."

That prompted me to bring up the subject I hadn't been sure how to broach, but she hurried past the moment by suddenly declaring that we should go to Six Flags on Saturday. "It'll be so much fun to spend the whole day there together."

"Good idea!" I exclaimed excitedly. "I haven't been there in years, not since the last time I went with you. I can't wait!"

It was the perfect thing for us to do to bridge the gap between then and now. It held the carefree memories of early adolescence, and we would naturally loosen up as we had fun. We could talk over the course of the day about anything that came to mind and dissipate any lingering hesitation or self-consciousness between us.

I left her house feeling happy, and I wanted to share that feeling. So, I called Zoey to invite her out for ice cream with me. I drove to the apartment building where she lived and picked her up. She dropped the unaffected tough girl act when she got in my car, and protectiveness surged up within me at the sight of her innocent smile. She was still a kid, happy to get a simple treat, and seeing her happy warmed my heart. I did feel like she was my little sister, and I often wished that she lived with me so that I could keep an eye on her every day. Logically, I knew that there was no guarantee that I could keep her safe, but I still had the illusion in my mind that I could protect her.

I knew better than to hug her in the parking lot of her apartment building, so I waited until we arrived at the ice cream shop. She had long since stopped pretending that she was reluctantly indulging me, and she hugged me back without rolling her eyes at me afterwards.

"Boy have I missed you," I declared. "How have you been?"

"You just saw me last week," she retorted.

I was startled to realize that it had been such a short time. "Yeah, well it feels longer. A lot has happened."

She focused her attention on me more intently. "Like what?" she questioned curiously.

Realizing my mistake in blurting that out, I tried to backtrack. "Oh, you know, just starting school and stuff," I said as I opened my door to escape her scrutiny.

Regrouping, I turned the focus on her when she joined me in exiting the car. "That reminds me, how is your first week going? I still can't believe you're in high school now."

"What happened?" she demanded. "Did that asshole start more shit?"

"Language," I admonished her automatically, as was my futile habit with her. I felt it was my sisterly duty to try to curb her of her swearing, and to watch my own language around her. She ignored my protests, but I had noticed that she didn't swear in front of her mom, so I knew the lady would want me to continue my effort.

Zoey wouldn't let up. "What the fuck did he do?"

I halted in front of the door to the ice cream shop. "Nothing," I said before turning to look at her. "Watch your language. There are little kids in there."

Her gaze narrowed on me. "Why won't you tell me?"

I was regretting ever mentioning Mason to her at all, but I had shared my own story of being bullied so that she would open up to me too. It had worked, and she had told me about what had happened to her. Besides her age, that was another reason that I avoided topics with her that involved anything sexual. I certainly wasn't going to tell her about Mason taking a naked picture of me.

"There's nothing to tell," I stated as I pulled the door open and held it for her to enter the cool interior of the ice cream shop.

She gave me a look that clearly conveyed that she wasn't buying my bullshit, but she let it go and allowed herself to become distracted by the goodies awaiting her at the counter. After we ordered, I pulled my wallet out of my purse to get out the money to pay.

"I've got it," a male voice spoke from behind me.

As I froze in shock and dread, he brushed against me as he moved up beside me to hand the cashier money. I glanced at Mason before my gaze shot toward Zoey in panic. She didn't even notice me, because her attention was riveted on him. It was disconcerting to see the look of female appreciation for an attractive male on her young face, and my head turned away only to be confronted by the sight of Mason watching me.

"I knew you wanted some," he said and smirked before adding, "ice cream."

I was beyond sexual innuendos at this point though, and my flushed skin was a result of my extreme nervousness over trying to prevent Zoey from finding out about us. "Uh, thanks sir," I said as my eyes pleaded with him to not say anything. "That's very nice of you."

I stepped sideways and gave Zoey a little push to move further along the counter to wait for our ice cream. To my distress, Mason joined us like we were together.

"You don't have to call me sir anymore," he told me before turning his attention on Zoey. "Hi, I'm Mason, and you must be Zoey. I couldn't wait to meet you after Ella told me about you."

She came out of her besotted trance as her eyes widened in shock before her gaze shifted to me. *"That's Mason?"*

"She's talked about me to you?" he enquired, sounding pleased.

Her gaze shot back to him in sudden fury. "You piece of shit asshole! You get the fuck away from her!"

Mason looked startled by her vehement outburst as the guy at the counter spoke awkwardly. "Uh, here's your strawberry sundae. Your banana split will be right up."

Zoey snatched the sundae out of his hand and flung it at Mason. It hit him in the chest and made a mess all over his shirt.

"Uh, you're gonna have to leave," the guy at the counter said.

Mason stopped staring at Zoey and turned to speak to the guy. "It's fine. Could you get them another strawberry sundae?" He pulled out more money out of his wallet and placed it on the counter. "Keep the change."

Pulling his t-shirt up off his abs to catch the ice cream dripping down from his chest, he faced Zoey. "I'm sorry you have the wrong impression of me, but I hope you'll give me a chance to change that just like Ella did. Especially since I'm her boyfriend now."

Zoey gaped at him in utter shock as he walked quickly toward the restrooms. My face was on fire with the heat of my humiliation, and I wasn't prepared to deal with her incredulous scrutiny. "It's true?" she accused.

The guy at the counter announced our banana split, and I turned toward him like a drowning person seeking a life raft. I handed the ice cream to her without looking at her. "Get us a table."

She didn't reply, but she disappeared from my peripheral vision. When the guy brought me my ice cream sundae, I couldn't put off facing Zoey any longer. Turning and spotting the table she was seated at, I slowly started walking toward her. She glanced up at me as I set my ice cream down, but my attention was caught by the sight several feet behind her.

"Hey," the frazzled guy who had served us our ice cream protested, "you can't be in here without a shirt."

"I know," Mason replied. "I'm leaving, but I had to rinse my shirt off first." He held up the wet fabric he had bunched in his hand.

"Hey, Ella," he said as he came near and smirked at me as my gaze shot up from his bare stomach to his face. "I'll pick you up for school in the morning."

Before I could recover my wits to protest, he was striding out the door, and I became distracted by the sexy sight of the tan skin of his back beneath the sun.

"Fuck, he's hot," Zoey said. "You didn't tell me he looked like *that*."

I closed my eyes in mortification as I braced myself to face her. My lowered gaze fixed first on the chair I was pulling out, and I sat down before forcing myself to look at her. "Um…" I began and trailed off without a clue of what to say to her.

"Yeah," she agreed like I had said something. "Wow, okay. So that's happening. I can see why."

I flushed. "No, it's not. He's not really my boyfriend."

"So, it's just sex," she stated matter-of-factly.

I emitted an embarrassing squeak as my face overheated. "No! We're not...no! That would never happen. Why would you think that?"

"Probably because you were looking at him like that," she replied.

"I was not!" I protested.

"It's okay," she assured me. "He was looking at you like that too."

I hastily grabbed a spoonful of ice cream in an attempt to cool down and regain my composure. It prompted Zoey to begin eating her ice cream too, so it worked as a momentary distraction to give me a reprieve from the conversation.

I used the opportunity to change the subject. "So, I'm going to a concert on Friday."

"With Mason?" she asked.

"No," I answered flatly before forcing a bright smile. "With my new friend, Erin! She had an extra ticket, and she asked me to go. It's Taylor Swift!"

Zoey studied me steadily. "Why are you being so fake?"

"I'm not," I denied in dismay. "I like Taylor Swift, and I'm excited about seeing her in concert."

"Maybe," she allowed, "but you were being fake happy. Is it because you don't want to tell me how you got with Mason?"

I sighed. "I'm not with him, honestly. He thinks I am, but I'm not." I leaned toward her conspiratorially. "I actually have a secret boyfriend. His name is Josh."

Her brown eyes widened in surprise. "You do? When did that happen? Why didn't you tell me that before?"

"Because we just started dating today," I answered.

"What about you and Mason?" she questioned. "Why does he think he's your boyfriend? And how did that happen anyway? When did he stop being an asshole to you?"

"I don't know," I lied. "He just apologized out of the blue, and now he thinks that I'll forgive him and go out with him. But I won't."

"He apologized," she repeated in astonishment. "And nobody made him?"

"No," I replied, "but that can't make up for what he did. Saying he's sorry doesn't change anything."

She contemplated that thoughtfully as she ate her ice cream. I again tried to engage her in conversation that didn't involve Mason. "So, tell me how you like high school. How's it going so far?"

"Good," she answered absently before continuing with the topic on her mind. "Saying he's sorry when he doesn't have to...well, that's something. And he didn't get mad at me for throwing ice cream on him. He was even nice to me."

"He better be nice to you, or I'll kick his ass," I responded on instinct, protectiveness rising up in me immediately.

She smiled at me, and happiness surged up within me. Her smiles always lifted my spirits and made me happy no matter how down I was feeling. Her resilience was an inspiration to me, but it was more than that. I had grown to love her while spending time with her, and I had real sisterly feelings for her.

"Hey, do you want to go to Six Flags on Saturday?" I asked on impulse.

She beamed at me. "Yes!"

I suddenly felt bad for not thinking of offering to take her before. Of course, a kid would want to go to an amusement park, but I had only taken her to the fair, which had less rides than Six Flags. She'd had lots of fun anyway, and seeing her carefree enjoyment had inspired that poem about her. I had taken her back to the fair the following summer, but it hadn't occurred to me to take her to a place with bigger, more thrilling rides. She obviously wanted to go, but she wasn't like the kids I babysat who voiced their wants. Zoey accepted what I offered her, but she had never once asked me for anything, even though she had a lot less than the spoiled kids I got paid to watch.

That made me want to give her things, but I realized that there was another person involved this time, and I hadn't consulted her. I forged on ahead anyway. "Um, do you have a friend you could bring along? My friend, Alice, is going with us, so it would be good to have another person to go on rides with."

"Alice?" she enquired with a puzzled expression. "I thought Addison was your only friend."

I couldn't hide my reaction to her name, and Zoey responded to the expression on my face with an exclamation. "Whoa! What'd she do?"

I shook my head. "It doesn't matter. I just found out that she wasn't really my friend, so that's that. Anyway, Alice was my best friend in middle school, and we're friends again now. She's really nice. I think you'll like her."

"I've never met any of your friends before," she said in a tentative tone that was unlike her. "I thought maybe…"

"What?" I prompted after she trailed off.

She shook her head as if to dispel the thoughts in it. "Nothing. So, um, Alice is okay with me going with you?"

"Yes," I answered confidently even though I hadn't run it by her yet. "But do you have anyone you could bring? It's okay if you don't," I hurried to assure her.

"Well," she began and dropped her gaze as she swirled her spoon around in the thin layer of melted ice cream at the bottom of the plastic container, "there's someone I can ask."

"Okay, good," I said and stood up. "I should get you home now that I've spoiled your dinner."

"I'd rather eat ice cream for dinner anyway. And for breakfast and lunch," she added as we threw away our trash.

"You'd get sick of it if you had it all the time," I told her.

"No," she disagreed. "Some things are too good to ever get sick of."

A memory of how it felt to kiss Mason flashed in my mind, and I berated myself for tainting her innocent words with my inappropriate thoughts. This thing with him was encroaching on too much of my life. At least before he had been just an annoyance at school, and only in my secret thoughts when I was alone at home. Now he was everywhere—coming over to my house, calling me on the phone while I was with Alice, showing up here to disrupt my time with Zoey. It had to stop.

I told him so when he called me that evening, even though hearing his voice made me want to see him. "How did you know where I was today?" I demanded. "I didn't tell anyone I was going out for ice cream with Zoey, so how did you know?"

"I followed you from Alice's house," he replied.

I was taken aback by that answer. "But you didn't know I was at her house until I told you."

"But I went there after you told me."

"I didn't see you there," I protested.

"I parked down the street and waited for you to leave," he informed me.

"But how did you even know where she lives?" I questioned in dismay.

"I found out everything I could about you when I moved here. Who your friends were, where they lived. You spent the most time at Alice's house, so I still remembered her address."

"Do you have a photographic memory or something?" I complained.

"Not photographic, but it's pretty easy for me to remember things when I set my mind to it."

"Great," I muttered, "the asshole gets beauty *and* brains."

I instantly regretted letting those words slip out and braced myself for his smug reply. He surprised me when he spoke though. "Except for the asshole part, you could be talking about yourself, Ella. It pissed me off when I found out that you were smart. I expected you to be a brainless bimbo getting D's and F's and, on your way to dropping out of school. I couldn't believe it when I saw you had mostly A's."

"I had to study like crazy for those A's, but...wait! How the hell do you know what grades I got?"

"You being on the honor roll was my first clue, and then I paid someone to show me your school records," he admitted.

"I can't believe they'd do that!" I exclaimed in outrage. "That is so wrong!"

"What are you so upset about? You have a record to be proud of."

"That's not the point," I railed. "They violated my privacy. They should be fired! Who was it?"

"You know I'm not going to tell you that," he said like he was speaking to an unreasonable child.

"You're an asshole!" I yelled at him in frustration. "Just stay out of my life and leave me the hell alone. Don't fucking follow me either! I don't want you around my friends."

"I like Zoey," he told me. "I like how she defended you. She's braver than most guys I've met. I respect that."

I couldn't help warming toward him over his praise of her. "She's amazing!" I gushed. "So resilient after everything she's been through. I would have been afraid of every guy I met." I stopped in horror at having revealed too much. I never spoke about what she had confided in me to anyone.

Mason's voice was tight and terse. "Who hurt her?"

"I shouldn't have said anything," I told him regretfully. "Please don't say anything to her about it."

"I need a name," he snapped.

That's when I realized that he meant to take some kind of revenge on the man who hurt Zoey, and my heart swelled with feeling for him. "Mason," I said with more warmth than I ever could have imagined speaking his name, "you're not really in the mafia."

"I don't need the mafia," he retorted. "I'll get that fucking asshole myself. What the fuck did he do to her?" His voice shook with rage. "Did he rape that little girl?"

"He tried to," I answered. "Luckily, her mom got home early that day and stopped him. He went to jail, Mason, so you don't need to do anything. Just please don't ever tell Zoey that I told you about it. She confided that to me in secret. I can't believe I said anything," I added in self-reproach. "I've never told that to anyone."

"You can tell me anything," he declared. "I've got your back, Ella."

It felt strangely true, and I didn't know what to do with that feeling. "Thanks. Um, I should go."

"Wait, I wanted to ask you out on a date this weekend. I know you're going to the concert with Erin on Friday, so how about Saturday?"

"I'm going to Six Flags on Saturday with Alice and Zoey," I replied.

"Oh," he responded.

"It's girl bonding time," I said, feeling oddly compelled to explain why I wasn't inviting him along.

"Right. But, uh, won't someone be left without a partner for rides?"

"Zoey is bringing a friend," I informed him, trying to shake the feeling that I was leaving him out.

"Oh. Yeah, that makes sense. That way you can ride with Alice."

"Yeah, girl time," I repeated, forgoing the opportunity to voice my resentment again over how much time I had lost with Alice because of him.

He mentioned it himself however. "I'm glad you're friends again. I'm sorry I kept her from you."

I couldn't tell him that it was okay, because it wasn't. Yet I didn't feel like refusing his apology either. "I know," I said in acknowledgement.

This unprecedented moment between us was too disconcerting for me, and I retreated from it after a pause that felt like a prelude to something. "Well, I have to go. Bye," I threw out hastily before ending the call.

I received a text from him a moment later. *Goodnight Ella. I'll see you in the morning*

I didn't respond, but I also didn't delete his text. I hadn't deleted any of his previous ones either, and I didn't know what I was saving them for. Setting my phone down, I walked restlessly around my room. I was in a strange mood, and I couldn't pinpoint exactly how I was feeling. Maybe I was just overwhelmed by how much I had going on all of a sudden.

Yes, that had to be what was stirring me up this way and making me feel almost like I couldn't quite catch my breath. I decided that I just needed some rest, but sleep eluded me for much of the night. Yet I wasn't tired when I awoke to the sound of my alarm clock. I sprang out of bed with a buzz like I'd already had a cup of coffee. That turned out to be my breakfast, because I found that I wasn't hungry.

I brushed my teeth and got dressed in an effervescent state of anticipation I hadn't felt in ages. I was actually looking forward to the day. When Mason arrived, I practically bounced out to his car. He had gotten out and stood waiting for me with his hands in his pockets and a neutral expression on his face.

I beamed a smile at him, and his posture relaxed as he responded with an answering smile. Warmth radiated through me to combine with the buzz in my veins, and I felt the high of happiness.

"Hey," he greeted me as he approached me and stood looking at me like he wanted to say more.

"Hey," I replied and gazed back at him.

He was the first one to rouse himself out of the trance we had fallen into. "So, uh…"

He moved to my side and took my hand to walk me the short distance to his car, and it gave me an extra surge of happiness to hold his hand. My state of euphoria only increased during the ride to school when he started singing along to the song playing on the radio. I joined him when he put on Believer, and we belted out the lyrics together.

He put the radio back on after that, but I took control of it and sampled through the stations until I squealed in delight when I hit upon Taylor Swift's Shake It Off. It was only a short way into the song, and I started singing along and adding as many sassy moves as I could while seated in a car. Mason kept glancing over at me with a permanent smile on his face.

When we arrived at school, we sat there grinning at each other after he parked the car. A knock on his window shattered the perfect bubble we were in as the sight of Tyler's face brought me back to reality with a shock of recognition. The idiot outside was part of the crowd that had treated me like crap, and Mason was their leader. And I had been sitting here feeling happy with him.

The realization hit me then that I had been excited to see Mason this morning, and it hadn't had anything to do with sex. I had actually smiled at him. Seeing him had made me happy.

Mason, my tormentor, my enemy, my blackmailer. That's who I had been happy to see. The sexual attraction had been twisted enough, but this was on a whole other level of unhinged. The sudden clarity brought the urge to flee, and I threw open the door and left it like that as I dashed away. I heard Mason calling my name, but I didn't look back.

This insanity had to stop.

Chapter 12

It wouldn't be long before I had to deal with him again, but I hoped to be in a more rational frame of mind. Whatever madness had possessed me was wearing off, and I was feeling incredibly foolish. Veering into the first bathroom I saw after entering the building, I stopped to catch my breath and collect myself.

"What's the matter? Can't keep up with him?" a female voice taunted.

I looked over to see Addison sneering at me. Great. This was so not what I needed right now. Sensing that she had me at a disadvantage, she sauntered toward me. "I'm starting to believe that you were actually telling the truth about being a virgin. I bet he's giving you more than you can handle. You should have left him to someone who could take care of his demands. I bet you don't even know how to give a good blowjob."

She laughed at my expression. "Oh, Ella! You won't even give him a blowjob, will you? I bet he's so fucking frustrated that he can't stand it. Serves him right," she declared with satisfaction.

Her taunts shouldn't have bothered me. I didn't care if I was lacking in sexual expertise. It wasn't like I was aspiring to compete with her in that area, especially not for Mason. "I don't care if he's frustrated. I could care less about him—or you. Go ahead and give him all the blowjobs you want. You two deserve each other."

A sly look came into her eyes before she laughed with delight. "You're not having sex with him? Holy shit, this is even better than I thought!" she exclaimed in glee.

"How did you know I'm not having sex with him?" I asked in surprise. "I didn't tell you that."

She smiled indulgently at me. "Besides the fact that you just confirmed it? You wouldn't have been telling me to do anything with him if you were sleeping with him. You wouldn't have been okay with that at all."

My mouth opened to tell her that I hadn't said anything about being okay with it, but the thought failed to form into words.

Addison bestowed another indulgent smile upon me. "Thanks for making my day, Ella," she said and walked past me with confidence.

She had somehow managed to make me feel like a kid who was completely out of her element. She had given Mason blowjobs, while I had given him karaoke in the car. I cringed at the memory and then shrank back self-consciously as other girls came into the bathroom. Their conversation stopped as they noticed me, and I quickly left to escape their scrutiny.

Looking for a place to be alone, I caught sight of the doors to the auditorium. I slipped inside and felt a measure of relief as the door closed behind me and shut out the sounds of people talking in the hallway. I moved further into the room and soaked up the silence before my ringtone shattered it. Seeing that it was Mason, I hit ignore, but he immediately called me again.

"What?" I snapped.

"What's wrong?" he asked. "Why'd you take off like that? Did Tyler do something? Did he mess with you?" he demanded, starting to sound angry.

"No," I replied. "It has nothing to do with him."

"Are you sure?" he pressed. "Because you were fine until he showed up. You were happy one minute, and the next you were running away like someone was chasing you. What happened?"

That was the crux of the problem. I had been *happy*. "Nothing," I said. "Just leave me alone."

"Damn it, Ella, talk to me! Where are you? I want to talk to you in person."

"What for?" I retorted. "You're wasting your time, Mason. I'm not going to give you sex or blowjobs, so—"

"Who said anything about blowjobs?" he cut in.

I fell silent. Shit! Why had I said that?

"Ella, who said anything about blowjobs?" he demanded.

"Uh, never mind," I responded nervously. "Um, I'm just going to hang up now, okay?" Not sure why I was asking permission, I nevertheless winced when I ended the call after he said no.

Completely flustered now, I paced around as I tried to calm down and let the silence soothe me. After several minutes, I was even more agitated than I had been after hanging up with Mason. Thinking about our conversation had me berating myself for even answering his call, letting alone for blurting out such a thing. What the hell was wrong with me lately? Why did Mason make me lose all my common sense?

With a sigh, I started trudging toward the doors just as he burst through them. Both of us halted at the sight of each other, but his gaze swept around the room before returning to me. "What are you doing in here?" he demanded.

"Trying to be by myself," I retorted in exasperation, "but nobody will leave me alone. First Addison bothered me in the bathroom. Then you kept calling me, and now you're here."

"So, you were here alone?" he questioned.

"I *was*," I stressed, "until you showed up. I guess I'll have to go to class to get away from you."

"I knew Alicia was lying," he said. "She said that she saw you come in here with a guy."

I rolled my eyes. "She still thinks I'm a prostitute. Thanks to your lovely rumors," I added.

"I told her that wasn't true," he reminded me defensively. "You heard me say it."

"Yeah, and I don't care what she thinks anyway," I said as I started to walk past him.

"Why'd you bring up blowjobs?"

I hurried toward the door without answering, but I stopped in my tracks when he sharply called out my name. I could feel my face heating up as he came up behind me and moved to stand in front of me again. I was too embarrassed to look at him, but he placed his hand beneath my chin to lift my downcast gaze.

"Ella," he said in a much gentler tone, "talk to me."

He let go of my chin and took a step back to give me space as he gazed at me with an open, encouraging expression, and I found myself telling him about Addison confronting me in the bathroom. "She's the one who brought them up. She said that's what you want, so…if you want to get back with her…"

My gaze slid away from his as I trailed off awkwardly. I shifted my weight to one side and fidgeted with my hands, feeling unaccountably nervous as I awaited his answer.

"Ella," he said smoothly, drawing my attention back to him, "ask me what I want."

I stared at him as my heart began to pound with trepidation. Did he really expect me to ask him if he wanted a blowjob? Did he think that he could demand that from me?

His gaze intensified. "Ask me...what...I want," he commanded with deliberate slowness to assert his implacable demand.

My voice shook with nervousness as I obeyed. "What do you want?"

"You," he answered. "I want you, Ella."

My breath hitched. "I'm not having sex with you."

"Did I ask you to?" he enquired.

I faltered at his smooth question. "Isn't that...ah, isn't that what you just said?"

"I said I wanted you," he stated. "I didn't say anything about sex."

"Um," I began in confusion.

"I want you to be my girlfriend," he clarified. "I told you that I can wait for sex."

His declaration lifted my spirits, but I tamped down on the feeling as I reminded myself that he was just saying that to win me over and get me to drop my guard so that he could trick me into sleeping with him. "What if I never have sex with you?" I challenged.

His confident amusement should have pissed me off, but it elicited an excited fluttering in my stomach as he spoke. "I don't think that will be a problem."

He stepped as close as he could without touching me, and my body started to anticipate the contact he was withholding. I was incredibly aware of the tantalizingly slight space between us. His mouth was just shy of my ear, and his voice heightened the sensation of teasing proximity. "Never is a long time, Ella, and I am *very* patient."

How he had made that sound so sexy was beyond me, but it sent a hot rush of excitement through me. My body thrummed with an electric pulse of possibilities that gave me a high I had never experienced before. It felt like a current was running between us and charging me up with this exhilarating feeling that I could barely contain.

He pulled back to look at me before slowly leaning in to kiss me. I closed my eyes as I rode that high of anticipation and excitement. His breath ghosted over my lips, and they tingled in response. "Very patient," he murmured, sending more heat rushing through my body like a wildfire.

My breathing became labored with the acute wait for him to kiss me, and I felt an electric spark when he took hold of my hand. My eyes opened to see that he was no longer standing in front of me but was beside me instead.

"We should get to class," he said.

His smirk conveyed his smug knowledge that he had left me craving the kiss he had made me think I was about to get. The denial of it didn't douse the thrilling effect he was having on me though. I was still flying high on feeling so incredibly alive, and I directed a spontaneous smile of happiness at him. He responded with a brilliant smile of his own and gave my hand a happy little squeeze.

We walked out of the auditorium together, holding hands like a couple who had that kind of connection. I glided through the halls with him without faltering until I saw Josh watching us. Guilty panic swept through me, and my eyes darted toward Mason to see if he suspected anything. He smiled warmly at me, and I gave him a weak smile in return.

He immediately noticed that something was off with me. "What's wrong?"

"Nothing," I replied, trying to quell my overwhelming nervousness. I forced a bigger smile.

He viewed it in concern and pulled me aside to stop and talk to me out of the flow of students. "What's going on, Ella? Why'd you run off earlier, and why are you upset now?"

"I'm not upset," I denied as I struggled not to look back and see if Josh was still watching us. I felt like a glance in his direction would give me away and reveal to Mason that I had cheated on him.

"You are," he insisted. "Tell me why."

Panic seized me for a second until I realized he was referring to me being upset and not to me cheating on him. I reacted by going on the offensive. "Gee, I don't know, Mason. Maybe it's because I don't know how you're going to act from one minute to the next. First you hate me, then you like me. You tell people I'm a hooker, but now you say I'm your girlfriend. You act like you're going to kiss me, but then you don't."

He moved so fast that he had me pressed back against the wall before I knew what was happening. "You made that rule," he retorted harshly, the patience he claimed to have seemingly on the verge of snapping. "Did you change your mind?"

I could see that it would only take one word from me for his mouth to come crashing down on mine. I wanted him to unleash that wild side of him and kiss me with all the passionate intensity I could sense he was barely holding back.

But my pride kept me from admitting it. "No," I said.

He eased back a bit and put a little space between our bodies, and I immediately missed the contact. "Then why are you complaining that I didn't kiss you?" he asked.

"I'm not," I denied, although I really had been. I was feeling contrarily resentful toward him for respecting my rules and putting me in the situation of having to ask him to kiss me.

"Then what are you complaining about?" he challenged.

I expelled an exasperated breath. "About you always changing your mind and playing games with me."

"I'm not always changing my mind," he refuted. "I didn't change my mind about you until I found out that I was wrong. My feelings for you haven't changed since then, and I'm not playing any games with you. I like you, I want you to be my girlfriend, and I want to kiss you."

His gaze was so intent as he spoke that it completely disconcerted me. I was suddenly looking anywhere but at him, which wasn't easy since he was standing right in front of me. "Ella," he said, compelling my attention back to him. "Do you want to be my girlfriend?"

My heart practically burst out of my chest with happiness. Everything else was forgotten as my girlhood dream came true. I rapidly surpassed the exhilarating high from before and rose to ecstatic heights of pure joy. "Yes!" I exclaimed as I left any semblance of rational thinking far behind me.

His response was as spontaneous as mine as he beamed at me and threw his arms around me in a joyful hug. The bell rang just then, and he gave me a quick peck on the lips before stepping back and taking hold of my hand to walk me to class.

I remained in that blissful, dreamlike state until I saw Addison smirking at me as we passed by her in the hallway. Then it all came back to me, and I felt a pang in my chest as I remembered that Mason had sex with her. He had been with her and touched her, and they had set me up together. And here I was agreeing to be his girlfriend because he had finally asked me like I had always dreamed he would.

It had felt so wonderful that I was reluctant to let go of it even now, but I forced myself to pull my hand away from his. "I have to go to the bathroom," I lied in answer to his questioning look. "You go on to class."

"I can wait for you," he offered.

"No, you go," I urged. "I'll see you there."

"Okay," he agreed and gave me another one of those warm, happy smiles that I wanted to bask in forever.

My heart contracted as I turned away and walked across the hall into the girls' bathroom. Thankfully, it was empty due to the prompting of the warning bell, and I slumped against the wall without having to hide my misery.

My life had been perfect for a moment until I came crashing back down into reality. Mason had done this to me. It was always Mason ruining everything, and I needed to get over it and move on. This time was different though, because I had my friends. And I had Josh.

For a minute there, I actually thought that I had Mason. How delusional could I be? Of course, he was just pretending to like me so he could have sex with me. Once he got what he wanted, he would drop me like he dropped Addison. And she had been able to keep up with his "demands" for a year. Since I wouldn't do half the stuff she did for him, he would tire of me much faster.

Not that I was planning to do anything with him at all, I assured myself. Just because I had let him kiss me didn't mean that I was going to let him do anything else. He had gotten the wrong idea from my sex poem. That was just a fantasy, and I had no intention of acting it out in real life. He was going to be very disappointed if he thought that he was going to seduce me with this approach. Forcing me to be his girlfriend hadn't worked, so now he was trying asking me instead. And he had almost fooled me.

Okay, he had fooled me, but only momentarily. I had come back to my senses, and I wouldn't let him get the best of me again. From now on, I would be the one fooling him. With that determined thought, I texted Josh and told him where to meet me.

I wasn't sure if he would take the chance, but he rushed in right before the bell rang to indicate the start of class. I approached him as he looked around anxiously. "We're alone," I said, pitching my voice into a seductive tone.

"This is crazy," he protested even as his dark brown eyes fixed on me with a heated stare.

"I know," I agreed, "but I couldn't wait."

I was speaking the truth, but not in the way I made it sound. I didn't want to see Mason again before I broke his hold on me. I was worried that I would fall right back under his spell as soon as I saw him, so I needed to have someone else on my mind to prevent that from happening. This was extreme, but that's why I thought it would work.

The recklessness of the situation and the threat of getting caught made this kiss with Josh much hotter than our previous one. We were both flushed when I pulled away from him. "We better get back," I said.

"Can I see you tonight?" he asked.

His eyes promised more hot kisses, and I wanted to keep this momentum going and push all thoughts of Mason out of my mind. I had been imagining him walking in on us while Josh was kissing me, so I hadn't yet succeeded in banishing him from my thoughts.

"Yes," I replied. "I'll let you know when."

He smiled in satisfaction, and I noticed how different it was from the bright, warm smile Mason had beamed at me when I agreed to be his girlfriend. Guilt dimmed the brief smile I mustered for Josh before leaving the restroom. I wasn't really Mason's girlfriend, I told myself. That had just been a moment of temporary insanity, and he was just playing me anyway. None of this was real, so I wasn't really cheating on him.

My stomach was tied up in knots by the time I entered the classroom though, and I almost hoped that the teacher would send me to the office for being late again. She just scolded me and told me to take my seat, so I avoided Mason's gaze as I walked with my head lowered and sat down. I could still feel his eyes on me as the rest of the class mercifully lost interest in me.

"Hey," he said.

I was worried that he would call out louder if I ignored him, so I reluctantly turned my head to look at him. The concern in his eyes was unexpected and made me feel worse than I already did. "Are you okay?" he asked.

"Upset stomach," I replied and added an unnecessary nervous gesture toward my belly before looking back down at my desk.

"Ella and Mason," the teacher snapped at us, "what is so important that you have to interrupt class? Again," she added, glaring at me.

"Ella doesn't feel well," Mason told her to my mortification. "That's why she was late. She might need to go to the nurse."

The teacher's expression softened. "Are you alright, Ella? Do you need a pass to go see the nurse?"

I didn't, but I wanted to escape their unwarranted concern for me. I could feel my face getting hotter with the guilty knowledge of the real reason I had been late to class. I was supposed to be feeling great about my secret rendezvous and finally taking something that had been denied to me, but I felt like I had done something wrong.

"Yes, please," I replied to the teacher.

She started writing out a pass, and I stood to walk up to her desk. I froze when Mason volunteered to walk me down to the nurse. "She looks like she's running a fever, and she could pass out."

The teacher glanced from him to me suspiciously. "Is this a ploy to cut class and make out?"

I was now utterly mortified, but Mason spoke angrily over the laughter of our classmates. "Can't you see that she's sick? Ella has never cut class in her life! She has a perfect record, so give her some damn respect."

I gasped in horror over how he was talking to the teacher. "I'm sorry," I apologized for him. "I just don't feel well." I moved meekly toward her. "If I could just get the pass for the nurse."

She handed it to me, but her gaze went past me and hardened as it fixed on a point behind me. "Go with her, but come right back."

"No," I protested. "He doesn't need to go."

They both ignored my objection however, and Mason followed me out of the classroom. When he took hold of my hand, it felt comforting despite my turmoil. "Can you make it?" he asked. "Do you need to lean against me?"

"I'm fine," I answered. "It's just my stomach. I'm not lightheaded or anything. You didn't need to come with me."

"I wanted to make sure you were okay," he insisted. "I would have waited for you to get out of the bathroom if I knew you were sick."

I thought about what I had really been doing in the bathroom, and I felt like such a fraud for pretending to be sick. It was all Mason's fault for putting me in this situation by telling the teacher that I needed to go to the nurse when I had just wanted to sit in class and be left alone. He could never just leave me in peace.

I lashed out at him in my resentment. "Would you have cared if I was sick when you hated me? What would you have done if you saw me pass out in the hallway?"

He looked at me with a troubled expression. "I would have gotten you help."

"Sure," I scoffed. "What you really would have done is laughed about it with your friends. So, I don't need you to help me now either." I pulled my hand free of his grasp.

"Okay, maybe I would have laughed about it," he admitted, "*after* I found out that you were okay. I would have gotten you help first, because I'm not a damn psychopath," he finished in an angry and offended tone.

Both of us were silent and tense after that, and Mason left without another word as soon as he escorted me to the nurse's office. Getting rid of him didn't brighten my mood, and I didn't feel any better after the nurse let me lie down for a while.

What did instantly lift my spirits was seeing Mason waiting for me in the hallway with a mylar smiley face balloon. "Where did you get that?" I exclaimed.

"I went to the store," he replied as he gave it to me. "I also got you this to settle your stomach." He handed me the plastic bag he was holding, and I peered inside and saw a bottle of ginger ale and a couple of packs of crackers.

"You left school?" I asked in dismay.

"Yeah, I just drove to the store real quick."

"I can't believe you did this," I gushed. "That was so thoughtful!"

He shrugged, but he looked pleased with my praise. "I wanted to make you feel better."

"That is so sweet!" I was filled with warm, fuzzy feelings as I smiled at him.

"How are you feeling?" he asked.

"Better," I replied with a twinge of guilt over my nonexistent illness.

"So, you're staying at school?" he questioned.

"Oh, yeah, of course. I wasn't sick enough to go home, and I'm fine now."

He responded with a beautiful smile. "Good. I'm glad you're better, and that I get to see you all day. I want to take you on a date after school if you're up to it."

"Again? We just went on a date the other day."

"It wasn't really a date since I forced you to go on it. This time I'm asking you out. I wanted to take you out this weekend, but I know you'll be busy. So, will you go out with me today, Ella?"

Giddiness surged up in me at being asked out on a date by him. "Yes," I responded with enthusiasm.

"Great! I'll walk you to your next class. This one's almost over."

Realization brought dismay. "Oh no! You were supposed to go right back. Now you'll be in trouble because of me."

"It'll be worth it," he said. "I had to try to make you feel better."

I smiled warmly at him for his caring and sweetness. He was such a wonderful boyfriend...

It hit me then right before the bell rang. I stood still as a statue as students started filing out of the classrooms. Mason glanced at them. "Time to go," he noted reluctantly.

"Well, that was good. I've got to give you credit for this one."

My sarcastic tone alerted him to the fact that my praise was derogatory. His gaze sharpened as he assessed the expression on my face. "What are you talking about?"

"All your concern," I replied derisively. "The care package was a nice touch." I lifted the bag for emphasis before dropping it on the floor. "But the balloon really clinched it. Everyone will be asking me about it, and I can tell them that my wonderful boyfriend gave it to me."

I let go of it and narrowed my eyes at him. "Nice try, but you're not going to win this bet. I'm going to step up my game and beat you."

"This was not about that stupid bet," he retorted in exasperation. "I did it because I care about you."

"You care about me," I scoffed. "Right. I believe that after all the shit you did to me. You've always been a real caring guy."

"I'm trying to make up for all that," he insisted. "If you just give me a chance, I'll—"

"No," I stated, interrupting him. "You didn't give me a chance, so I'm not going to give you a chance."

"Then why'd you say yes when I asked you to be my girlfriend?" he queried.

"I was just playing along for the bet," I lied.

"No, you weren't. You said yes on instinct, without thinking about it. That was your first response, because that's what you want. I don't know why you're trying to deny it now."

I didn't want to admit that he was speaking the truth, and I shook my head in denial. "It can't go like this," I blurted.

"Like what?" he questioned.

"Like this," I repeated. "It can't be this easy. You start acting like this, and all of a sudden, we're a happy couple. It doesn't work like that."

"Why not?" he demanded. "You were happy just now, Ella. I saw it. You were happy in the car with me this morning too. So, if you're happy being with me, then why can't it be that easy? Why make it complicated when it's not?"

I could feel the temptation to succumb to his reasoning and just let everything else go. It would be so simple and effortless to accept what he was offering, but I couldn't let myself do that. If I disregarded his past transgressions, then he would win. I wasn't going to let that happen.

He exhaled and spoke before I could form my thoughts into an answer. "Okay, I'll back off and let you have some space to adjust to things. Spend some time with your friends, and then we'll talk next week after you've had a chance to get used to everything being different."

He bent down and picked up the bag I had dropped and extended it to me. "Do you want this? It might help you feel better."

"No," I replied. "I'm fine."

"Okay," he said. "I guess I'll leave you alone now."

I could see his reluctance to do that though, as he lingered there. "Will you still go on the date with me today?"

"That's not really you leaving me alone," I said.

"Right," he replied, sounding disappointed. "Okay, then I hope you have fun this weekend. Call me if you need anything."

"Okay," I agreed, although he would be the last person I would ever think of calling for help with anything. "Bye."

I set myself in motion and took the reprieve he had unexpectedly given me. It would finally give me a chance to contemplate everything and figure out what I was doing.

Chapter 13

My life still felt like a whirlwind though. I had so much going on now that I had forgotten about Josh until I saw him in class. The heated look he gave me made me remember our kisses with a jolt. How could I forget about our wild interlude in the bathroom? It had been at the forefront of my mind after it happened, and it was supposed to replace all thoughts of Mason. Yet here I was obsessing over him again. He'd managed to do something so unexpected that it distracted me from what I had done with Josh. My kisses with him were suddenly not much of anything in comparison to Mason asking me to be his girlfriend.

He had changed tactics on me again by asking instead of demanding, and that had made a huge difference to me. The impact on me was even stronger than kissing him had been, and I didn't know how Josh could make me react to him that way and make me forget about Mason. I seemed to be even more susceptible to Mason's romantic gestures than I was to the physical attraction I felt for him. I could only hope that Josh would do something more romantic and become the only guy on my mind.

Getting some distance from Mason should also help me clear my head. I was surprised that he had volunteered to leave me alone for awhile and give me some space. It wasn't like him to be so thoughtful and considerate, and it made me wonder what was going on in his mind. I couldn't see how this could be a trick though. Unless he was going to use this as an opportunity to cheat on me.

That thought slithered its way through my mind and left me in an unpleasant state of suspicion. I started obsessing about which girl he would hook up with. That led to me going to sit with him at lunch so that I could spy on him. He was surprised to see me approach his table but quickly asked the girl sitting next to him to move so that I could have her seat. She obliged without protest, but my scrutiny narrowed in on her.

I had been introduced to her the previous day but had forgotten her name. "Thanks, uh…"

Mason supplied her name just as I knew he would. "Madison."

"Madison," I repeated, taking in her long brunette hair and sultry dark eyes.

She appraised me coolly as she took a seat across the table from me. Her dislike of me wasn't blatant, but nothing about her was. She was more understated in how she dressed than most of the other popular girls who showed off their figures to their best advantage. That was why she had slipped under my radar at first glance, but I saw that she was very pretty upon closer inspection. The girl was a stealthy threat, and I knew that Mason was discerning enough to notice her lithe, graceful beauty.

She actually looked like someone who would fit right into his former wealthy neighborhood. Even her name sounded upper class. And it fit so well with Mason. Madison and Mason. She was the kind of girl he could bring home to meet his mother, the kind of girl he could marry. Madison Sumner. I tested the name out in my mind.

Suddenly, I felt like the hookup, and Madison seemed like the girlfriend. All Mason ever wanted to do was see me naked. There had been the picture, and now there were the terms of the bet. He had made me clean his house in that skimpy maid uniform, which I couldn't imagine him doing to Madison. He would probably take her to fancy restaurants in a limo, and...

"Here," Mason said, cutting into my thoughts. "I got it back for you."

He was pulling the smiley face balloon out from under the table, and he tied it to the handle of my backpack, which I had placed on the floor beside my chair. My level of happiness over him giving me back that balloon was out of proportion for such a simple gift, but it reaffirmed that I was his girlfriend. He was acknowledging that in front of everyone with a visual reminder, and my spirits soared.

I beamed at him. "Thank you."

He responded with a dazzling smile. "You're welcome."

"That's so cute!" Erin exclaimed with her signature sunny enthusiasm.

That girl was quickly endearing herself to me, and I smiled warmly at her. Mason drew my attention again as he set the two packs of crackers he had bought me on the table in front of me. "I see you only have water again. At least eat a few of these," he urged.

I had gotten only a bottle of water, because I had been in a hurry to get to his table and observe him to see which girl he wanted to hook up with. I had been too riled up to feel hunger, but my appetite stirred at the sight of the crackers. They were a perfect snack for my nervous stomach, since my awareness of Madison had returned when Alicia made another comment about me being on a diet. I had looked in her direction but caught Madison's gaze instead. She was seated right next to Alicia, who was still running her mouth, but neither Madison nor I were paying any attention to her.

After a moment of studying me, Madison's gaze shifted to Mason as she appeared to lose interest in me. "That was so thoughtful of you, Mason," she praised him in her calm, cool tone.

My attention snapped back to him as she spoke to him, and I watched him make eye contact with her as he responded. "Well, I have to take care of my girl."

His cool tone matched hers, and they gave off the impression of being adults speaking about a child. My confidence plummeted, and the balloon now made me feel embarrassed. My childish delight over it was as immature as my little temper tantrum in the hallway earlier this morning. No wonder Mason could manipulate me so easily.

In my agitation, I ripped open a pack of crackers and shoved one in my mouth before realizing how uncouth that looked. Madison would never stress eat like that in public, and I doubted she did it in private either judging by her slim body. I chewed my mouthful awkwardly and took a sip of water after swallowing it down. Sitting up straighter in emulation of Madison, I delicately nibbled on another cracker.

"Thank you for these, Mason," I said, affecting a cultured, cool tone.

I saw him regarding me with amusement, but he replied with the same civil politeness. "You're welcome, Ella."

"We don't want you to starve," Alicia said. Apparently not caring at all about manners, she grabbed a hot dog out of the bun on her boyfriend's plate and flung it at me. "Here, put that in your mouth." She snickered as it hit me in the chest and landed on the table in front of me.

"Hey!" her boyfriend protested.

I looked down at the mustard on my shirt in dismay. Erin jumped up out of her seat and brought me some napkins to wipe it off.

"Alicia," Mason said in the calmest voice I had ever heard him use, "you don't sit here anymore."

He sounded so neutral and nonthreatening that it took her a moment to comprehend that he was kicking her out. "What?" she asked, still not quite understanding.

"Leave," Madison said in that same unconcerned tone that Mason had.

Alicia stared at her before her gaze swept around the silent table looking for someone to help her. Nobody did, and they all averted their gazes from her. Even her boyfriend didn't say a word.

"Seriously?" she demanded incredulously.

"You were mean to Ella," Erin spoke up.

"Are you kidding me?" Alicia raged. "You're going to take that slut's side over mine? She's—"

She cut off abruptly as Mason shot to his feet, but Madison spoke coolly before he could react further. "People who live in glass houses shouldn't throw stones, Alicia. Slut shaming is so hurtful. How would you feel if my brother called you a slut?"

All the color drained from Alicia's face, and her gaze flew to her boyfriend's suddenly suspicious expression. "What does that mean?" he demanded. "Did you fuck her brother?"

"I...no! I don't know what she's talking about," she said unconvincingly.

"She's always had a crush on him," Madison commented, "even though he's such a player. I warned her, but she said she had to go for it before he left for college."

"You are such a bitch!" Alicia exclaimed.

"Again, people who live in glass houses shouldn't—"

"Shut up!" Alicia yelled. "This is all because of Ryan, isn't it? Well, I can't help it if he likes girls with boobs instead of flat—"

Alicia's tirade came to an abrupt halt when her boyfriend scraped his chair back as he got up and stormed off. "Connor!" she called out in distress and ran after him.

Mason relaxed and patted Erin on the back. "Thanks for helping Ella," he told her before sitting back down.

She turned from gaping at the couple who had just left the cafeteria and replied to him. "Yeah, of course." Glancing at my shirt, she shook her head. "That was crazy."

She was probably referring more to the rest of the incident than Alicia throwing a hot dog at me. Mason spoke then and drew my attention. "Thank you too, Madison, for standing up for Ella."

"Yeah, thank you," I said.

She barely glanced at me, and her eyes were on Mason as she responded. "Of course. We have to take care of your girl."

I might have been paranoid, but that sounded ominous to me. I had just seen her "take care" of Alicia, and I doubted she had done it for me. While I had no sympathy for Alicia, Madison had obviously betrayed their supposed friendship by revealing that dirty secret in front of everyone. She was cold and calculating, and I didn't trust her. At least Alicia had been upfront about her dislike of me, and I knew what to expect from her. Madison was nearly impossible to read. I wasn't sure if she disliked me or had simply dismissed me as of being of no interest to her whatsoever.

"Man, I thought that was going to be more of a girl fight," Tyler complained. "You should have fought back, Ella."

I shrugged like the incident hadn't bothered me. "All she did was throw food at me. I guess I could have thrown my crackers at her, but I don't think it would have made much of an impact."

"No," he agreed. "You needed whipped cream. And bikinis."

I laughed, because by this time I'd come to the conclusion that Tyler was harmless. He was actually more ridiculous than sleazy with his sexual innuendos and comments. "Next time," I joked.

He grinned. "You're alright, Ella."

I didn't realize how pleased I was with his approval until I realized that I was grinning back at him. "So are you, Tyler."

I felt an arm drape around my shoulders and looked over to see Mason scowling at Tyler. He felt my gaze and glanced at me, and I smiled at him as I relaxed in the comfort of his arm around me. His expression smoothed out, and a smile slowly formed on his lips.

"Bro, you are so whipped!" Tyler exclaimed in what sounded more like amazement than teasing.

Mason glanced in his direction, but my focus was all on him. His skin seemed to be slightly flushed, and I had the thought that he might be embarrassed. My heart started an erratic beat at the possibility. Could it be true? Was Mason really into me?

His gaze returned to me and took my breath away. It was too much, too overwhelming. Becoming incredibly flustered, I looked away from him and happened to catch Josh watching us suspiciously. Heat flooded my face as I felt like he had just discovered my secret crush on Mason. Telling myself that he couldn't possibly know just from looking at me, I nevertheless averted my gaze from his.

That's when I saw Mason watching me, and my heart went into overdrive with panic. He doesn't know, I told myself as I tried to quell my paranoia. He didn't know that I had kissed Josh. Nobody did, so there was no reason that he would. Yeah, the thought came, because you were so discrete kissing him in the bathroom at school.

Anyone could have seen him come in there. But they hadn't, I assured myself. We had been alone in the restroom, and the hallways had been empty due to classes being in session. Our secret was safe as long as I didn't give myself away. With a tremendous effort that strained my nerves to the max, I managed to sit there and produce a smile for Mason.

His unnerving scrutiny continued for several more seconds before he smiled back at me. I didn't dare look at Josh again for the rest of lunch, and I was very glad when it was over. Mason, however, wasn't done with me.

"What's going on?" he asked as we walked out into the hallway.

My heart leapt up into my throat in alarm, but I tried not to show my nervousness. "Nothing. What?"

"You know what I'm talking about," he insisted with a sideways glance at me. "What were you doing there at lunch?"

I defended myself by turning it around on him. "What were *you* doing? Were you making plans with Madison for this weekend? Did I interrupt something?"

"I knew you were jealous!" he declared with a smirk.

"I am not jealous," I huffed. "In fact, I think she's perfect for you. Go ahead and be snobs together and look down on everyone else. Take her home to meet your mother. What do I care?"

I halted and turned to glare at him as he started laughing at me. I almost fell into him when someone knocked into me, and Mason laughed even harder before grabbing my hand to pull me aside out of the way of other students.

"I'll cancel my exciting plans to be a snob with Madison," he told me in amusement. "But only for you."

"You don't have to do anything for me," I snapped. "I told you I don't care what you do."

"You do care," he said as his expression became heated. He stepped closer and lifted a strand of my hair to run through his fingers as he spoke. "I like that you got jealous, and that you don't want me to be with anyone else."

His intense gaze fixed on mine. "That's how I feel about you too, Ella, and I'm so glad that you said yes to being my girlfriend."

I opened my mouth to protest, but he spoke first. "I know I said I'll leave you alone for now, and I will. Let me just walk you to class."

I couldn't argue with that, so I allowed him to take my hand as we walked together to my classroom. It felt so nice, and it was the most natural thing in the world for me to give my boyfriend a brief kiss in parting.

I didn't really realize what I had done until I pulled back with a soft smile and saw his intense expression. "Ella," he said in a voice that conveyed things I didn't dare hope for.

His gaze held mine with intense emotion before he dipped his head and pressed his lips to mine in a brief but powerful kiss that left me staring after him in a daze as he decisively strode away.

Chapter 14

I was still in a trance as I drifted into the classroom and took my seat. Impressions of Mason lingered in my mind. The look in his eyes, the sound of his voice, the feel of his lips on mine. I was intoxicated by him, and the realization came slowly that I had fallen under his spell again. It felt exactly the same as when I first saw his picture and became captivated by him. I should have known better by now, but I felt the same magnetic pull toward him and had the same yearning in my heart to be with him. That's when I knew that my feelings for him hadn't been destroyed when he trampled on them. They had only gone dormant, and they were rising to the surface now.

The troubling thought that I might never be able to rid myself of them worried me, but I rejected that idea. It was just a crush, and of course it would end eventually and be replaced by a new crush. I just had to keep my wits about me until then. What had I been thinking when I went to stake my territory at lunch today, which was what I now realized I had been doing. I should have walked away when I saw Madison sitting with him instead of going to claim my spot beside him. If he cheated on me, he would lose the bet. That was exactly what I wanted, but I had been overcome with jealousy and sabotaged the opportunity.

Not that he couldn't still cheat on me with her. All I had really done was make it more humiliating for myself if he did. I had made it obvious to him that it would bother me, when I should have been indifferent. I had to focus on the fact that it would free me from him.

It would be good to gain some distance from him this weekend and concentrate on other people. Connecting with my friends would help me disconnect from Mason. I was probably only feeling this attachment to him because he was my entire social life right now. Once that changed, I would stop feeling so possessive of him. After all, I didn't even miss Addison anymore, and I had spent a lot more time with her. Mason would also fade into the background of my life after we went our separate ways.

I ignored the fact that I couldn't imagine him ever fading into the background. He commanded attention whenever he stepped into a room, and I wasn't sure if that had more to do with his looks or the way he carried himself. Maybe it was just because he had come from a life of privilege and felt entitled to be deferred to by people with less money.

Whatever it was, people reacted to it. He was always noticed. I could ignore him, however, if he left me alone. My awareness of him stemmed from the antagonism between us, but that was gone now. All that would be left was the memory of kissing him, but I would be more focused on new experiences. He would be living his life, and I would finally be living mine.

That had yet to happen though, because he insisted on driving me home after school. "This is it for the week," he promised. "Since I drove you to school, I should drive you home. Besides, I have something for you."

I felt a jolt of excitement over his words. Had he decided to give me my poem back? I didn't dare voice that thought in the fear that appearing too anxious about it would prompt him to change his mind. Instead, I docilely went with him to his car.

I was on pins and needles as he made small talk during the ride home, asking me if I was excited about going to the concert and about what other concerts I wanted to go to. I engaged in conversation with him as best I could, but he noticed my distraction.

"What's wrong?" he asked as he pulled into my driveway and turned off the car.

"Nothing," I replied and forced a smile to convey that everything was fine.

"Ella," he said in a warning tone.

"Nothing," I repeated. "It's just, um, you said that you have something for me?"

"Oh," he responded as his tense expression relaxed. "Yeah, I've got the pictures."

He turned and reached into the backseat to grab his backpack. Pulling a large envelope out of it, he handed it to me. "Cassie sent them to me yesterday, and I went and had them developed. I made some of them larger so you can put them in your modeling portfolio. I'll send you the digitals too."

"Oh. Thanks," I said.

Apparently, I didn't manage to hide my disappointment well enough, because he questioned me again. "What is wrong, Ella? Tell me," he demanded.

"I thought you were going to give me back my poem," I admitted.

He studied me in silence for a moment as I dropped my gaze to the envelope in my hands. "I'll give it back to you soon," he said.

My gaze shot back to him in surprise. "You will?"

"Yeah," he answered. "I think we—"

"Mason!" my mom's voice interrupted him as it carried to us through his open window.

We both looked and saw her approaching the car. "Come inside," she urged. "You don't need to sit out here."

He glanced at me uncertainly. "I was just dropping Ella off," he told her.

"Can't you stay just a little while?" she asked him in a disturbingly flirty voice. "You took off so fast yesterday that I hardly got a chance to thank you for the ice cream."

"That was for Ella. *Everything* is for Ella," he emphasized as he looked at her with a flat expression in his eyes.

She glanced at me, and I could tell that it was more out of nervousness than to acknowledge my presence. Mason had managed to unnerve her, which I had never seen happen to her before. She always had men eating out of her hand, but he wasn't reacting to her in the way she was used to.

At the same time, his declaration had done something entirely different to me. I felt strangely grounded and secure even as my heart soared in elation.

"Did you give it to her?" he demanded.

"I...well, it was just so tempting that I couldn't help myself. I know I don't need the calories," she said and gestured toward her beautiful body, recovering her confidence in the knowledge that she still possessed perfect curves.

Mason's hard gaze remained on her face though. "Don't you ever take anything that belongs to Ella."

She was startled by his harsh tone. "I'm sorry. I didn't think that—"

"It's okay," I cut in, wanting to end the conflict. "I wasn't going to eat it anyway. I went out for ice cream yesterday with Zoey."

"See? She had ice cream," Mom told him brightly. "Everyone is happy."

He regarded her in stony-faced silence until she became so uncomfortable that she looked to me in desperation. "How was school today, Ella?"

"Good," I replied awkwardly, knowing that she had no real interest in hearing about my day.

I decided to get out of the car so I could end this confrontation. "Okay, thanks for the ride, Mason," I said as I opened the door and made a quick exit without waiting for a reply.

He got out too though, seemingly unwilling to leave yet as he came to stand beside me. Mom noticed the envelope in my hand and seized on it as a distraction from the awkwardness. "What's that?"

"These are the pictures," I replied.

That cheered her up. "Oh! Yes, the pictures! Let me see them."

I reluctantly handed them over to her. She pulled them out and set the envelope down on the hood of Mason's car without giving a thought to how he might react. I glanced warily at him, but he said nothing. Curious to see the pictures myself, I moved closer to look at them with my mom.

I was surprised by how good they looked. I never stopped to take myself in this way, but my image in those pictures was eye-catchingly attractive. Even Mom exclaimed over them. "These are perfect! You look beautiful, Ella."

Her praise was wonderful to hear. I got so little validation from my mom that it affected me more than it should considering that I tried not to focus on my looks.

"She *is* beautiful," Mason spoke over my shoulder, and his compliment had even more of an impact on me.

When your boyfriend tells you're beautiful, it means a lot more than when your mom says it. Or maybe it was just how close he was standing to me. I sensed him behind me, radiating heat and warming me like the sun on my skin. It had the potential to be blazing hot, but right now it was blissfully warm, and I soaked it up like sunshine. I settled back against him, and his arms came around my waist in an embrace that was perfect comfort and support. The electricity was there too, buzzing beneath my skin, but in latent mode right now.

It began to spark when Mom came to the picture of us beside Mason's pool. She stopped and stared at it. I did too at seeing how evident the sexual tension between us was in the photograph. It was so obvious that it was embarrassing— but also discomfortingly arousing—for me to look at.

Was that what people saw when they looked at us? Was the attraction between us that obvious all the time? My face went hot at the thought of it, and I suddenly wanted out of Mason's arms. He let go of me in that instant and stepped away from my body.

"This is amazing! I didn't know that you're a model too," Mom said. "The agency will love this! I bet they don't get a lot of people applying together, so you'll stand out."

"I'm not applying," Mason told her. "These are just for Ella. I already sent them digital ones of her."

Mom balked and dropped the pictures before spinning around to look at him. "You applied for her? Which agency did you send it to?"

"All the top ones," he replied. "Might as well go for it if you're going to go for it."

"What?" I exclaimed. "How could you do that without asking me? You heard me tell her that I don't want to be a model."

"What did you put for her height?" Mom asked, seemingly as upset as me.

Mason answered her first. "Five six. I checked her driver's license to make sure."

He then began to speak to me. "It doesn't hurt to try, Ella. You can always tell them no if—"

"You shouldn't have done that!" Mom interrupted him in distress. "They want tall girls, so I was going to put that she's five nine so they'd give her a chance. They told me I was too short, but I was hoping that maybe Ella could—"

I whirled on her as I cut her off. "Wait, they turned you down? You said that you couldn't go because of me."

"Of course, I couldn't go on modeling shoots with a baby," she retorted.

"But they turned you down anyway," I said. "All this time you made me feel like it was my fault, like I kept you from your dream, when it had nothing to do with me at all."

"I would have tried again," she insisted. "I would have gone there and seen them in person, and I would have talked them into giving me a chance. Just like you'll have to do now that he screwed this up for you." For the first time, she cast a disapproving look at Mason.

"Sorry I'm not a liar," he shot back. "How would that have made her look when they found out she lied about her height? Don't you think they would have noticed she's not five nine when they met her?"

She waved his logic off in exasperation. "That wouldn't matter once she got her foot in the door. Other short models have made it big. It's just about making the right connections."

"And how do you expect her to do that?" he asked.

"There are ways," she said. "A lot of doors will open for a beautiful girl if she knows what she's doing. I'll just have to make sure she meets the right people."

"This is over," I declared and stepped over to scoop the pictures up from the hood of his car and return them to the envelope. Just because I didn't care about modeling didn't mean that I didn't want to keep these photographs for myself. "I never wanted this anyway, and I'm not going to beg anyone to make me a model."

"What ways?" Mason pressed with an edge to his tone that made me take notice. His hard gaze was fixed on Mom.

She didn't appear intimidated in the least, and she let out a bitter laugh. "Look at you getting all possessive like you care. You want to be her one and only, but *you* still get to play around, don't you? And if she comes to you when she really needs you, where will you be then? Sorry babe," she said, pitching her voice lower in imitation of a masculine tone, "but I'm still in high school. I don't know what you expect me to do."

Her own gaze hardened. "You have to look out for yourself in this world. That's what I found out, and that's what Ella's gonna do."

His expression became unreadable as he regarded her, and I was fascinated to know what he might be thinking. He revealed nothing as he spoke though. "Seems we both want to look out for Ella," he replied crisply. "I'm just wondering what your version of that is."

Her eyes sparked with anger, and she sneered at him. "My *version* has her becoming rich and famous. What are *you* gonna do for her besides get in her pants?"

"Mom!" I exclaimed in embarrassment, but both of them ignored me as they continued their standoff.

"Does that bother you?" Mason challenged. "Me getting in your daughter's pants."

"No," she answered nonplussed. "I've had her on the pill since she was fourteen, so I'm not worried about it."

My face flamed in mortification at her revealing that to him. She made it sound like I'd been having sex since I was fourteen when in reality, I'd never needed birth control at all. Unbeknownst to her, I'd never taken one pill and had thrown them all away instead.

"And are you worried about guys wanting to get in her pants in exchange for making her rich and famous?" Mason asked so smoothly that he could have been talking about any neutral topic instead of me trading sexual favors for fame and wealth.

Mom shrugged like it was no big deal. "That's how it works. It's called the casting couch."

Mason stiffened. "No, it's called sexual harassment."

She rolled her eyes. "That's just ugly girls bitching about being stupid enough to believe they could get anywhere by spreading their legs. Maybe that would work in business or somewhere boring like that, but not in Hollywood. You still have to have the right look, and Ella does."

Mason smiled, but in his eyes was the look of a predator. "Ella," he said in a tone that could almost pass for pleasant, "we're leaving now."

He spared a brief glance at me. "Bring your bathing suit."

I debated for all of two seconds before realizing that he wasn't going to leave without me, and that I needed to get him away from my mom before he snapped. I wasn't sure what he would do if he did, but I didn't want to find out. I had assured Alice that Mason would never hurt me physically, but my faith in his control of his temper didn't extend to my mom's safety around him. She might be a trigger for him, so I tried to get her to come into the house with me, but she shook me off.

"I won't steal your boyfriend," she threw out with a careless laugh that set me on edge.

Gritting my teeth, I stomped off into the house and up to my room. Setting the pictures down on my desk, I yanked open my dresser drawer and pulled out my one-piece swimsuit. Despite thinking that my mom would deserve what she got if she tried to put the moves on Mason, I hurried back outside to them.

To my relief, Mason was sitting in his car with the engine running. His window was closed, and he wasn't looking at my mom who stood beside him watching him. She appeared unharmed, and she glanced at me with a smirk.

"Well," she said, "I'm glad you're on the pill. That boy is all man."

Before I could even try to guess her reason for saying that, Mason's voice snapped at me like a whip. "Ella! Get in the car."

It startled me since I hadn't heard him put his window down. My gaze shot toward him, and I saw his hard expression fixed on me. It prompted me to move and quickly get in the car. Mason started backing out as soon as I shut my door. He came to an abrupt stop at the end of the driveway.

"Seatbelt," he commanded tersely.

He spun the car out onto the street as soon as I complied and peeled off with a screech of tires. Adrenaline surged through me even after he eased off the gas and settled into a normal, steady speed. Mason remained tense, and I didn't dare ask him why he was so angry. He drove in silence to his house and directed me to change in a spare bedroom.

"Come out to the pool when you're done," he told me.

There were no heated looks and no sexual tension between us this time. I wasn't worried about him trying to see me change out of my clothes, but I walked out to the pool in wariness of his mood. He was swimming laps back and forth from one end of the pool to the other. I stood and watched him for a couple of minutes before he noticed me.

"Come in," he urged and went back to swimming laps without another word.

Feeling freed to take advantage of the opportunity presented to me, I indulged in having the pool practically to myself. Swimming laps until I tired, I then floated lazily on my back as I gazed at the blue sky and basked in the sunshine.

To my surprise, Mason joined me and floated beside me in peaceful silence. The tension that had been emanating from him earlier was gone now, and I relaxed into a near trance until he spoke and drew my attention.

"You're welcome to use the pool any time you want. You can invite Zoey too."

"Thanks," I replied. "And thank you for inviting me today. This is so much nicer than going to the Y. I love swimming outside."

He stood up and came over to me. "Why haven't you been going to the rec center then? They have an outdoor pool."

"People from school go there," I answered. "I try to avoid them as much as I can."

He looked pained. "Because of me. I'm sorry, Ella. I had no idea what you were dealing with."

I gave him a disbelieving look. "Uh, you didn't know that they would harass me after you told them all those nasty lies about me and my mom?"

His gaze sharpened, and his voice sounded softly dangerous. "How did they harass you?"

"They called me all kinds of names and treated me like dirt," I told him. "I didn't want to hear it, so I avoided places where I knew they went."

"Did anyone ever touch you?" he asked.

"No," I responded.

Feeling too agitated by this conversation to relax any longer, I stood up too. The water was up to my nose though, so I swam over to the side of the pool. Mason followed me and stood beside me as I held on to the edge.

He expelled a big breath as he gazed at me with a troubled expression. "I actually felt sympathy for her for a minute when she was talking about her asshole boyfriend leaving her to deal with her pregnancy on her own."

As I realized that he was referring to my mother, he took a shaky breath before his expression hardened. "Then she started making plans to prostitute you, and I wanted to strangle her."

I gaped at him. "Prostitute me? Do you really believe that escort stuff you've been telling everyone?"

"The casting couch," he snapped. "Do you know what that is? She wants you to trade sexual favors for modeling jobs."

"Oh," I said dismissively, "I don't want to be a model anyway, so I don't have to worry about it."

"But she wanted you to do it! She actually wanted you to have sex with guys for money. What kind of mother is that? I thought mine sucked, but yours is even worse!"

I looked away from him uncomfortably, reluctant to acknowledge that as truth. "She has crazy ideas sometimes, but she's not so bad."

"You're a very forgiving person," he said. "I'm not, but I'll tolerate her for you."

I turned to look at him in surprise. "You will?"

He gave me a pained smile. "If I want to be with you, then I have to put up with her, don't I?"

Something lightened in my chest, causing a tentative smile to surface on my face. I knew how much he hated my mother, but he was willing to put up with her for me? He wanted to be with me that much?

His expression turned serious. "That whole casting couch thing. I would never do that."

"Uh, okay," I said, slightly bewildered with the direction of his thoughts. "Yeah, of course you shouldn't do that to get a job. It's not worth it." I shuddered at the thought of being molested by some sleazy, middle-aged pervert.

He reacted in bewilderment himself before barking out a laugh. "No! Not me on the casting couch." His amusement was brief, though, and his smile quickly faded. "I meant I wouldn't do that to you—to anyone. I wouldn't use my power to get sex. I want you to know that I wouldn't have tried to blackmail you into it."

"I wouldn't have let you," I declared. "I would have let you post the picture before I would do that."

"Good," he said, sounding like he meant it. "I'm glad to know you won't go for something like that, even if your mother pressures you into it."

I looked at him in dismay. "Of course, I wouldn't let her talk me into having sex with someone for a job! I can't believe you thought I would."

"With all that pressure on you from your own mother," he began, looking troubled. "I wouldn't blame you for that. I would blame her and whatever perverted asshole took advantage of you." His jaw clenched at that imagined scenario.

A fluttery sensation gained momentum in my stomach in response to his protectiveness and understanding for me. "You don't have to worry about that," I told him, instinctively reassuring him without giving any thought as to why I would need to.

"I *was* worried about it," he said. "I would go crazy if someone had sex with you. I would go out of my fucking mind."

My pulse jumped and then skittered at his admission, and the butterflies in my stomach went into a frenzy. "Mason," I said, my voice sounding so shaky that he had to know how he affected me.

"Ella," he responded as his gaze became electric.

His touch sent a charge through me as he took hold of me and pulled me into him. My legs wrapped around his waist in the cool water as he brought his hot mouth to mine. It was so sexy that I moaned as his tongue caressed mine.

"I'm glad I caught you before you got naked this time."

I gasped in shock and quickly unentangled myself from Mason at the sound of the woman's voice. Clinging to the side of the pool again, I looked up at her and got another shock as I recognized her.

"Mom," Mason said flatly. "I didn't know you were coming home."

There was nothing in his expression to indicate that he had missed her or was glad to see her. Her own gaze showed mild fondness as she looked at him. "Yes, well, my plans changed suddenly. And I missed you," she threw out like it was an afterthought. "I decided I might as well come see you and catch up with you."

"Might as well," he agreed.

She apparently mistook the sarcasm in his voice for aggravation over her interruption of our kiss. "Sorry I interrupted your little tryst, but you can see your girlfriends any time. I'm only here for a week, so it's not too much to ask for you to spend this time with me."

"It's not much at all," he stated.

Once again, his criticism of her went right over her head. "Good. Now go shower and get dressed. We have dinner reservations at six."

I had moved down away from them as they spoke, and I tried to unobtrusively pull myself out of the pool and quietly slip away. Mason pulled himself out in a flash with his strong arms though and bypassed his mother to come and help me to my feet.

"Mom," he said as he kept hold of my hand and turned to face her, "I'd like you to meet my girlfriend, Ella."

Surprise showed on her face before her gaze shifted to me. Then her mouth dropped open as she stared at me in complete shock.

"This is Ella, Mom." Mason's voice sounded like he was urging her to accept that rather than stating a fact. "She's not...she's Ella," he finished, seemingly at a loss for words.

Her gaze snapped toward him. "Her daughter?"

"Yeah," he confirmed uncomfortably.

The horrible realization hit me then, and my stomach sank. Never in my life had I hated looking like my mother as much as I did in that moment. Knowing that she had seen the spitting image of the woman her husband had cheated on her with when she looked at me made me ashamed to be standing in front of her. My gaze dropped to the cement at my feet, and I pulled my hand out of Mason's grasp.

"Sorry," I expelled inadequately and backed up before turning to hurry away.

"Ella," Mason called after me, but I fled into the house.

I went immediately upstairs and put my clothes on right over my wet bathing suit in my hurry to be gone from this place. I was flooded with renewed shame as I thought about the position Mason's mom had caught us in. Even if she hadn't known who I was, I had already made a bad impression on her. The only thing I could do now was remove myself from her sight.

As I clamored down the stairs in my haste, Mason moved into view at the bottom of them. "You didn't have to rush off like—Jesus, Ella, you didn't even change!"

I glanced past him anxiously, looking for his mom.

"She left," he told me.

I halted in dismay. "Left? Where did she go?"

"Back to her hotel. She's going to send a car for me, but we have time. You can go back up and change out of your bathing suit before I drive you home."

I had forgotten that he had driven me here, but that barely registered through my bewilderment. "She went to a hotel?"

He responded with a cold smile. "You didn't think she'd slum it here, did you?" he questioned derisively.

I gaped at him. "She doesn't stay here with you?"

He gave me another thin smile. "My mom is used to five-star treatment. She's not going to rough it here without maid service and a staff to cater to her."

But she just said she wanted to spend time with you, I almost protested. I closed my mouth instead to prevent myself from pointing that out. I didn't want to make Mason feel any worse than he already did, but anger at his mother flared to life within me. Her selfishness hurt her son, and I was starting to hate her for it. She left him alone most of the time, and then she couldn't even make a small sacrifice for him for the short time that she was here.

Composing myself, I attempted a joke to lighten the mood. "No wonder you said she's a terrible housekeeper."

"Yeah," he said flatly. "She doesn't keep house at all."

"Well," I said, going into my default mode of making excuses for her like I did with my mother, "heiresses aren't known for their housekeeping skills. When you grow up with maids doing everything for you, like someone I know," I added with a pointed look at him, which was more playful teasing to get him out of his funk than actual criticism.

He scoffed. "My mom's not an heiress. She grew up in a suburb like this, but she acts like she came from the ghetto the way she carries on about *never going back*. I grew up with a housekeeping staff, but I'm handling this better than she is. Granted, I have maids come clean once a week, but I pick up after myself from day to day. It's not like I can't lift a finger to do *anything*."

I didn't know which of these surprising revelations to tackle first. "But you had a bunch of dust and dirt!" I exclaimed.

He gave me a sheepish smile. "Yeah, I cancelled maid service for a couple of months so you'd have more to clean." He shook his head. "I really was an asshole to you."

I didn't know what to do with that statement besides feeling a general sense of satisfaction that he had acknowledged it without any prompting from me. Feeling no need to belabor the point he had already stated, I moved on to the other thing he had told me. "Your mom didn't grow up rich? How did she meet your dad?"

"She was his secretary," he replied with another thin smile. "Isn't that a cliché," he remarked. "But I guess she knew what she was doing since she became his wife."

I bristled at that comment. "You make it sound like she planned it. Maybe she fell in love with him! Did you ever think of that?"

"She made it pretty clear she didn't give a shit about him," he retorted. "She was always going somewhere without him. No wonder he..."

"Cheated on her?" I demanded. "You think it was okay for him to do that? Did you see her face when she saw me? Did that look like a woman who didn't care that her husband cheated on her?"

"It was just the shock," he said defensively. "You look so much like your mother that it just stunned her for a minute."

"Why would she even remember my mom's face if she didn't care about who he slept with?" I challenged.

His jaw clenched before he replied. "He died in bed with her. That's not something you forget."

That pretty much killed the conversation, and Mason offered to drive me home after a moment during which neither one of us said anything as we avoided looking at each other.

It wasn't until I was alone in the shower washing off the chlorine from his pool and thinking about everything that had happened there this afternoon that my mind focused on what his mom had said about catching him before he got naked this time.

The realization that she had caught him naked in the pool with another girl in the past brought a clarity that I didn't want to face. What could be sexier than being half-naked in a private pool with Mason? I wondered how many girls he had seduced there. That was why he had brought me there, and it had worked on me just as easily as it had on the others. If his mom hadn't interrupted us...

I tried to imagine what would have happened, but I wasn't sure. Would I have stopped him or succumbed entirely to desire? The fact that I didn't know troubled me greatly. I couldn't predict my own actions around him, and that was scary.

At least those other girls had presumably known what they wanted. They knew they wanted to be with Mason, but I kept telling myself that I didn't. Did I even know what I wanted anymore? I kept losing myself in him and forgetting everything else, and that was going to ruin me.

I had to break his hold on me, even if it took drastic measures.

I texted Josh after my shower. *Is there anywhere where we can be alone?*

He responded almost immediately. *My house. When can I pick you up?*

Now

I was only slightly nervous after I sent that text, which told me that I recognized Josh as a safe choice. I knew exactly what I wanted from him, and I could picture step by step how it would all go. It was simple, easy, and uncomplicated. I didn't have all these conflicted feelings about him, and the attraction between us wasn't too intense. I could handle it without losing control. Without forgetting who I was or what I was doing.

Conversely, I needed him to affect me enough to replace Mason in my thoughts. Which meant that I needed to take it further with him than I had with Mason.

Exposed to you
As I breathe your name
Hoping, wishing
That you feel the same

With every heartbeat
I reveal to you
That every kiss
Is real and true

Lost behind smoky eyes
I search for you and try to see

A text message alert startled me, but I froze when I saw what I had written on the piece of paper I had earlier been doodling on as I waited for Josh to let me know he was on his way. He had told me that he was going to take a quick shower before picking me up. I grabbed my phone and saw that he had texted me. Replying to him with a simple ok, I shoved the poem I had been writing into my desk drawer and hurried downstairs.

I didn't want to think about what it meant or why I had pulled it from my subconscious. I tried to focus on my plans with Josh and get in the right mood for what I was about to do. Since my mom and dad weren't home, I didn't have to deal with my dad interrogating Josh before I could leave with him.

We could have stayed here, but I didn't want to take the chance of my dad catching Josh here alone with me. I couldn't have him making a bad impression on my dad when he was the boy that I could bring home to meet my parents. Mason wasn't ever supposed to play that role.

Josh showed once again that he wasn't the smooth operator that Mason was. The nervous excitement emanating from him was exactly what I would have expected from a teenage boy about to spend private time alone with a girl. Mason, I now realized, had the cool, sexy confidence of a man. That boy is all man, I remembered my mom saying, and I understood what she meant. I wondered what had made her come to that conclusion though.

"Uh, are you okay, Ella?"

Josh's voice roused me from my thoughts, and I blinked at him. "Yeah. Why?"

"You looked kind of mad," he replied. "Did you...um, did you still want to come inside?"

I glanced out and saw that we had apparently arrived at his house. "Oh. Yeah, okay."

I could see the excitement surge within him again, and his voice was shaky with it. "Okay." He pushed open his door and got out quickly.

I was slower, but he came around and took my hand to pull me out of my seat. "Your parents aren't home?" I enquired, double checking to be sure.

"Business trip," he told me. "They won't be home until Monday."

"My parents aren't home either, but they only went out to dinner for their anniversary," I said, glad that he had the house to himself for a longer time, and that I wouldn't have to worry about his parents coming home at an inopportune time.

"We have all night," he confirmed with that mixture of nervousness and excitement.

I knew that I couldn't stay all night, and I wasted no time once we were inside his house. Initiating a kiss, I hoped that he would take over since I had no experience beyond this. He did after leading me up to his room.

It looked exactly like I had always imagined a teenage boy's bedroom to look, messy with posters of bikini clad models on his walls. His bed was unmade, but it didn't matter to me when he gradually laid me down on it after we kissed for a while seated together on it. He stretched out beside me on his side as he resumed kissing me. I made no protest when he placed his hand on my breast, and his kisses became more passionate as he fondled it. He grew bolder and moved his hand beneath my shirt to touch me through my bra.

He soon removed both my shirt and my bra, but the thought that he wasn't the first guy to see me this way flitted through my mind. Mason had seen more, and his gaze had affected me much more intensely. It was the worst possible time for thoughts of him to intrude, and I tried to push them out of my mind and focus on the lust in Josh's eyes as he stared at my breasts.

When he reached out to touch one, there was a new sensation to distract me. Until I began to imagine that it was Mason touching me.

Chapter 15

The concert turned out to be a much better distraction. My excitement level was much higher even before the opening act took to the stage. The arena was so big, and there were so many people. I had never experienced anything like it, and being able to share it with a friend made it even better. Erin was as thrilled to be there as I was, and the mood of the crowd was also infectious. Everyone was there to have a good time, and that intensified to near euphoria when Taylor Swift came onstage.

The energy was incredible as we sang along to the songs I knew by heart. It was such a rush to hear her sing them in person, but my biggest high came when she sang Shake It Off. I was singing at the top of my lungs and dancing like a maniac. It was absolutely the most fun I had ever had, and I was still fizzing like a soda pop as we walked toward the parking lot.

"That was amazing!" I gushed. "Thank you so much for inviting me to go with you!"

"Thank you for coming with me!" she replied just as enthusiastically. "I would have hated to miss it, but I wouldn't have come by myself. And all the other girls would have talked about Josh. And I know that I just brought him up myself, but thanks for not mentioning him tonight."

I stopped in my tracks as dread replaced my happy mood. "Josh?" I questioned.

She halted and turned to look at me in surprise. "You didn't know he was my boyfriend? Ex-boyfriend," she amended firmly.

The dread turned into a sickening feeling in my stomach. "Josh Connors?" I asked, desperately hoping that she was talking about another Josh.

"Yeah," she confirmed, sending me into a tailspin. "I felt so lucky when he asked me out," she added bitterly. "He seemed so perfect, and I couldn't believe he wanted me to be his girlfriend."

I looked away from her as terrible guilt overwhelmed me over what I had done with him last night. If only I had known that he was her ex-boyfriend, I never would have started anything with him. I didn't pay attention to who was dating who though. Except for Mason, my mind supplied derisively. I had always noticed who he was dating.

"Why am I even talking about him?" Erin chided herself. "I'm sorry, Ella," she apologized, making me feel even worse. "You don't want to hear me mope over my ex. Forget I ever mentioned him," she said as she resumed walking.

I fell into step beside her again. "You can talk about him if you need to," I offered even as I prayed that she wouldn't.

"No," she stated firmly, "he isn't worth another minute of my time. I'm much better off without him."

"You are," I confirmed, finding the conviction to speak even as I felt like a fraud.

"He told me that I was nothing without him, and that I'd be shunned by everybody. But Mason made sure that I wasn't. I always thought he was so intimidating, but he was so nice to me. I'm so glad he finally found a nice girlfriend like you."

I managed a brief smile at her before lapsing into silence. I wanted to go crawl into a hole somewhere and hide from everything, but I had to pretend like nothing was wrong. Erin bounced back and began talking about the concert. I tried to feign the enthusiasm I had felt only moments before, but Erin noticed my change in mood.

"What's wrong?" she asked.

"Nothing," I lied. "I'm just tired. I guess all that singing and dancing wore me out."

"Yeah," she agreed, believing my explanation. "Can you imagine what it's like for the singers and the bands? I bet it's exhausting sometimes."

"Yeah," I acknowledged, wondering how they performed when they were dealing with emotional devastation. I could barely muster up enough energy for a conversation.

Somehow, I managed to make it through without falling apart, even when Erin thanked me again for going with her and happily suggested that we should both wear the concert shirts we had bought to school on Monday. Fortunately, I had driven her to the concert, so I got to drop the act after dropping her off at home.

I drove myself home in a stupor, too weary from my huge mood swing to even think anymore. I wanted to block it all out anyway and sink into the oblivion of sleep. I would have to deal with it eventually, but I couldn't face it right now. Parking the car in the driveway so that I wouldn't wake anyone with the sound of the garage door opening and closing, I slowly began to trudge toward the house.

"Ella," a male voice called out to me in a hushed tone.

I turned and saw Mason approaching me. "Hey," he greeted me. "How was the concert?"

"Good," I replied.

"What's wrong?" he questioned in sudden concern. "What happened?"

"Nothing," I answered, still unable to find any energy to liven up my voice. "Just tired."

He scrutinized me in the dim light, but my expression was probably as empty as I felt. "Night," I said and turned back toward the house.

"What's wrong with you?" he demanded, stepping in front of me to halt my progress again. "You didn't even ask me why I'm here. Why are you acting like somebody died? What the hell happened?"

I was too despondent to even try to make another attempt to convince him that nothing was wrong. "I have to go to bed now." All I craved was to collapse on it.

"Hey," he said and gently cupped my face to tilt my chin up. "Ella. Talk to me."

His tender touch cracked the shell encasing me from my feelings. "Please," I pleaded.

He slowly dropped his hand and let me pass. With a heavy heart, I resumed my melancholy walk into my house without looking back at him. When I got up to my room, I collapsed hopelessly on my bed without bothering to remove my clothes. I wasn't sure how long I stared blankly into the darkness before my eyelids closed in the oblivion I sought.

Chapter 16

Things did actually look better in the morning. My cell phone alarm woke me from a dead sleep, and I could see a bright, clear day outside my window. I was glad that I had thought to set my alarm beforehand so that I wouldn't forget after the concert, because I certainly would have forgotten in my distress last night.

So now I knew that Josh wasn't the guy I thought he was, and that I had made a mistake. Lots of girls trusted the wrong guy and made mistakes like mine. I wasn't the only one, and this wasn't the end of the world. I just needed to put this behind me and move on.

That turned out to be pretty easy during my fun day with my friends. My thoughts didn't stray toward Josh once, but I did begin to wonder why Mason had shown up at my house. That wasn't at the forefront of my mind either though, because I was too distracted by Zoey's crush on her "friend." I alternated between exchanging looks with Alice over their cuteness and worrying about him taking advantage of her.

Devon appeared to be kind of nerdy though rather than a player in training. He was cute enough that I could see the potential for him to grow into being a serious hottie however. If he ever realized that—and how much Zoey was crushing on him—he could end up breaking her heart. Right now, they were adorable together as they acted like they were only buddies but would have moments of awkwardness during which it was obvious to Alice and me that they liked each other as more than friends. I hoped that they figured it out later rather than sooner. I wanted Zoey to remain innocent as long as possible.

"Puppy love is so cute," Alice gushed as we watched them waiting in line to get on the log ride.

She and I had opted not to get wet, so we were skipping it and eating ice cream instead. "Yeah," I said. "Too bad it can't stay that sweet and cute."

"Kids are having sex so much younger now," she sighed.

I glanced at her in dismay at that statement. "They don't even look like they've had their first kiss."

"I don't think they have," she agreed. "I meant just in general. They caught this boy and girl having sex in the bathroom last year at the middle school my mom teaches at. Middle school!"

"Wow, that's young," I agreed. "And at school! I'd be mortified."

She gave me a sideways glance. "So, have you and Mason—not at school of course, but have you…"

The memory of our hot kiss in the pool heated my cheeks. "No, but his mom caught us together in his pool. We weren't naked," I hastened to add, "but it was embarrassing. I think she assumed we were about to have sex."

"Were you?" she questioned.

My gaze flew to hers. "I don't know," I admitted. "It seems like I can't predict what I'm going to do when I'm with him. I actually kissed him first."

"You did?" she asked in surprise. "Wow, I never could have imagined you doing that."

"Me either," I told her in distress. "It's like I lose my mind when I'm around him."

"Passion," she stated, apparently without judgement.

I looked at her curiously. "Did you feel that with…"

She shook her head as I trailed off in deference to the dead. "I loved him, but it wasn't overwhelming passion like you're talking about. It was this feeling when I saw him, like he brightened my whole day."

"So, did you ever…"

"No," she said. "I wanted to, but he wouldn't. He said that I was special to him, and that he wanted to do everything right."

"You wanted to?" I asked in surprise.

She blushed. "Well, yeah. I had a hot jock boyfriend."

I gave her a tentative smile, unsure if it was okay for me to joke back with her about him. Had she recovered enough from his death to be able to handle that?

Her attempt at levity was short-lived, and her expression sobered. "I wanted to feel closer to him," she admitted. "It was like there was a part of him I couldn't reach, something below the surface, you know? There were times when his eyes would go distant during a lull in the conversation or when we were watching TV. He would always make some kind of joke when I asked him what he was thinking about and be all happy and fun again, but I knew that he was avoiding telling me what was on his mind. I felt like I needed to get closer to him for him to tell me, and sex seemed like it could be the way to get him to let me in."

She sighed deeply. "If only I had known that something was bothering him that much. He never seemed depressed."

"That's what Mason said too," I told her. "I don't think anybody knew."

"No," she acknowledged. "He didn't share those feelings with anyone. He covered them up with his fun personality, but I wish so much that he would have told me about his depression. I could have talked him into getting help."

"Yeah," I agreed. "But that doesn't always work either. My mom's one boyfriend was a psychiatrist, and he had a patient commit suicide."

My gaze shot toward her as I realized that I had spoken the taboo word, but she didn't seem inordinately affected by it. "Yeah, I know. My mom's cousin was on antidepressants, and she committed suicide too."

"I didn't know that!" I exclaimed. "When did that happen?"

"When I was in fourth grade," she replied. "It was the first funeral I ever went to. I didn't know until a few years later that it was suicide. At the time, my mom told me her cousin got sick and died."

"Wow, I'm sorry," I said, thinking how awful it was for her to lose two people to suicide.

"I only saw her once a year at our family reunion, so it didn't affect me as much as Chase. I was sad for her of course, but—"

My ringtone interrupted her, and my focus went to my phone as I pulled it out of my purse. I answered it without thinking when I saw that Mason was calling me. "Hello?"

"Are you okay?" he asked urgently.

"Yeah," I responded, starting to feel embarrassed about my behavior last night. "I'm fine."

"Erin told me that she was with you the whole time and nothing out of the ordinary happened, but you just seemed so depressed."

"You talked to Erin?" I asked in surprise.

"Yes. I called her because I was really worried about you."

That was so unexpected and nice that guilt pricked at me. "It was PMS," I lied as Alice observed me curiously.

"PMS?" he repeated doubtfully. "Isn't that supposed to make you bitchy? You seemed really down and depressed."

"It's not just bitchiness. We get emotional too," I told him, "but I'm fine now. Thanks for calling though."

There was a pause during which I nervously waited for him to say something in parting so I could hang up. "What's going on, Ella?" he asked.

My anxiety spiked. "What do you mean? I'm out at Six Flags with my friends. I told you that's where I was going today."

"I wasn't questioning your whereabouts, but now I'm wondering why that was your first thought and why you sound so nervous. Also, thanks for calling? That's very general and polite, which you never are with me. So, I repeat, what's going on? What are you hiding from me?"

"Nothing!" I exclaimed. "Do you need proof that I'm telling the truth? I'll send you a picture of me and Alice right now."

I hung up before he could reply, and leaned closer to Alice to take a selfie of us to send him. I stared at my phone afterwards, anxiously waiting for a response from him. He sent me a text. *You could have taken that anytime. I'm going to FaceTime you right now*

I positioned my phone so he could see both me and Alice as I spoke to him. He watched me suspiciously even after exchanging greetings with her. "Do you believe me now?" I prompted.

"I'll talk to you later," he said as his eyes continued to scrutinize me. "Call me when you get home."

"Okay," I agreed and tried to lift that intense expression from his face. "Do you want me to get you a souvenir? I can get you a t-shirt or an awesome souvenir cup. How about your name written on a grain of rice? That's something you probably don't have."

"I don't," he replied, his expression unreadable now.

It made me even more nervous than when he had been studying me like I was under a microscope. "Okay! Well, I will rectify that immediately. I'll get you one right now before they run out. Gotta go. Bye!"

"Bye," he stated in a monotone.

I tapped my screen to end the call and took a shaky, anxious breath.

"What is going on with you?" Alice asked. "Why are you so nervous?"

"Is it that obvious?" I questioned. "Do you think he noticed?"

"I would say so," she retorted. "What with all the rambling about grains of rice."

"I was trying to be funny." I covered my face with my hands and groaned.

"Tell me, Ella," she urged. "What's got you so frazzled?"

I dropped my hands and looked directly at her as I began to speak. I didn't even have to think about whether I could confide in my best friend. Although we had been apart for years, I knew that I could trust her to keep my secret. She listened somberly, but I didn't feel like she was judging me. In fact, the comment she made after hearing the whole story confused me at first.

"So, why are you nervous about Mason finding out?"

She stumped me for a moment, although I had thought that it was so obvious that no explanation was needed. "Uh, well..."

"I mean, if your relationship isn't real, and you don't really care about him being your boyfriend."

"I don't," I confirmed automatically as I gathered my thoughts. "I just...well, uh...the bet," I finally supplied. "I'll lose the bet because I was cheating." Saying that now made me feel queasy and wrong, like I had actually cheated for real.

"So what?" she threw out like it didn't matter.

"I'll lose the bet," I repeated more emphatically to impart the seriousness of the consequences.

"So. What." She repeated the words slowly for emphasis. "I know you won't do anything you don't want to do just to stop him from showing people a *poem*, so what is this really about?"

I stared at her. "You don't know what I—"

"I don't care!" she interrupted. "They're words on a paper, Ella, so stop pretending that's why you're with him. I could understand the naked picture." She paused with a shudder. "But not this."

I was taken aback. I had been worried about what she would think of me after I told her about what I had done with Josh, but she was grilling me about Mason instead. I didn't really understand her reasoning though. I guessed that I had been too vague for her to grasp the mortifying impact of those words she was disregarding. "It's an erotic poem," I admitted. "About Mason."

"Now we're getting somewhere," she said. "Okay, so why is Josh even in the picture if you want Mason?"

I was extremely surprised about how she took that in stride and wasn't scandalized by my revelation of having sexual thoughts about Mason. "Because I shouldn't want him," I blurted. "I should want a nice guy like Josh. Except I was wrong about him too."

"But you didn't want him, so that one doesn't count."

"What?" I asked in confusion.

"Your instincts about guys," she explained. "Josh doesn't count, because you never wanted him. You just thought that you *should* want him. So, Mason is the only one you can use as an example about being right or wrong about guys. At least that I know of. Has there been anyone else?"

"No," I said, deflating with that answer.

"So, you still want to be with him. That's why you're using the poem as an excuse to stay with him, and that's why you're so nervous about losing him if he finds out about Josh."

I gaped at her. "No...that's...no. I'm not using excuses to stay with him, and I'm not afraid of losing him! Why would you even think that?"

"Because it's true, Ella. You still like him. That whole thing about putting his name on a grain of rice? That's the kind of corny stuff you do with someone you really like. That had nothing to do with blackmail or your poem. You just like him."

I opened my mouth to argue but closed it again. The feeling in the pit of my stomach overrode my denial. My anxiety had nothing to do with the bet. When I imagined Mason finding out about Josh, all I could think about was him walking away from me.

"I like him," I admitted in despair. "I tried not to, but I can't help it. It's never gone away, and it's gotten worse since we've been...together."

"You're falling for him," she stated.

That hit me like a punch to the gut. "No." It sounded more like a plea than a denial.

She gave me a sad smile. "You don't get to decide that. It happens on its own whether you want it to or not. You can't control it, but you can control what you do about it."

"What should I do about it?" I asked her desperately.

She sighed. "Tell him everything. Tell him to stop with all the blackmail bullshit and be honest, and you do the same."

I recoiled from that advice. "I can't tell him about Josh! Besides, that's over. I'm not going to have anything to do with him anymore."

"If Mason finds out you were lying to him, it'll be worse than if you tell him yourself."

"I thought you didn't like Mason. Why are you on his side?" I complained.

"I'm not on his side. I would *never* be on his side," she insisted. "I wish that you weren't in love with him, but since you are—"

I cut her off as the denial burst forth from me. "I'm not in love with him! That's crazy!"

"It is crazy," she agreed. "I can't explain it, and I don't think you can either. Regardless, it's true. You've been in love with him the entire time I've known you. Now you have the chance to find out once and for all if you can be with him or not, and I don't think you can do that with this hanging over you."

I was still reeling from her thinking that I was in love with him.

"You need to clear the air and start fresh," she continued. "Hash it out with him before you do. Call him on all his crap too."

"I have been," I replied absently. "He's been saying he's sorry."

"Doesn't seem like enough," she said, "but I guess there's no way he can make that all up to you. You either forgive him for it or you don't."

"I'm not in love with him," I said, speaking at a normal volume now.

"Then why do you care if he finds out about Josh?" She pinned me with an intense look. "Are you afraid of him?"

"No." I shook my head for emphasis. "No, I'm not afraid of Mason."

She relaxed after a moment, seeming satisfied with my answer. "So then?" she enquired.

I swallowed, my nervousness returning. Fortunately, Zoey and Devon came up to us then and got me out of this conversation. They were soaked from the water ride and laughing about it. Zoey's face was lit up with happiness and youthful excitement, and it was wonderful to see. My mood instantly brightened, and I could see that it affected Alice in the same way. She smiled the brightest smile that I had seen on her face in a long time.

A happy sense of nostalgia overtook me as we began to walk toward the next ride on this sunny day. The sights and sounds of the amusement park were so familiar, and they brought back impressions of carefree days spent here having fun with my best friend. That magical mood stayed with us as we rode roller coasters and ate funnel cakes and cotton candy. All the walking and standing in line combined with the sugar coma to leave us all pleasantly mellow by the end of the day as we browsed the gift shop.

Zoey had refused my offer to buy her something. "You already paid for my ticket, and I know it wasn't cheap. I have enough money to get something small, and all that matters to me is that it has the name of the park on it. I just want a little souvenir."

My conversation with Mason came back to me then, but I didn't admit to myself what I was browsing for after Zoey opted for a refrigerator magnet with both her name and Six Flags written on it. I had drifted over to the keychains and hesitated only a second before grabbing one with Mason's name. Alice said nothing as she followed me to the register. Zoey and Devon were ahead of us and went to wait outside together after paying for their souvenirs.

Alice left the shop empty-handed. "I'm waiting to use Madison's employee discount wherever she gets hired," she explained. "I've got lots of stuff from when she worked here."

I was glad that she didn't comment on my purchase. "Yeah," I replied lightly. "How many souvenirs could you need from the same place?"

"If she gets a job at Disney, I'll break the record," she declared. "I'll have all the Mickey Mouse ears in existence."

I laughed, and we joined Zoey and Devon to stroll toward the exit of the park. I got the inspiration to ask someone to take a picture of the four of us together, and we posed with big smiles on our faces to commemorate the end of a wonderful day. This was the only picture we had of all of us together, since we had taken turns snapping photos of each other throughout the day in pairs or with the three girls posing together while Devon took our picture.

As we walked to the car, I sent our most recent photo to Alice and to Zoey, knowing that she would send it to Devon so he could have it too. I also sent it to Mason and put my phone away. I dropped Zoey and Devon off together at her apartment building, and they both thanked me again for taking them.

I checked my phone before taking off and laughed at the text I had received from Mason. *Who is that boy band reject with Zoey? Tell him I'm watching him. Hint that she has an uncle in the mafia*

I showed it to Alice and put it away with a smile as I began to drive to her house. "I see," she said. "I didn't know he had a side like that."

"Like what?" I asked as I glanced at her.

"A fun, joking side," she replied. "I didn't know he could be like that. Now I see how you can like him if he's fun like that with you. He seemed kind of cold earlier."

"I guess he got in a better mood," I said. "I know I did. It was a really good day."

"Yes, it was," she agreed, her tone warming.

"Thanks for letting Zoey come with us," I told her. "I promise it'll be just you and me next time."

"No, she was great. They both were, and it worked out that we could still talk and catch up."

"Yeah," I acknowledged. "I'm so glad to have you back."

"Me too. This year is going to be the best."

I felt that wonderful optimism too before my life started to unravel.

Chapter 17

It began that evening when I kept my promise to call Mason. Thinking that everything was fine after his humorous text, I greeted him in a teasing tone. "I got you something. I bet you can't guess what it is."

"You called," he stated.

"Yeah, you told me to," I reminded him. "Are you busy right now? Should I call back later?"

"I told you to," he repeated. "And you didn't argue, didn't complain that I was calling you while you were out with your friends, *thanked me* for calling you but acted like I caught you going out with another guy, and you were practically in tears last night with no explanation. You are hiding something from me, Ella, and I want to know what it is."

My heart had almost stopped when he mentioned catching me with another guy, and I was glad that he couldn't see my face. "I'm not hiding anything," I said, but my voice sounded nervous and unconvincing.

"I'm going to come over there right now, and you're going to tell me," he said in a threatening tone.

"I love you," I blurted in panic.

My heart hammered in my chest during the ensuing silence. I couldn't believe that I had said that to him, and my shocked mind couldn't think what to do now.

"You love me?" he questioned in surprise and disbelief.

"It's why I've been so messed up and stuff. Because it's crazy. I know it is, and Alice said so too, but she knows I didn't decide to. She wishes that I didn't, and I do too, because we can't ever get a fresh start like she says, because—"

"Ella," he said, halting my rambling. "We can get a fresh start."

"We can?" I asked in a daze.

"Yes," he confirmed, his voice sounding smooth and seductive. "I'll give you back your poem, and we'll start anew. Can I do that now? Can I come see you, Ella?"

"Yes," I said, expelling the word on a shaky breath of nervous excitement.

I couldn't wait to see him, and I knew that it wasn't because of getting back my poem. I had told him that I loved him, and it was like saying the words to him had freed the feeling inside me. I was soaring on it and the knowledge that I would soon be in the presence of the one who made me feel this way.

Fortunately, my parents were at a wedding for the daughter of dad's best friend, so I was able to greet Mason with all the enthusiasm I was feeling. "Hi!" I exclaimed, the exhilaration of seeing him giving me the same high I had experienced at the concert.

"Come in," I urged, practically bouncing in my excitement as I stepped back so he could enter.

An amused smile played over his lips, but his gaze was locked on me as he stepped inside. I handed him the little bag from the gift shop. "I got you this."

He peered inside but didn't take out the keychain. His eyes returned to me with that same intensity. "Thank you." His gaze stayed on me as he pulled a folded piece of paper out of his pocket. "Here's your poem."

I took it and shoved it into my pocket to look at later. "Thanks," I said, starting to feel like his intense stare was stealing my breath.

He moved in closer and reached out to caress my cheek as he spoke. "I want to hear you say it again."

His seductive voice was like an intimate command, and I obeyed it even as sudden shyness softened my voice. "I love you."

His potent gaze held mine captive, but his voice shook. "You own me, Ella."

His words sent an electric thrill through me. Then his mouth claimed mine in a possessive, bone-melting kiss that consumed me completely. When it ended, I was immediately drawn in again by the magnetic pull of his lips, but he stepped back from me.

"You told me you love me today. That's what I want to remember." Heat smoldered in his eyes. "I'll kiss you again tomorrow, and every day after that."

It was a promise that made happiness surge in my heart and burst forth into a happy smile on my face. Mason smiled back at me with dazzling brightness and warmth. "Goodnight, Ella," he said and walked toward the door.

"Goodnight, Mason," I responded as I followed him.

He opened the door and gave me a parting look before walking out. I watched him get in his car and back out of the driveway. With a brief wave that I returned, he drove off. I shut the door in a blissful daze and leaned back against it with a happy sigh.

Everything felt new and wonderful and perfect. The exhilaration returned and had me going upstairs to crank up some music in my room and dance in sheer joy. After expending some of the energy coursing through me and working up a sweat, I took a shower.

It wasn't until much later that night that I remembered to retrieve my poem from the shorts I had thrown into the

laundry hamper after undressing for my shower. I saw that Mason had indeed returned
my poem to me just like he said he would. There was nothing hanging over my head anymore, and it felt good not to have to keep anything hidden anymore.

My feelings for Mason had been my secret shame for so long, and I'd tried to suppress them to no avail. Deep down inside, I'd still had hope that he would change his mind about me. A part of me had still believed that fate was drawing us together, and that he eventually wouldn't be able to resist its pull. The fact that I had lived in his house and found him years ago and that we were now going to school together despite being born into vastly different circumstances, had validated that destiny wouldn't allow us to be apart. Now I had discovered that Mason had sought me out himself, and the feelings I had been fighting had only gotten stronger as he pursued me.

Discovering that Alice didn't fault me for how I felt, and that she would stand by me no matter what had changed my perspective. I didn't care what anyone else thought if I had the support of my best friend. She had liberated me from my shame and gave me confidence. That had been the catalyst for accepting my feelings for Mason, but it was the absolute failure of trying to deny them and be with someone else that had taken the fight out of me.

That was a mistake that was better forgotten. Telling Mason about it would serve no purpose. No good could come from it, and it didn't matter anymore anyway. It happened before Mason became my real boyfriend. I marveled at that amazing fact. Mason was really my boyfriend. We weren't together because of a bet or some twisted game of blackmail, but because we wanted to be. His reaction to me telling him that I loved him had been to relinquish his hold on me by giving me back my poem so that I was with him of my own free will. All it had taken to claim me as his was a kiss.

I knew that there was no turning back for me now that I had declared my feelings for him. By opening my heart and making myself that vulnerable to him, I had given him power over me. Taking that risk had turned out to be so thrilling that I was no longer afraid. The incredible rush kept me from realizing how bad the fall could be from this height, and why I had always played it safe before.

Chapter 18

Those three days were the most amazing, most memorable of my life. Experiencing the concert, giving Zoey a perfect day with the added bonus of me getting to spend it with Alice, telling Mason that I loved him and getting that thrilling reaction from him, and being woken on Sunday by a phone call from him.

"Tell me last night wasn't a dream. I woke up fucking happy, Ella. Like in some damn movie."

The happiness was bubbling up inside me as his voice instantly brought me out of my sleepy state. "Mason!" I exclaimed like a little kid. "You're calling me," I gushed happily.

"I know it's early, but I couldn't wait. I needed to hear your voice and know it was real, that last night really happened."

"It did," I said, giving him the assurance he seemed to need. A spontaneous, happy laugh burst forth from me.

"God, I wish I was with you right now," he declared. "But I promised my mom I'd spend the whole day with her before she leaves. I'm just about to go play tennis with her, but I had to call you first before she monopolized my whole day."

"She's leaving already?" I asked in dismay. "She just got here a few days ago!"

"That's why she set aside the whole day for me," he explained in a mocking tone.

"I'm sorry," I told him.

"Hey, don't worry about it," he said. "I'm just bummed that I can't spend the day with you. But my mom thinks that concentrated doses of time with her will make up for her absence the rest of the time, and I'll be the bad guy if I cancel on her."

"No, of course you should spend today with her," I assured him. "We'll have lots of time together after she leaves."

"Yes, we will," he agreed. "I'll still be thinking about you all day and wishing I was with you. I actually can't wait for school tomorrow so I can see you. I'll be picking you up in the morning, just so you know. All that giving you space crap is going out the window."

"I don't need space now. That was just because I was in denial about wanting to be with you," I admitted.

"I'm glad you're not anymore," he said. "And that I can kiss you," he added. "I can, right? That's not a rule anymore?"

"No," I said. "No more rules."

There was a pause. "Don't tell me that, Ella," he warned. "I need rules—lots of rules—to keep me from doing everything I want to do to you."

My stomach dipped at the thought of him doing some of those things, but there was also a pang of guilt, even as my body enflamed as I replaced the fleeting image of Josh with Mason in my mind and pictured him touching me instead. I wouldn't have stopped him, I realized. If it had been Mason, I wouldn't have stopped him.

"Maybe I want you to do everything," I dared to say.

He sucked in a breath. "Ella," he said in a tight voice, "you're going to fucking kill me."

A thrill of pure feminine power went through me at knowing that just the thought of having me was affecting him so strongly. I didn't often delight in my affect on men, but it was pretty damn great at the moment.

"Okay, now that you've made me unfit to go out in public, I have to go meet my mother."

I giggled in response. "I'm sorry."

"You would be if I was there," he said with a laugh.

"What would you do?" I goaded him.

"You'll find out one day," he promised. "But not today. I seriously have to go now, Ella. I'll call you tonight."

"Okay. I hope you have a good day with your mom," I told him sincerely.

"Thanks. I hope you have a good day too. I'll talk to you later."

I lay there with a smile on my face after getting off the phone. When I finally glanced at the clock after coming out of my blissful trance, I saw that it was only six-thirty in the morning. There was no way that I could go back to sleep though after talking with Mason. I was too happy and excited.

Getting out of bed, I got dressed and went downstairs. My thoughts were on Mason playing tennis, so I decided to do some exercise too. Leaving the house, I started walking down the sidewalk before picking up the pace to turn it into a jog. My feet found a steady rhythm that focused the energy surging through me. I wanted to go see Mason but couldn't, and that had made me restless. I didn't normally run, but I went around the block twice before tiring.

Taking a shower to wash off the sweat, I put on fresh clothes and went downstairs again. I was surprised to see my dad in the kitchen. "What are you doing up so early?" I asked.

"I could ask you the same question," he replied. "Aren't teenagers supposed to sleep until noon on the weekends?"

"I decided to buck the trend," I quipped.

"You always do," he said. "We're so proud of you, Ella. We couldn't have asked for a better daughter."

His praise always made me emotional, because it meant so much to me. "I couldn't have asked for a better dad," I told him.

He held my gaze for a moment before looking away and clearing his throat. He wasn't demonstrative with his affection, but he showed that he cared about me by taking an interest in me and looking out for me. "Your mother showed me the pictures Mason took. Very nice," he commented. "I'm very impressed that he chose wedding photography. That's sensible and pragmatic."

Mom had obviously known better than to show him the provocative pictures taken beside Mason's pool. I was relieved, especially since I now wanted him to approve of Mason. "Yes. There are always people needing wedding photographers. How was the wedding by the way?"

"Good, but I just can't believe that Katie is old enough to get married. But then I think of you going to college soon, and that's even more mind-blowing. Where has the time gone?"

I shrugged, but time hadn't gone that fast for me. It had been a relief to make it to my last year of high school, but now I no longer wanted to rush through it. I couldn't think past it to college, when it had been the opposite until recently. I had *only* been looking forward to college and starting anew somewhere else. Having Alice back in my life had changed that, and so had my evolving relationship with Mason. This year was suddenly special.

"I'm going to make breakfast," I declared and pulled a package of bacon out of the fridge.

"Of course, I knew you were growing up," Dad said. "But at the same time, it's kind of hit me all at once. Those pictures. You've never brought a boy home before, but I can see that you're a couple."

I froze at first before realizing that he was talking about Mason and I posing together in the park. "Yeah we are," I confirmed, hoping that my dad was okay with that.

"Then why did you tell us that you were only friends?" he asked. "You know that you don't have to hide things from us."

"I know," I replied. "We *were* just friends at the time, but now..."

I trailed off since I had already confirmed that we were a couple, and I didn't feel that comfortable discussing my love life with my dad. Fortunately, I was facing away from him as I cooked the bacon when he asked a question that unraveled my composure.

"How is Addison handling you two dating?"

I stiffened as her name brought back her betrayal, and the awful knowledge that Mason had slept with her. It took me a moment to remember that my dad knew none of this.

"Uh-oh," he said. "Is she interested in him too?"

I turned to stare at him in shock.

He smiled wryly. "It wasn't that hard to guess. You're not the first girls to fight over a guy."

"She fought over him. I didn't."

"Because he was interested in you," he remarked. "I could see it, but I was hoping that you didn't return his feelings."

That distracted me from thoughts of Mason's interest in Addison. "You think he had feelings for me?" I asked.

"It was palpable," he replied, looking none too happy about it. "I've seen guys and girls be friends before, and he had none of that in his demeanor. I was about ready to warn you away from him, but the way he looked at you when he said you're beautiful..."

I waited desperately for him to continue as he trailed off and his gaze went distant while remembering. "I could tell he had it *bad*," he finished.

My heart started thumping in excitement and exhilaration. This observation coming from my dad held weight. He wasn't given to flights of fancy or exaggeration. He thought that Mason had it bad for me in a way that was more than lust. I didn't dare yet try to put a name to what that might be, but the possibility of it surged through me.

My life was damn near perfect, which was why I had not even an inkling that anything bad was going to happen.

Chapter 19

The next day continued in the same wonderful way when Mason picked me up for school. Seeing him caused my stomach to flutter in anticipation of his kiss. A warm smile preceded it, and it was very brief and gentle. Even that pressing of lips together gave me a heady rush, although it was a much tamer kiss than we'd ever had before.

When we arrived at school, he parked the car and pulled me into a much more thorough and passionate kiss.

"I'm happy to see you too," I quipped after we finally pulled apart.

"I had to act like a gentleman when I picked you up, just in case your dad was watching," he told me. "I can't take a chance of him banning me from seeing you."

"He wouldn't do that," I said, although I had also been anxious for him to approve of Mason.

"You've never had a boyfriend before, so you don't know what he would do. I'm not taking *any* chances of screwing this up," he declared fiercely.

I felt those butterflies in my stomach and the lightness in my chest that I used to have when I was in middle school and imagining him asking me on a date. "You're my boyfriend?" I asked with a touch of the innocent awe I would have had back then.

"Of course I'm your boyfriend," he responded, looking a bit taken aback. "I've been your boyfriend."

"That wasn't real," I said. "That was just for the bet."

"I never gave a crap about that stupid bet," he retorted. "That was just a way to hold onto you, but it was real for me since the moment you kissed me. You can't tell me it wasn't real for you too, because I felt how much you wanted to kiss me. And you wouldn't tell me that you love me if it wasn't real."

With the realization that he was right, unease slithered through me. But I wouldn't entertain the thought that I had cheated on him for real, so I pushed it to the back of my mind. "I wasn't sure of your feelings," I admitted instead. "I thought you were just messing with me. I mean, you were still blackmailing me."

He grimaced. "I know I should have given that poem back to you right away, but you were so resistant to giving me a chance that I used the only thing I knew would work on you."

"I should still be mad at you for that," I said, leveling a pretend look of ire at him.

"You should still be mad at me for everything," he said, looking genuinely troubled. "If any other guy had treated you that way, I'd be kicking his ass right now. But it was me."

"I can kick your ass for you," I offered teasingly, wanting to lighten the mood.

"Ooh baby, I like the sound of that," he bantered back. "Tell me more about what you want to do to my ass."

A blush crept over my cheeks as I imagined my hands sliding down over his butt as he kissed me. Mason laughed, but his gaze became heated. His voice dropped to a quietly seductive volume when he spoke. "I didn't get to see your ass when you were naked. You were so fucking hot that I had to leave the room."

Lust shot straight down to my core, and I wanted to be naked with him again.

"Fuck, don't look at me like that." He took an uneven breath. "We better go in before I start making out with you right here in the parking lot."

He flung open his door and got out of the car like he really was in danger of succumbing to the temptation. The charged sexual tension between us remained even as we walked among our classmates and past throngs of students in the hallways. Giving into it, Mason pressed me back against the wall and kissed me hungrily. His breathing was as heavy as mine when he pulled back.

He took a step away from me. "Okay, wow, I need to…"

He began to angle his body to turn in the opposite direction. "I'll see you in class, okay?"

"Yeah," I managed, still feeling intoxicated by that kiss.

I watched him walk off down the hallway and vaguely thought about going to my locker.

"Are you giving him blue balls too?"

My stomach plummeted as I turned to face the guy who had spoken. His gaze was hard, nothing at all like it usually was. "That was all just for show, right?" Josh mocked me.

I glanced around nervously, but nobody seemed to be paying any attention to us. My gaze returned to him. "Things have changed. I'm sorry," I added, although he really didn't deserve it now that I knew how he had treated Erin.

He smiled, apparently amused. "I'm not making you choose, Ella. You didn't have to lie to me to get something on the side."

"I wasn't lying to you," I insisted. "We weren't together like we are now."

He shrugged. "It doesn't matter to me one way or the other."

"Then what was all that about not going behind his back?" I demanded.

He shrugged again. "That was how you came at me with it, so I played along. Now I know that I don't have to pretend with you anymore."

"Right," I agreed carefully, "because we're not—"

"We're not keeping it a secret anymore?" he interrupted me with false surprise.

I stared at him as dread spread through me. The look in his eyes told me that he knew he had me. "I don't think it's a good idea to tell him, Ella. Do you?"

"Josh," I said, not knowing how to appeal to him for his silence.

He didn't smirk or mock me or make anymore veiled threats. "Once," he told me in a straightforward manner, "and then it will stay a secret."

He walked away like the matter was settled. I stood there in utter horror until panic began to set in, and I walked quickly toward the exit in a mindless rush to flee from the situation. The sound of the warning bell brought me back to my senses as I realized that I couldn't just leave school. I would be marked absent, and the office would notify my parents. Mason was also expecting to see me in class and would want to know why I wasn't there.

I had to act normal until I figured out a way to deal with this. Maybe Alice could help me, I thought hopefully until I remembered that she had advised me to tell Mason everything. I knew that she would just encourage me to tell him myself before Josh did, but I couldn't see him taking it well. Especially after he had insisted that our relationship had been real the entire time. He would view it as cheating, and it was starting to feel that way to me too.

The guilt that twisted in my gut along with the anxiety when I saw him waiting for me outside the classroom was a strong indicator of it, and it got worse when he smiled at me. Class failed to distract me from the panic that was building inside of me.

"Let's get out of here," I pleaded desperately as we left the classroom.

He was startled by my plea. "Why? What's wrong?" he asked in concern.

"Nothing," I told him as I willed myself to calm down. "I just…"

I took a shaky breath and moved closer to him. "I just can't focus on anything. I want to be alone with you."

The heat flaring in his eyes was able to actually distract me enough for my desire to be with him to be more than just wanting to escape from Josh. "I'm having the same problem," Mason said, "but it's probably not a good idea to be alone right now."

I knew that he was right, and that I shouldn't make any rash decisions. I'd already learned that lesson the hard way with Josh. Even so, I was desperate to get away somewhere with Mason. Leaving him behind would make me paranoid about Josh talking to him.

"We can go to my house," I suggested. "My mom is home, so that will keep us from going too far."

He gave me a perplexed look. "Won't she mind that you're skipping school?"

"No," I answered. "She'll think that I finally have a life. Besides, I've never skipped before."

"Okay," he said. "Let's get out of here before the bell rings and somebody sees us standing here."

"Are you okay with skipping?" I asked belatedly as we hurried toward the exit.

"Yes," he said as we pushed open the doors and burst outside. "I've never skipped either."

I turned my head to look at him in surprise. "You haven't? Not even one class?"

"I had to stay out of trouble so they wouldn't call my mom, remember?"

"Oh, no!" I exclaimed. "We have to go back. You can't—"

"Relax," he urged. "I've stayed out of trouble long enough for her not to flip out over this. I'll probably just get detention."

I exhaled in relief. "Okay, as long as you're sure you won't have to move."

"Would you miss me?" he asked in a teasing tone.

"I never thought I'd say this, but yeah, I would."

He stopped me as I was walking toward the passenger side of his car and stood facing me with a serious expression on his face. "I deserved that."

I hadn't meant it as a dig at him, and I started to tell him so, but he interrupted me. "It's true. You would have been glad to get rid of me. As pissed as you should be at me, I'm even more pissed at myself. I wasted so much time being an asshole, but I'm going to make it up to you, Ella. I swear it."

"I believe you," I told him.

He smiled in response, and it was a beautiful, warm smile that gave me a warm, fuzzy feeling inside. That sense of wonderful contentment stayed with me as he drove to my house. It was easy to forget everything else when it was just the two of us.

As I unlocked my front door, I wasn't even stressing about Mom flirting with Mason. She wouldn't stop me from taking him up to my room, so my plan was to keep moving and get past her as fast as possible. I came to a complete standstill, though, when I entered the house and saw her kissing our neighbor's twenty-five-year-old son. He had her pressed up against the wall, and her legs were wrapped around his waist.

He broke off the kiss when he heard us come in and turned to glance back at us with a fearful expression before setting her down. She didn't appear fazed at all as she walked toward us. "Well," she said, "I won't tell if you won't." She even smiled and gave us a wink. "Have fun and don't do anything I wouldn't do." She followed that with a throaty laugh and walked back toward her boy toy.

I stood rooted to the spot as she led the young man upstairs—apparently to continue her tryst with him. "C'mon, Ella," Mason urged me gently. "Let's go."

Still in shock, I let him take my hand and lead me back to his car. The horror was trying to seep through, but my mind blocked it out until we arrived at Mason's house. We had just stepped inside when everything came crashing down on me. "My dad," I gasped.

Mason embraced me, and I clung to him for support. Tears started falling down my cheeks. "I'll lose my dad," I sobbed.

"No, you won't," he said. "He loves you. This isn't going to change that."

I cried as he held me and ran a hand soothingly up and down my back. Eventually, my sorrow turned to anger, and I pulled away in agitation. "She ruins everything!" I wailed.

I stomped around as bitter tears fell. "I hate her! She always ruins everything."

Mason spoke in a calming tone. "It'll be okay, Ella. You're not alone. You've got me, and I'll help you make it through this."

The words must have had an affect somewhere deep inside, although I paid them no conscious attention right then. I cried and paced around until I was spent, and then I just sat on the couch staring blankly at nothing.

Mason placed a glass in my hand, and I automatically sipped the liquid inside. It was cola, and it restored some of my depleted energy. I came out of my semi-catatonic state as my eyes focused on Mason sitting across from me.

"It's over," I stated emotionlessly. All the feeling seemed to have drained out of me. "I've lost my dad."

Something flared in his eyes, and his composure slipped. "He's alive," he bit out. "He's fucking alive, so you haven't lost him. I know you're upset, and this sucks, but your dad is still here."

His emotion penetrated the numbness separating me from him, and sympathy rushed through me. "I'm sorry, Mason. I wasn't thinking."

"You're upset," he repeated, this time as an excuse for my insensitivity.

It put things somewhat in perspective. As awful as this was, nobody had died. I briefly imagined finding out that my dad was dead, and it hit me for the first time how horrible that must have been for Mason. At the time, I hadn't had a dad, so I couldn't relate to his loss on such visceral level.

I stared at him with the horrible realization of his devastating pain. "I'm so sorry, Mason. I'm so sorry about your dad."

Intense emotion crossed his face, and he looked away. When his gaze returned to me, it softened. "Thank you."

I felt something lift, some barrier that I didn't even know was between us until it was gone. A connection seemed to form between us unimpeded now, and I took comfort and strength from it. Mason stood up and came to sit beside me, angling his body toward me and taking hold of my hand.

"You'll be okay, Ella, I promise. You can stay here tonight if you don't want to go home."

"I don't," I said, unable to imagine being able to pretend like everything was normal when my dad came home from work.

"Okay," Mason said. "We can go buy you a change of clothes for tomorrow. And something to sleep in tonight."

"I'll ask Alice to go to my house and get clothes for me," I decided.

"You're going to tell her that you're staying here?" he asked, looking surprised.

"Yes. She won't tell anyone, and I'll say that I'm staying at her house. She'll cover for me if she needs to."

He regarded me intently. "You know that even though you haven't talked to her yet? You're that sure of her?"

"Yes," I stated unequivocally.

He appeared to be puzzling over something as he studied me. "You've secretly kept up your friendship with her?"

"No," I replied. "Last week was the first time I've talked to her since—well, since I saw her in the park after Chase died, but before that it was since freshman year."

"But you have total faith in her?" he questioned. "You have that much trust in her even though you've hardly talked for years."

"Yes," I said. "She's the one friend I know I can count on no matter what. Time doesn't matter with her."

"What does that mean?" he queried. "How could time not matter?"

"It means that she's still Alice, and that she's still my friend. I don't know how to explain it, but it's never gone away. I still care about her, and if she asked me to help her, I would no matter how much time had passed since we talked. And I know that she would do the same for me. That's just how it is with us."

He regarded me pensively. "I don't have anyone like that."

"They're rare," I acknowledged. "I've never had another friend like Alice."

Melancholy overtook me again. "I just got her back, and now we're going to be separated again."

"Why are you going to be separated?" Mason asked.

"When my dad finds out about my mom, he'll—"

"Who's going to tell him?" Mason interjected.

That stopped me cold. I stared speechlessly at him as I grappled with the realization that my dad didn't have to find out. He could remain completely unaware that his wife was cheating on him, but that would mean that I would have to keep the secret of what was going on behind his back. Not that I could imagine telling him, but I also couldn't fathom acting like nothing had happened.

Yet what else could I do? I couldn't stand the thought of hurting him, and he would be so terribly hurt to learn of

Mom's infidelity. I didn't know how she could do that to him. He was such a good husband to her and a great father to me. What more could she want in a man? Why could she never be satisfied with what she had? Why did she have to ruin everything everywhere she went?

"He doesn't have to know," Mason said. "I know it's a shitty situation, but telling him won't make it better. You're upset, but you'll deal, and then you can just ignore it. It's only for a year, right? And then you'll be going to college."

"Yeah," I replied. "I guess."

"You guess you're going to college?"

"I guess I'll have to ignore it," I clarified listlessly. "My mother with Jeremy. Addison was always lusting after him. Guess my mom beat her to him."

He said nothing in response to that and just softly stroked his thumb over my knuckles as he continued to hold my hand. I stared off into space as my thoughts shut down, and I wasn't aware of anything until Mason asked me what I wanted for lunch.

"I'm not hungry," I replied.

"Well, I am," he said, "and I'd like to get something that you might eat too. What do you prefer? I can get something delivered or go pick up some fast food for us."

"Get what you want," I told him. "I don't want anything."

"I guess I'll order pizza," he decided. "It'll still be good if you feel like having some later."

I heard my ringtone go off, and I pulled my phone out of my purse. "It's Alice."

"Talk to her. I'll go get the pizza myself so you can have some privacy. Call me if you need anything."

"Okay," I said before answering the phone.

"Where are you?" Alice asked as Mason left the room. "You're going to miss lunch if you don't get here soon."

I recalled that we had planned to sit together at lunch. That seemed much longer ago than yesterday. "I went home."

"Why?" she questioned.

I could hardly remember why now. "Something happened," I told her. "I caught my mom cheating on my dad."

"What?" she exclaimed.

I filled her in on everything that had happened and asked her if she could pick up some clothes for me after school. "I don't want to go back there today. I'm going to tell my parents that I'm staying over your house, if that's okay."

"You can," she offered. "I can sneak you in."

I knew her mom's rule about not having anyone sleeping over on school nights, and I didn't want to cause problems for her. I also didn't want to rehash everything with her tonight. Best friends were great when you needed to talk, but I didn't feel like talking. Mason hadn't pushed me to, and that was what I needed right now.

"Thanks, but I'm fine here," I told her.

There was a pause. "Ella," she began tentatively, "I don't think this is a good time for you to be there. I know you're upset, and you want comfort, but—"

I let out a harsh laugh. "Believe me, the last thing I want right now is sex. Seeing my mom with her boy toy was not sexy. I wish I could erase it from my mind."

"Of course I didn't mean it was sexy," she exclaimed in a horrified tone. "I just meant that it's natural to want comfort when you're upset, and it might just start with him putting his arms around you, and then little by little..." She trailed off before adding, "I'm just worried that he'll take advantage of you when you're vulnerable."

"He won't," I assured her. "He hasn't done anything except hold my hand. He's actually been giving me my space even though I'm in his house. That's what I need," I admitted. "So being here is perfect right now."

"Okay," she said, "but you can call me to come get you if he tries anything."

"He won't," I replied with total confidence.

My faith in him took a nosedive that night when I couldn't sleep and he suggested I go for a swim in his pool. I hadn't thought to ask Alice to bring my bathing suit, and I told him that.

"You don't need one," he replied. "It's dark, and nobody will see you."

"Except you," I retorted as the realization of what he was suggesting sank in.

Instead of assuring me that he wouldn't look, his reply left no doubt that he would. "I've seen you naked before."

A spark of anger ignited within me and contrarily prompted me to goad him rather than protest his inappropriateness at a time like this. "That's right, you have."

I swiftly removed my pajama shorts and top right in front of him before strutting past him completely nude. Pulling open the patio door, I walked out into the darkness. I felt a sense of freedom as it swallowed me up, like I had left behind the daily world. Entering the water was a special treat at night. It was something I had never done before, and neither had I ever gone skinny dipping. I couldn't deny how sensual and forbidden it felt, but I was alone in the pool. That freed me further and relaxed me. I leaned back and gazed at the night sky as I floated in the dark silence.

Awareness prickled back to life in my nerve endings, and I turned my head to see Mason at the edge of the pool. I didn't know how long he had been standing there watching me, but he lingered a moment longer before moving from his spot and diving into the water furthest away from me. My body tensed in anticipation, but he began to swim laps rather than approaching me. As the realization set in that he wasn't going to touch me, I broke my pose and started gliding through the water.

We swam laps, keeping to opposite sides of the pool. I almost forgot he was there as I got into the zone of smooth, even strokes pulling me through the water. When I finally tired and stopped, I remembered to look for him and saw that he was floating on his back now. Swimming over to him, I leaned back to float on my back beside him.

After a moment of gazing at the sky, I glanced at him. "It's unfair that you told me to come out here naked, but you've got your swim trunks on. We should be equal."

His eyes slid down to my breasts before returning to my face. "We could never be equal. I can't compare to how beautiful you are."

"You have to know how gorgeous you are," I scoffed. "All the girls want you."

"But I only want you," he said.

"Really?" I challenged. "You've had other girls. Right in this pool in fact. Isn't that what your mother said? She caught you naked in here with another girl."

"That was before you," he retorted.

"Well," I said blithely even as anger roiled through me, "I guess it's my turn now."

Letting my body sink down into the water, I turned toward him and moved in close. I placed my hand on top of the bulge in his swim shorts, and he hissed out a breath. "Let me see it," I told him boldly.

"Fuck," he swore. "Stop it, Ella."

"You can be naked with her, but not with me?" I argued.

He dropped his body into the water to dislodge my hand. "You have no reason to be jealous. I've never wanted anyone as much as—"

"I'm not jealous," I cut in. "Everybody's having sex. I get it. You, my mother. I might as well do it too. Why the hell not?"

"Ella," he said, sounding like he was struggling to speak in a patient tone, "you need to get some sleep. Go up to bed."

"No, you need to get naked," I replied obstinately. "I'm sick of this shit. I told you I want us to be equal."

He glared at me as I stared him down. "Fine," he said through gritted teeth.

His arms moved from his sides to his front, and then back to his sides as his shoulders dipped into the water. He leaned back as his legs sprang up, and he pulled his swim trunks off his feet and flung them onto the cement surrounding the pool. I got just a glimpse of what was between his legs before he submerged it beneath the water.

"I want to see you. Float on your back," I demanded.

He let out an exasperated breath but complied and brought his body up out of the water. I stared at his erection. There wasn't much moonlight, but there was enough for me to see the size and shape of him jutting up into the air. Without thinking, I wrapped my hand around it in curiosity to know how it felt.

Mason sucked in a sharp breath. "Oh fuck," he groaned.

"It's hard but soft," I marveled as I moved my hand up to the tip.

He moaned. "Ella," he protested in a strangled voice, "let go."

I liked the power I had discovered I had over him, so I moved my hand back down over his length to elicit another tortured moan.

I lost my grip on him as he quickly dropped his body into the water and moved so fast that I found myself pressed against the side of the pool before I knew what was happening. His mouth was on mine in the next instant in a hungry, demanding kiss.

Now I moaned as his tongue plunged into my mouth and his naked body pressed against mine as the sensual feel of the water enveloped my skin. Mason devoured my mouth before pulling my body out of the water to sit me on the edge of the pool in front of him. Before I could completely register the cool air on my wet skin, his hot mouth closed over my nipple. I moaned as my head fell back in surrender to the intensely pleasurable sensation. As he continued to suck on my nipple, I felt his hand touch me between my parted legs, and I stiffened. I pushed against his shoulders, and he stopped immediately and pulled away from me.

"Shit!" he exclaimed. "I'm sorry."

I took a shaky breath. "I want to," I said, but the insistence was gone from my voice.

"Go to bed," he pleaded. "Please, Ella."

This time, I left without arguing. As I got up, he turned away from me, and he didn't look up from the water as I made my way around the pool. With a final glance at him, I walked away toward the house. My back prickled, and I imagined that I could feel his eyes on me, but I resisted the urge to look back and see if he was looking at me.

He didn't follow me into the house, and I was relieved to be alone again. When I reached the bedroom he had put me in, I saw my pajama top and shorts laid out on the bed. Remembering that I had dropped them on the floor when I had stripped them off in the kitchen, I realized that Mason must have picked them up and brought them to my room for me.

It was considerate, I noted absently as I thought about taking a shower. Deciding that I needed to wash the chlorine off, I walked back out into the hall and down to the bathroom where I had taken a shower earlier in the evening. It wasn't until I was standing under the warm spray of water that what had happened in the pool came back to me in vivid detail. Embarrassment warred with arousal within me. I couldn't believe how I had acted, but remembering how everything had felt was incredibly erotic. I nearly gave in to the sudden ache between my legs before realizing that Mason was probably in his room just down the hall by now. I couldn't masturbate in his house, with him so nearby. Embarrassment flooded through me again, and I hurried up and finished showering.

Wrapping a towel around me, I walked out into the hallway and halted when I saw Mason walking toward me from the direction of the stairs. His eyes swept over me before he fixed a heated look on my face. I clutched the towel tucked into my cleavage as he approached me. His swim trunks were back on his body, but I was keenly aware of what was beneath them. My pulse jumped in anticipation of what he would do now, but he surprised me.

"Did you leave me any warm water?" he asked in a playful, teasing tone.

"Uh," I responded, "I think so."

"If you keep standing here in that towel, I'm going to need to take a cold shower anyway," he said as his eyes dropped to my cleavage.

My breath hitched, and his gaze snapped back up to mine. "Are you turned on again too?" he asked in a sultry tone.

"Again?" I repeated as I blushed.

Surprise flashed in his eyes. "Didn't you get off in the shower?"

My eyes widened as my blush deepened. "No!" I exclaimed in a scandalized tone like I hadn't been tempted to do what he had just said.

"Why not?" he questioned.

"Because," I huffed without explaining further. Sidestepping him, I took off toward my room.

His low laugh was followed by a taunting parting. "Goodnight, Ella. I'm going to get off in the shower now."

"I don't care," I threw back at him.

That was a lie, because I was imagining him in the shower as I put on my pajamas and tried to go to sleep. I remembered how he had reacted when I gripped him and moved my hand up and down, and I knew that he was probably doing that. He was in there naked beneath the spray of water. I rolled onto my side and tried to push that thought out of my mind.

I did manage to drift off to sleep, and I only realized in the morning how much Mason had distracted me from my depressing thoughts about my mom cheating on my dad. Daylight brought back the realization that I would have to go home today.

"I wish you could stay here," Mason told me, echoing my thoughts.

"Me too," I said.

"We can get an apartment together at college," he suggested. "Where are you planning to go?"

That shook me out of my subdued state, and I stared at him, my uneaten cereal forgotten. "You want to live with me?"

"Yeah," he replied like it was obvious. "I'd rather live with you than some annoying roommate. Don't tell me that you would rather live in some tiny college dorm than in your own apartment."

"You're planning to be with me in college?" I asked, completely stunned.

"Well yeah. We just got together, and I don't want to be separated from you so soon. You don't have to move in with me, of course, but it would be great if you did."

I was still trying to wrap my mind around this. "You think you'll still want me after high school?"

He seemed taken aback. "Why wouldn't I?"

"I just thought…"

I trailed off uncertainly, and his gaze sharpened. "You thought what?"

My eyes looked past him as my hand ran nervously back and forth over the smooth tabletop in front of me. "I don't know."

"You don't know?" he demanded. "You obviously thought something, and I want to know what it is."

I shrugged helplessly, and my gaze lowered to the table.

"Look at me," he commanded.

I slowly lifted my eyes to meet his intense stare. "What do you think this is?" he questioned. "I asked you to be my girlfriend. This isn't just some casual hookup. I let you stay over my house, and nobody does that. I'm here for you, Ella. Do you get that?"

I got that fluttery feeling, but it was tempered by caution. "Yeah," I agreed, just to end the discussion.

He exhaled heavily and leveled his gaze on me again. "Are you planning to break up with me, Ella? Is that why you can't see us together in college?"

"You said that I'm not allowed," I replied.

He stiffened, and his expression froze for a moment before settling into complete neutrality. "You're allowed now," he said. "Break up with me if that's what you want."

Everything in me stilled as his words reached me through my apathetic fog. They brought me back to full awareness and to the realization that something was happening right here, right now.

"It's your decision, Ella," he said, his neutral expression giving way to an intent look that underscored his words. "I'm not forcing you to stay with me. I just wanted you to give me a chance, but I don't want you to stay with me another minute if you don't want to."

I wanted to retreat from this conversation and not deal with anything right now, but his gaze held mine insistently. "Can't we talk about this later?" I pleaded.

"There's nothing to talk about. You either want to be with me or you don't. Which is it?" he demanded.

I wrung my hands in agitation at being put on the spot. "Mason," I protested.

"Answer me, Ella. Do you want to break up with me?" He leaned in closer over the table with a fierce look. "No more blackmail, no more bullshit. It's all up to you. I just want to know how you feel. Do you want to be with me?"

I exhaled slowly before answering him. "Yes."

His expression became guarded as he pulled back. "Yes to which question?"

"Yes, I want to be with you," I told him in exasperation.

A happy smile spread across his face, and he sprang up out of his chair. Coming up behind me, he leaned down and wrapped his arms around my waist as he pressed a kiss to the top of my head. "Eat your breakfast," he urged. "We have to leave for school soon."

It felt wonderful to have his arms around me, and I still felt that warm comfort as he let go and left to get ready. Finishing my breakfast, I cleared the table and placed our bowls and spoons in the dishwasher before going upstairs to brush my teeth.

Mason and I didn't talk during the drive to school, but the atmosphere between us was mellow and content. The classical music he chose to put on was also soothing and calming. It allowed my mind to drift smoothly without the distraction of words.

Once we left the serene cocoon of his car, the noise of the other cars and students in the school parking lot intruded upon my peaceful state of mind. I wanted to escape from all of it again and steal away with Mason, but I couldn't keep cutting school.

Then I saw Josh and remembered everything that had happened with him, and my blood ran cold.

Chapter 20

I stood there like a deer in the headlights as Josh sauntered toward us. The next thing I knew, Tyler had his arm around my shoulders and pulled me slightly off balance as he dragged me into his side. "How's it going, Ella?" he boomed.

"What the hell are you doing?" Mason demanded. "Get your hands off her!" he exclaimed and gave Tyler a shove.

"Hey!" Tyler protested as he removed his arm from my shoulders. "I'm not trying to steal your girl. Ella and I are buds."

Mason scowled at him. "Since when?"

"Since I found out that she's like this cool assassin. She's been upgraded from hot babe to badass."

Mason appeared to be mollified and slightly amused. "Badass is better than hot babe?"

"Yeah," Tyler confirmed, seeming to be completely serious. "There are hot babes everywhere, but not many girls are badass. I've always wanted to be friends with a girl like that."

"You've never been friends with a girl in your life," Josh said. "You don't talk with a girl longer than it takes to hook up with her."

At least he doesn't pretend like he wants to date her, I thought as I avoided looking at Josh. Tyler had distracted me enough to compose myself, but I was still on edge. I didn't really think that Josh would say anything in front of everyone, but the threat hung over me.

"That's because I've never met a girl like Ella before," Tyler said. "She's the first one I haven't wanted to hook up with."

"You tried to pick her up at Mason's party," Josh pointed out.

He'd actually tried to solicit my "services" while under the impression that I was a prostitute, but Mason had forbidden them from ever calling me that again. Since Josh had phrased it in a way that avoided mentioning that word, he must have taken Mason's threat seriously. That realization gave me hope that he wouldn't dare tell Mason about him and me.

"That was before I knew how cool she was," Tyler told him.

Mason laughed. "Your logic makes no sense, but it works for me as long as you keep your hands off of her."

Tyler raised his hands palms out. "I swear. We'll fist bump only." He made a fist with his right hand and held it out to me.

It made me smile, and I bumped fists with him. He smiled back, and it seemed like such a genuine, friendly smile. I marveled again at how different he was from the sleazy, obnoxious guy I had always assumed him to be. Amazingly, I could actually picture myself being friends with him.

Mason took hold of my hand, drawing my attention back to him. He smiled at me too, but his smile gave me that fluttery, excited feeling. It was so obvious to me now that he was the guy for me. I had tried to fight my feelings for him, but I didn't want to anymore now that I had discovered the side of him I had always wished for. He had been there for me when I needed him without expecting anything in return, and he was including me in his future plans. He was turning out to be the boyfriend of my dreams, and I allowed that to become my focus so that I could avoid thinking of the part of my life that had derailed. It seemed that whenever something went right for me, something else went wrong. I didn't want to dwell on that though, so I ignored the negative in favor of the positive.

At least until Josh accosted me after class later that day. "What's your answer?" he demanded.

I decided to call his bluff. "My answer is no."

He shrugged. "I guess you don't care if he dumps you."

He simply walked away then. Having expected him to try to coerce me with more empty threats, I was thrown into a tailspin when it appeared that he meant to actually follow through. I rushed to catch up with him. "Wait!"

He stopped and turned to face me. "Well?" he demanded after waiting for me to say something.

"Aren't you afraid of what he'll do to you?" I asked desperately.

"I've been thinking about that," he replied coolly. "You told me yourself that he wasn't really in the mafia, and then he admitted that he lied about you and your mom. So, he's probably been lying about the mafia thing too."

I tried to get him to second-guess himself. "Are you sure about that?"

He smirked at me. "You seem awful eager all of a sudden to convince me that your boyfriend is in the mafia. Why is that Ella?"

I dropped the pretense and appealed to his honor. "You said that you would never force a girl. You told me that story about your dad beating up that rapist and how proud you are of him. Was that all just bullshit?"

His eyes narrowed at me as anger flared in them. "I'm not forcing you, Ella. I'm not some filthy rapist, and you're not any kind of victim. You came on to me behind your boyfriend's back, and now you want to play innocent. I know you're not, but he doesn't have to. It's all up to you."

"That's blackmail," I retorted.

He shrugged. "It's a deal. You get what you want, and I get what I want."

"Please don't do this," I pleaded. "Please, Josh. Please be the good guy I know you are."

He was completely unmoved by my plea. "Yes or no?"

"Josh," I begged.

"Yes or no?" he demanded again.

"I can't," I said as tears sprang to my eyes.

He gave me a cold smile. "You see? I can take no for an answer."

He walked past me then, and I didn't try to follow him this time. There was no point since he wouldn't be swayed by anything I said. I held out the tiniest bit of hope that he wouldn't go through with it, and that's what kept me from completely panicking. I needed to keep it together and get through this day so that I could seek advice from Alice after school. At least I wouldn't have to sit at the same table with Josh during lunch, since I had already told Mason that I was going to sit with Alice.

I wanted to tell her everything right now, but I couldn't do that at school. I had assumed that Josh couldn't tell Mason at school either, but I had badly misjudged him again. Since I wasn't expecting it, Mason was able to ambush me.

I heaved a sigh of relief as I walked out of my last class before lunch. My mind was on meeting up with Alice, so I was slow to react when I saw Mason standing outside my classroom. "Oh," I responded, starting to realize that he was going to walk me to the cafeteria despite our agreement to sit separately.

"Josh told me about you and him."

His words froze me in my spot, and I stared at him as all the blood drained from my face. He watched me, his neutral gaze sharpening into that chilling, predatory stare. "It's true," he stated.

"Mason," I said, his name a plea on my lips.

He stiffened, and the feral look went out of his eyes. They turned icy cold. He had never looked at me like that before, not even when he hated me. There had always been a spark between us, whether it was anger or lust, but now there was nothing.

"Well," he said, "that's it then."

His gaze shifted away from me, and he walked past me without a backward glance. My heart seized up, and I gasped out a choked breath. I had lost Mason just when he had finally become mine.

Chapter 21

The tears didn't come this time. They remained trapped behind my brittle façade as I sat alone in the library. I had texted Alice that I couldn't make it to the cafeteria today, and that I would explain later. I was numb at this point, but I felt like it wouldn't take much to make me crumble. I needed to avoid seeing Mason so that I could make it through the rest of the day.

My mind slingshot in the opposite direction by the time I got to the last class of the day, which Mason was in with me. Whether from desperation or insanity, an idea of how to get him back had formed in my mind, and I was in no condition to think clearly.

He ignored me during class, just like I knew he would. Undeterred now that I had latched onto my crazy plan, I followed him out to his car afterwards. His glacial gaze finally focused on me. "Take the bus," he snapped in a harsh tone that belied his icy exterior. He was furious beneath the unnatural calm.

The glimpse of emotion only encouraged me, because he was not as indifferent as he pretended to be. I still affected him, and I was going to use that to get him back. It still took herculean effort to say the words. "I lost the bet."

Mason went as still as a statue. He had looked away from me dismissively, but now he slowly brought his eyes back to me. The look in them almost made me run away. His fury was no longer hidden but focused all at me with frightening intensity. If looks could kill...

With my heart in my throat, I fought the panic threatening to overwhelm me and stood my ground.

His jaw clenched as he seemed to also be fighting some internal battle. After a heart pounding moment, he appeared to have subdued the fury, and the icy mask was back in place. He gave me a cool appraisal. "You ready to pay up?"

I swallowed thickly. "Yes."

He clicked the button to unlock the doors and gave me a curt nod. I got into his car and sat stiffly in the passenger seat. He drove to his house in silence without sparing me another glance.

My nervousness built steadily until my knees were so weak with it that I could barely walk into his house. He didn't make anything easier on me when he sat down on the couch as I stood before him and gave me a terse order. "Strip."

It was completely humiliating and demeaning, but I obeyed with trembling hands as I removed my t-shirt and shorts. Hesitating, I took a shaky breath before taking off my bra. My face flamed as I stared at the floor.

"Keep going," Mason commanded in a harsh tone, but I heard something more than anger in it.

Not daring to look at him, I pulled my underwear down and heard him take a sharp breath. Stepping out of them with a little more confidence, I took a peek at Mason's lap and saw the bulge between his legs. Heat flared within me and flushed my skin.

"Come here," Mason snapped, and my gaze shot up to his.

I saw a volatile combination of desire and anger that drew me and intimidated me at the same time, but I went toward it like a moth to the flame. The heat inflamed me as I stood close enough for him to touch me while his eyes roamed over my naked body.

"Spread your legs," he ordered in a rough voice.

Burning with both embarrassment and lust, I stepped so that I stood with my feet wide apart. It made me aware of the mortifying wetness between my legs, and I gasped when he swiped a finger over it.

"Did you get this wet for him?" he demanded.

"No," I said.

"But you let him fuck you."

My mouth opened in shock. "No!" I denied.

Mason scowled. "Don't lie to me. I saw the truth on your face when I confronted you about it."

"I didn't, I swear! He only touched me up here." I pressed my hands to my breasts to show him before dropping them to reach out to him.

He flinched away from me. "Get dressed, and get the fuck out of my house."

"Mason," I pleaded. "I didn't have sex with him, I swear. I'm still a virgin."

His gaze chilled me like a gust of cold air. "Are you willing to prove that?"

My throat went dry. As much as I wanted Mason to be with me, I wasn't ready for that.

He sneered at the expression on my face. "That's what I thought."

Pulling his phone out of his pocket, he dropped his gaze to it and started swiping at the screen. "I'm ordering an Uber to take you home. Don't ever come back here."

Anger rose within me. "I guess you're just like Josh. You give girls ultimatums to have sex with you, and if they don't, you get mean. No wonder you're friends."

Before I could react, he had dropped his phone and grabbed my arms to get in my face. "I have never given you an ultimatum to have sex with me. Never! And I wouldn't touch you right now if you begged me, so get the fuck out of here."

He let go of me so roughly that I stumbled back. Shooting up out of his seat, he stalked out of the room even as his phone clattered to the floor. The noise drew my gaze, and I saw it lying next to my discarded panties. I had momentarily forgotten that I was naked, and shame overcame me as I realized how pathetic my ploy to get him back had been. I had humiliated myself by taking off my clothes and trying to entice him with my body, and he had rejected me. It hit me that this was something my mother would do, and that shamed me even more.

I sure am her daughter, I thought bitterly as I got dressed. The only difference was that I hadn't had sex with him as she surely would have done, but that was little consolation to me right now.

When my Uber arrived, I asked the driver to drop me off at a different address from the one Mason had requested. Since it was only a few streets over and wouldn't change the fare, the driver agreed. Alice was home by now, and she answered the door just in time to be my shoulder to cry on. Because the tears came easily when I saw her sympathetic face.

I told her everything in between crying jags, and I felt emotionally drained by the time I was done. Both of us sat glumly in silence, me on the couch and Alice on the coffee table in front of me. I smiled sadly as I noted her little quirk, but something inside me loosened a bit. The feeling grew stronger even as I sighed. I might have lost Mason, but I still had Alice.

I straightened up in determination. "He's not going to take you away from me again."

Her eyes widened in realization, but she bravely agreed as she sat up straighter too. "No, he won't."

He didn't even bother though. Instead of taking revenge on me, this time Mason acted like I didn't even exist. He walked by me in the halls at school like I wasn't there, but he did trade seats with other people so he wouldn't have to sit next to me in the classes we shared. None of his friends made comments about me or harassed my friends. Alice and I were left in peace to enjoy our friendship. Mason had left me alone, just like I had always asked him to in the past.

While I was glad that he wasn't bullying my friends or me, I was miserable that he was completely ignoring me. I wished that I could block him out just as easily, but I was always intensely aware of him even as I avoided looking at him. I hated that he could still affect me so much, and it infuriated me that he had completely cut me off while allowing Josh to remain part of his crowd.

"He's a sexist asshole," I vented to Alice. "He blamed my mom for his dad cheating on his mom, and now he's only blaming me and not Josh. I guess it's always the woman's fault."

Yet I felt like an asshole myself when Erin asked me why I broke up with Mason. "He broke up with me," I admitted. "He didn't tell you?"

"No," she answered. "He refuses to talk about it, or you. He won't let anyone mention your name. I thought you broke up with him, but...what happened?"

I glanced around at the students passing us in the hallway. Nobody was paying attention to us, but I felt uncomfortable to have this discussion at school. "I can't talk about it here. Can we talk after school?"

"I have cheer practice," she replied, "but I'll call you later?"

"Okay," I agreed, feeling relieved that I could tell her over the phone instead of in person.

I had no idea how she'd react to finding out that I had made out with her ex-boyfriend, and it would be easier if I didn't have to face her. She seemed more confused than upset though when I talked to her later that evening. "You had a crush on Josh, but you were going out with Mason?"

"I swear I didn't know you dated him," I repeated. "I would never have gone near Josh if I knew that. I would have picked someone else." I winced after saying that.

"To have a crush on?" she asked in bewilderment.

"I never had a crush on him," I admitted. "I mean, not really. He just seemed like a nice guy to go out with, and I was trying to get over Mason."

"But weren't you already going out with Mason?" she questioned.

"I didn't think it was real." I expelled a breath. "I know it's hard to understand, but he hated me for so long that I didn't really believe he liked me. It seemed too good to be true, and then his mom made me feel like just another girl he was hooking up with."

"You were jealous," Erin said, "and you wanted to make him jealous."

"No," I denied. "Well, I was jealous. I hated thinking about him being with those other girls, but I wasn't trying to make him jealous. I was trying to like someone more than I liked him, and Josh seemed like a good choice for a boyfriend. But he turned out to be worse than Mason. At least Mason never tried to blackmail me into having sex with him."

"So, you didn't?" she asked.

"No. We just kissed and made out." Telling her that brought back my shame. "I didn't know about you and him until you told me at the concert. That's why I felt so bad."

"Oh," she responded like she was having an epiphany. "I wondered what happened all of a sudden. You were having such a great time, and then..."

"Yeah," I confirmed glumly. "I'm so sorry, Erin. I feel so awful about going out with him after the way he treated you. I never would have done it if I had known."

"It's okay," she said. "I just feel bad that you lost a great guy like Mason over him."

I exhaled heavily. "It wasn't meant to be. Anyway, I'm sorry. Thanks for being so nice to me. I loved going to the concert with you, and I wish we could have been friends longer."

"We're not friends anymore?" she asked in a hurt voice.

"I...thought that you wouldn't want to be," I replied hesitantly.

"Because of Josh?" she scoffed. "I'm not going to let him ruin anything for me. He's not worth it."

I was delighted and grateful that she still wanted to be friends with me, but I was stunned when Tyler did. "Do you know Krav Maga?" he asked me one day in the hallway at school.

"Uh, isn't that some kind of martial arts?" I responded as I wondered what he was up to, and if Mason had sent him to bully me.

"It's a combination of fighting techniques. My brother teaches classes in it. You should sign up."

This seemed so random that I didn't know what to say. "Um...I—"

"C'mon, Ella," he urged, "I know that you can be as badass as you want to be. You can go with me, and I'll help you. Here," he said, pulling out his phone. "Give me your number."

I wasn't sure if this was some kind of prank, but Mason had my number anyway, so I couldn't see any harm in giving it to Tyler. He later texted me his number, and the information about the Krav Maga classes. I looked up the facility, and it was a real place.

I tentatively asked my dad about taking classes, and he thought it was a great idea. "It's smart to learn self-defense. Hopefully you'll never need it, but it's good to be prepared."

I had never thought about doing anything like that before, but it turned out that I loved feeling "badass." To my surprise, Tyler was genuine when he claimed he wanted to be my friend. He was actually a lot of fun, and I marveled that such a player could be a great guy friend.

"Why do you think women love me?" he asked when I voiced that aloud. "I charm the pants off of them," he quipped.

I laughed and swatted his arm. "You'd actually make a great boyfriend if you could stay with one girl."

"Don't get any ideas," he warned playfully.

"I'll try to control myself," I joked.

"I know it's hard," he bantered back. "And by hard, I mean *hard*," he emphasized suggestively.

"Gross," I complained and swatted his arm harder.

"Ow," he cried out, pretending to be hurt.

I rolled my eyes at him before asking casually, "So, what does everyone think of us being friends?"

"And by everyone, you mean Mason," he retorted.

I opened my mouth to protest, but he continued. "He's jealous as hell."

"He is?" I questioned before I could stop myself.

Tyler grinned at me. "Oh yeah. It's killing him that I get to hang with you but he doesn't. He kept telling me to shut the fuck up whenever I mentioned you, but now he just glares at me."

"Oh," I responded in disappointment. "That just sounds like he hates me."

"No, he hates Josh. He never says a word to him anymore, but he watches him like a cobra watching its prey." He slid a glance toward me. "So, Josh fooled you with his nice guy routine."

It was spoken more like a statement than a question, and my embarrassed face was confirmation enough anyway.

"I should have warned you about that guy," Tyler said like he was at fault for my mistake.

I dared a glance at him. "You don't blame me? I'm the one who cheated," I admitted.

"I don't judge people," he replied. "Monogamy is hard. And by hard, I mean—"

He broke off laughing as I shoulder bumped him, laughing myself. He always lightened my mood, but I was tense at home as I waited for the other shoe to drop. I felt guilty around my dad, like I was deceiving him too by not telling him about my mom cheating on him. Yet I couldn't bring myself to hurt him with the truth, and I also didn't want to destroy our family.

As the weeks passed, I learned to live with keeping my mom's secret. So, I was completely blindsided when she told him herself. I came home from school one day to find her waiting to talk to me right when I walked through the door.

"I'm leaving Charles," she told me without preamble. "I'm going to tell him tonight."

"What?" I exclaimed. "You're leaving Dad for Jeremy?"

She scoffed. "He was just for fun. I have a man who wants to marry me."

"There's another man?" I yelled. "You've been cheating with two guys? How could you do this to Dad? He loves you!"

"You have two boyfriends yourself," she retorted, "so don't give me that attitude."

That brought me up short. "I don't have any boyfriends, Mom. I made a mistake, and I lost Mason because of it. Don't you lose Dad. He's the best thing that ever happened to you."

She ignored my plea. "It's too bad you lost Mason. It seemed like he had money. Craig has lots of money though, so you'll be meeting some rich boys once we move in with him. Wait until you see the neighborhood he lives in!"

"I'm not going with you," I declared.

"He knows about you, and he's fine with you moving in with us," she assured me. "He lives in a mansion, so there's plenty of room," she added with a girlish giggle.

I looked at her with all the disappointment I felt. I had already cried before over her cheating, and I had yelled. Now I just spoke wearily. "I'm staying here with Dad. I love him even if you don't."

She couldn't seem to comprehend how I felt. "You don't want to live in a mansion?"

I sighed, completely disheartened. "No, Mom. I don't."

She shrugged. "Suit yourself. You might change your mind once you see it. Anyway, I'll be leaving later tonight after I tell him."

After she told him. Like it was no big deal, like it wouldn't rip his heart out.

I did have more tears left in me after all, and I went to my room and cried for Dad. And for everything else that was lost.

Chapter 22

Dad survived, just like we all did. Even though heartache ripped your heart out, it didn't kill you. Alice, Erin, and I had all lost our boyfriends, and we were now united in what we called the single ladies club. We had a couple more members, who were Alice's friends. They had filled the void for her when she and I were separated, and I became friends with them too after I started sitting at their table at lunch. Lauren had never had a boyfriend, and Sarah was in love with her stepbrother.

"He's only been my stepbrother for a year," she explained. "We didn't grow up together, and I've never thought of him as my brother. It was love at first sight. You know?"

Yes, I did know. But I didn't want to reveal that I had fallen in love through a picture. I also didn't want to talk about Mason. I had gotten pretty good at blocking him from my mind when I was with other people, and I was able to have fun with my friends. I still spent entirely too much time thinking about him when I was alone though, but I hoped that it was only because I saw him at school. I still had my hopes set on putting him out of sight and out of mind when I went to college.

Having Mom out of sight didn't seem to be helping my dad, but it had only been a few weeks since she'd left. He had smiled sadly when I suggested that he should take Krav Maga classes with me and told him that they had helped me feel better after my breakup.

"You make me feel better," he told me. "It means the world to me that you chose to stay here with me." He grimaced. "I know I'm not supposed to say that and put that kind of pressure on you, but I can't help it."

"You didn't put pressure on me. I made that decision on my own before you even knew that she was leaving." I winced. "She told me before you came home," I explained.

"Yeah, she told me," he said. "You don't know what a difference it made to me, knowing that I still had you, that I wasn't alone. Just knowing that you were still in the house."

We hadn't seen each other that evening. I'd had no appetite for dinner and stayed in my room. Judging by the lack of dirty dishes the next morning, Dad had also skipped dinner. It was the weekend, and he had stayed in bed most of the day—which was something he hadn't ever done since I'd known him.

"I'm so sorry about Mom," I told him now. "I'm so sorry she did that to you."

He sighed. "A part of me always knew it was too good to be true. When I first met her, I couldn't believe that she was talking to me. She was the most beautiful woman, and she was talking to *me*. You're not going to believe this," he joked self-depreciatingly, "but I was a nerd in high school. I know, look at me now."

I smiled, glad that he was still able to joke and smile, however fleetingly.

"She was my dream woman," he said, "and dreams don't last."

"Yeah," I agreed, thinking of Mason.

I decided to write him a letter for closure. In it, I told him about my mom leaving, and the conversation I'd had with my dad. I told him how he was my dream guy, and how it had seemed too good to be true. I explained how Josh had seemed safer, because I knew he couldn't break my heart. But it had been too late, because I'd already fallen for Mason, and my heart was broken anyway. I'm sorry, I wrote. I know it doesn't make up for anything, but I'm sorry.

I mailed it to him the next day, but he didn't acknowledge to me that he had received it. I hadn't expected him to, but I hoped he had at least read it before throwing it away. He continued to act like I didn't exist, so he certainly hadn't forgiven me even if he had read my apology.

While I hadn't forgiven my mom either, I caved to her incessant requests for me to visit her. My dad had also encouraged me to go. Whether I liked it or not, she was still my mother. I suspected that her wanting me to visit was more about showing off her new lifestyle rather than missing me, but I went to stay the weekend with her.

The mansion wasn't the grandest one I'd been in—Mason's former mansion held that distinction—but Mom was still living in a mansion. She had definitely snagged a man with money. Seeing them together pissed me off, because they looked like Barbie and Ken. Why did Craig have to be attractive too? It wasn't fair that she had gotten everything she wanted while breaking my dad's heart in the process.

To top it off, Craig seemed nice. He was friendly and welcoming, but I refused to like him. I was polite though, but reserved. Until I saw my future stepbrother. Then my jaw dropped open as I stared at him.

He was the result of Craig's relationship with a Brazilian model, and he was one of the hottest guys I had ever seen. Craig's blue eyes stood out vividly in his son's face, offset by thick, jet black hair.

"Lucas models," Mom told me excitedly.

"No kidding," I remarked drily.

Lucas responded with a sexy laugh and winked at me.

When I told the story to my friends during lunch at school, I couldn't stop laughing. "I have a hot stepbrother too!" I said gleefully to Sarah.

"Did you fall in love at first sight?" she asked.

"No," I replied, "but he sure made the weekend more fun."

"Did he kiss you?" Erin asked, looking all wide-eyed over my story. She had taken to sitting with us since we all became friends.

"No," I said with a laugh. "He's a big flirt though. Kind of like Tyler, except smoother."

"I resent that," Tyler said from behind me. "I'm very smooth."

I turned in my seat to look at him. "What are you doing here? You're not a member of our club. No boys allowed."

He smirked at me. "What are you, twelve? You girls were having so much fun that I had to come see what was going on."

"Ella has a hot stepbrother," Erin told him.

"It's hilarious," I said in agreement.

He laughed. "Right. Because I always think it's hilarious when someone is hot."

"It is," I insisted. "It's like a scenario from one of those romance novels I used to read. Get this, not only is he insanely hot, but he's a model. How hilarious is that?"

Tyler no longer looked amused. "Do you have a picture of this guy?"

I looked toward Alice, who still had my phone instead of passing it around like I had instructed her to. They had all already seen my personal picture of Lucas, but I had pulled up some of his professional photos to show them. She handed me my phone, and I gave it to Tyler.

"Holy shit," he exclaimed. "You can't live with this guy! He'll sex you for sure."

I rolled my eyes. "Sex me? And I'm not living with him. He doesn't even live with his dad. He's a professional soccer player, so he's out on his own. He just came for a visit, like I did."

"Wait, how old is this guy?" Tyler questioned.

"Twenty," I replied.

There was a collective sigh from the other girls before Tyler exploded. "Oh, hell no! He's a freaking man? You can't stay in the same house with that guy ever again."

"Well, I hate to break it to you, but we'll be staying at the same house again for the wedding. My mom is going to be a winter bride," I added, the bitterness creeping into my voice.

Erin darted around and snatched my phone out of Tyler's hand. "Wow!" she exclaimed.

Sarah and Lauren crowded beside her to look too while she gazed at Lucas's modeling photos. "Now I think I'm in love," Lauren proclaimed.

Tyler affected a disgusted expression and left us to our fun. While the girls were occupied with my phone, I indulged the habit I had been unable to break and snuck a glance at Mason.

He was staring right at me.

The unexpected shock of it sent a jolt through me. My pulse raced, and I couldn't look away. It had been so long since he had looked directly at me, but it riveted me like always. The realization that nobody else had ever affected me this way was starkly apparent to me when he looked away. I felt the loss of his gaze and his attention, and it took me a moment to regain my equilibrium.

He shattered it again when he ambushed me in the hallway after my friends and I parted ways after lunch. Suddenly he was there and pulling me aside to stare at me with that intense gaze of his. "Are we even?" he demanded.

My brain was still wrapping around the fact that he was speaking to me. "What?" I asked in a daze.

"Are we even now? Have you had your revenge on me?"

My mouth gaped open. "I never wanted revenge on you."

"But you got it," he told me tersely. "I went through hell thinking about him touching you."

He expelled a harsh breath. "As you said in your letter, being sorry doesn't make up for anything. So I want to know if we're even now, or if you're still going to hold the past against me."

"I'm not," I told him. "I'm over that now. After everything that's happened, it's not even on my mind anymore."

"Good," he said, "because you're all that's on my mind. I tried to get over you, Ella, but I can't."

Hope blossomed in my chest. "I can't get over you either."

He smiled in response, but his eyes blazed with heat. "That does sound like we're even."

"It does," I agreed as I burned with the desire to kiss him.

He leaned in, seemingly pulled toward me like a magnet before his lips crashed down on mine. He groaned like he had gotten something he had long been denied, and then he was kissing me with a hunger that matched my own.

A few minutes later, we were both late for class but extremely happy as we parted. Because we were back together, and we were in love. We'd both said it spontaneously at the same time after our passionate kiss. "I love you."

My heart swelled with happiness, and this time I had no doubt that we both meant it.

Epilogue

I opened the door and took in the sight of Mason in his tux. It brought back the memory of the first time I'd seen him wearing one. He still looked like my dream come true, and now he really was. This time he was wearing a new tux for prom, and he was going with me.

His eyes swept over my dress—my mom's contribution to the evening. I had at first resisted the idea of getting a dress at the expensive boutiques where she had taken me shopping, but I had succumbed when I saw this champagne and silver elegant beaded beauty. It had an elaborate jeweled bodice and a simple chiffon skirt, and it looked lovely on me.

"My God you're beautiful," Mason exclaimed as he gazed at me.

"She certainly is," Dad said from behind me. "I told her she looks like Grace Kelly in that dress. Not that she knew who that was, but when I told her she was a princess that was all she cared to know."

I was blushing from all the compliments, and I felt too shy to voice my own in front of my dad, but Mason was absolutely gorgeous. At times like these, I was astounded that he was really my boyfriend. "I can't believe you're mine," I told him once we were alone in his car.

Mason looked at me. "Me too. I mean, I can't believe you're mine, Ella. I've wanted you for so long, and now I have you. Sometimes I feel like I'm dreaming."

"Me too!" I exclaimed excitedly. "And tonight is like my ultimate dream fantasy."

He quirked his lips. "I can't say it's my ultimate fantasy about you, but..."

I flushed and worked up the courage to say what I had been thinking about for the last few days. "Maybe we can fulfill your ultimate fantasy tonight."

Mason had been about to put the key in the ignition, but he stilled and slowly looked toward me. "I thought that we were going to wait until we got to college."

That had been the plan I had presented to him, although he had never once brought up the subject of when we would have sex. He was set on getting his own apartment even though I had decided that I wanted to live in a dorm. I had been worried about him being able to afford the apartment by himself, but he had reminded me that he had already been able to access his trust fund when he turned eighteen. I had therefore been able to take finances out of my decision and base it solely on what I thought was best for us. Alice had also weighed in and advised me that living together might complicate things. I had agreed and decided that each having our own space would be good for us.

I did, however, see the advantages of him having his own apartment where we could be alone. Both of us would be adults, and we would have the perfect place to unleash the passion that we felt for each other. Yet we already had that now. We were both eighteen, and Mason had an entire house to himself. We also had the whole night to ourselves, since I wasn't expected home until morning due to after parties.

"I've changed my mind," I told Mason. "I don't want to wait that long. I want to be with you now—tonight."

He expelled a breath. "Shit, I feel like your dad is about to come out here with a shotgun."

He shoved the key in the ignition and turned it to start the car and pull out of my driveway. Once we were driving away, he threw a glance at me. "Don't buy into any bullshit about tonight, Ella. I don't care what other people are doing. I'm going out with my girl, and that's all that matters to me."

I smiled. "Mason Sumner, you are a romantic and exactly the boyfriend I always dreamed you would be."

He glanced at me with a smile before returning his attention to the road, but his smile disappeared when I placed my hand on his thigh. "But tonight," I continued, "I want you to be my silver-eyed devil."

He sucked in a sharp breath. "Ella," he protested.

"I've been thinking about you constantly," I confessed. "When I'm in the shower, in bed at night." I looked at my hands clasped in my lap as my face heated in embarrassment. "I want you to be the one to touch me."

"Ella," he said, his voice sounding hoarse, "you have to stop talking like that. I won't be fit to be in public."

I looked at the bulge in his pants and slid my hand up toward it. Mason's hand shot off the wheel to grab mine. "Stop," he ordered, but twined his fingers with mine.

"That's the problem," I told him. "I don't want to stop. I never want to stop anymore. I don't think I can wait all summer to be with you, Mason."

He exhaled slowly. "Let's just calm down and go to prom. If you still feel the same afterwards, we'll see. But no pressure, okay?"

"Okay," I agreed.

There might not have been any pressure to have sex, but there was plenty of sexual tension. I only lasted an hour at the dance before I suggested to Mason that we get out of there. This time, he didn't argue.

He affected a casual tone as we walked toward his car. "Where do you want to go?"

"Your house," I told him unequivocally.

We didn't speak again until we were in his bedroom. "Tell me if you want to stop," he said.

"I won't," I replied.

"Ella," he admonished me sternly, "tell me if you want to stop."

"Okay," I agreed.

Then my romantic and erotic fantasies melded as my tuxedo-clad boyfriend kissed me with heated desire. He carefully removed my expensive dress and draped it over his desk chair before turning to look at me. Although he had seen me naked before, he took the time to appreciate the view of me in my white bra and panties.

"So beautiful," he said

Loving the way he was looking at me, I walked toward him and pressed myself against his body. He kissed me hungrily as his hands moved down my back to grip my rear. I moaned into his mouth and began to shove his tuxedo jacket off his shoulders.

He pulled back to allow me to push it down his arms and onto the floor. "Do you want to stop?" he asked.

"No," I replied impatiently. "Take off your shirt."

I watched him undo all the buttons one by one, seemingly purposely taking his time as he watched me. When the last button was undone, I moved in with anticipation and slid the shirt off his shoulders and down his arms, letting it drop to the floor as I pressed myself against his bare skin. He groaned and took my mouth in another hot kiss.

Lust consumed us, and it all felt so good that I didn't even think about stopping until Mason asked me that question again as I lay naked on his bed. He was naked too, and my hands had been all over his body before he halted his exploration of mine and got up off the bed.

"Do you want to stop?"

"No," I answered. "Do you?"

"No," he replied, "but I will if you want me to. We can still wait until another time. It doesn't have to be tonight."

"I don't want to wait," I told him. "I'm ready now."

"Are you sure?" he asked.

"Yes," I answered.

His gaze held mine a moment longer before he opened his nightstand and took a condom out of a box inside. Tearing the wrapper open, he unrolled it and put it on before returning to the bed. I tensed in preparation for the loss of my virginity, but Mason gave me a long, deep kiss that I melted into. He repeated the foreplay he had already given me before stopping to get the condom, and he worked my body up into such a frenzy of lust that I was out of my mind with wanting him.

When he hesitated after positioning himself between my legs, I spoke before he could say a word. "Yes please," I pleaded in encouragement without a shred of self-consciousness.

He slipped inside me, and I gritted my teeth at the sudden pain as he pushed further in. He tensed and stopped.

"Don't stop," I demanded through clenched teeth.

His expression was so tense that he looked like he was in pain too. "Hurting you," he ground out. "Have to…"

He began to pull back, but I dug my nails into his back. "No, don't stop."

His hissed and thrust forward, tearing through the barrier that had halted him. His loud groan mingled with my cry of pain. "Oh fuck, I'm sorry," he said as he stilled completely.

I took shallow breaths as the pain subsided. Then I gasped when I felt his finger rubbing that spot between my legs. It felt even more incredible with him inside me, and the pleasure built quickly. "Oh," I moaned. "Oh, yes."

"That's it," he encouraged.

As soon as my orgasm overcame me, Mason moaned and began to thrust. I was still sore, but he was done within a few thrusts and pulled out to collapse on the bed beside me.

"Are you okay?" he panted.

"Yeah," I breathed.

He took a few more breaths before speaking. "I'm sorry. I didn't want to hurt you."

"It's okay," I assured him. "It didn't last that long, and then you made me feel good."

"Oh, I'm going to make you feel much better," he promised. "And I'm going to last much longer next time."

Heat spread over my face. "I meant the pain didn't last long. I wasn't saying that you didn't last long."

He smiled at me. "You are so cute. I know what you meant." His gaze intensified as his smile faded. "No more pain. Only pleasure." His gaze skimmed down my body, making desire flare in me again. "Do you want to take a shower with me?"

I had fantasized so often about him when I was in the shower that I was instantly aroused. "Yes."

He gave me a sultry smile and got up off the bed. I happened to glance down at myself as I sat up. "Oh," I said in dismay, realizing why he had suggested a shower. Scooting off the bed, I looked back and saw that a little blood had gotten on the sheets too. "Oh, I'm sorry."

Mason barked out a laugh. "Fuck, Ella. You just gave yourself to me, and you're sorry about my sheets? I'm the luckiest fucking guy in the world to have you."

His gaze was fierce with emotion as he looked at me, but his kiss was gentle and tender before he took my hand and led me to the bathroom. Letting go, he discarded the condom and turned on the water in the shower. When we stepped inside, he gently lathered soap on me and washed me off.

Then he pulled me back against his body as his hands joined the spray of water on my skin. He touched and teased until I was crazed with lust again. "I've been fantasizing about this ever since I read your poem," he said into my ear. "Is this what you imagined when you touched yourself in the shower?"

"Yes," I moaned as he stroked me, too far gone to be embarrassed about admitting it.

"So fucking hot," he rasped.

He held strong as I collapsed against him with the force of my orgasm. When he helped me out of the shower, he wrapped a towel around me before grabbing one for himself. Instead of going back to his room, he led me to the guest bedroom where I had slept when I spent the night at his house.

When he pulled back the covers, I took his cue to get into bed and dropped the towel. He dropped his own towel, and my eyes went to his erection. I thought that we were going to have sex again, but he cuddled against me instead. Wondering if I should try to do for him what he had done for me, I moved my hand down tentatively to reach for him, but he stopped me.

"It's okay," he said. "Just relax. I know you're tired out."

I actually was, but I felt bad to leave him unsatisfied. "But you're still—"

"It's okay," he assured me. "This happens all the time when I'm around you," he joked. "You just don't notice since I'm not usually naked."

"I like when you're naked," I told him before a yawn escaped me.

He laughed softly. "Go to sleep now, Ella."

I drifted off, feeling totally content. When someone shook me awake, I tried to snuggle back into sleep. "It's morning," Mason said and placed a kiss on the back of my head. "I need to take you home."

I opened my eyes and saw the pale light of dawn. "Can't believe I slept so long," I mumbled.

"Because I wore you out," he said with a note of male pride. "Mm," he added as he skimmed his hand over my hip.

"I like waking up with you naked in my bed. Too bad you have to go home."

He sprang out of bed just as I was anticipating where his hand would go next. "Get dressed. I'll wait for you downstairs."

I turned to see that he was already dressed. "You put your tux back on?"

He paused in the doorway and glanced at me. "It'll look like we went straight from prom to the after party. I don't want your dad to get any ideas about me taking off my clothes. Or yours." His eyes trailed down my body before he turned and walked quickly away.

I felt the buzz of arousal as I got up and padded naked to Mason's bedroom. Glancing at his bed, I saw that he had changed the sheets, and I flushed at the thought of him coming in here to get his clothes and seeing the stained sheets. I wondered what he had thought as he looked at them.

Sex. That's what I was thinking about. I'd had sex with Mason, and I wanted to do it again. I was getting hot just thinking about it, and standing here naked in his room wasn't helping. Crossing to the chair where my dress was draped, I saw my bra and panties laid out on top of Mason's desk.

"You better put them on before I shove everything off that desk and fulfill another fantasy of mine."

His voice startled me, and I turned to see him in the doorway watching me with that predatory stare. My breath hitched, and a heatwave rushed through my entire body. "What fantasy?" I asked in a voice weak with desire.

He gave me a slow, wicked smile. "I'm not going to reveal everything to you all at once. I have to have something to entice you back here with." His eyes did a slow sweep over my body. "Now get dressed."

"Make me," I challenged, apparently afflicted with a wickedness that surpassed his.

His gaze snapped up to mine as he straightened and prowled toward me. My pulse jumped but I held my ground as he approached. Wild, half-formed thoughts of what he might do to me had my breath coming fast. Tension held me taut as he came close and loomed over me. Reaching past me, he grabbed my panties off the desk and sank down onto the floor.

"Step into them," he instructed as he held them out.

I did, and he slowly pulled them up my legs and inched them over my thighs deliberately slow so that dressing me was just as erotic as undressing me. His gaze followed the path of my panties and lingered at the juncture between my legs after he covered it up. He smiled in satisfaction as moisture pooled there and dampened the fabric.

My blush deepened as he looked up at me. I felt both aroused and embarrassed, and my gaze shifted away from his.

He stood up and took hold of my chin to make me look at him. "Nothing is hotter than knowing you're wet for me," he said.

He let go and stepped away. "Now please get dressed before your dad hunts me down."

I responded with a shaky laugh that was a mixture of arousal and amusement. Mason closed the door behind him as he left, and I grabbed my bra and put it on. After putting on my dress, my sense of propriety returned, and I went into the bathroom to make sure my hair was smoothed down.

When I went downstairs, Mason was waiting for me by the front door. "Sorry we don't have time for breakfast," he said.

"I'm too nervous to eat right now anyway," I replied. "I just need to get past my dad without him suspecting anything."

"That's what I've been trying to get you to do," he retorted. "But I couldn't get you to put your clothes on," he added with a smirk.

"Shut up," I huffed but laughed.

"I love my nudist girlfriend," he said as he pulled open the door.

"Shut up," I said laughingly.

He faced me directly, and his expression turned serious. "I love you, Ella." His smile returned. "Even with your clothes on."

Happiness surged through me. "I love you, Mason. Even without your clothes on," I teased.

His grin was something that I hadn't ever expected to see directed at me. Nor had I ever imagined that I could be joking with him. Being with him was more than what I had pictured in my romantic dreams, and more than what I had imagined in my erotic fantasies. Being in love was all that plus a special kind of friendship too that was a lot of fun. I felt like I had everything with him now and couldn't ask for more.

Yet more kept coming. It was like fate decided to make up for all the years that we had been at odds, because Mason kept surpassing my expectations. When I expected to see only his new apartment at college, I saw Mason get down on one knee and propose to me. Of course I said yes, and I started off college with a fiancé rather than a boyfriend.

I had expected him to be into the party scene, but he was a focused student and a great study partner. Unlike me with my undecided major, he knew exactly what he wanted.

That's when I found out that he was planning to run his dad's company. "I thought that was all gone," I said. "Didn't you say that your mom was going through his fortune?"

"She sold the rest, but she couldn't sell my share in his company. I'm a major stockholder."

"Oh," I responded, not understanding the enormity of that statement. "That's good."

"Yeah," he agreed as he pulled me closer, "but not as good as this."

He then proceeded to prove how very good it was.

After college, the day arrived that was the culmination of all my girlish dreams. My dad walked me down the aisle where my handsome prince awaited me. I had a surreal moment when I flashed back to seeing his photograph and knowing that he was the one I'd marry. I didn't know what the odds were of being correct in that assumption about a boy I hadn't even met, but I knew they had to be astronomical.

Yet the odds didn't matter, because destiny wouldn't be deterred. All I had done was look at a photograph, and the rest had just happened. Now I was in the photographs with him, and it was like I had stepped straight into my dream.

It was true that most dreams ended, but mine didn't. I got to live in it for the rest of my life, and it far exceeded its simple beginnings. The boy in the photograph had become my husband, my lover, and my friend. He knew me in ways that no one else did, and he loved me. Right now he was looking at me like I was his dream come true.

"Do you have any idea how beautiful you are?" he asked.

"Yes," I retorted. "With this huge belly and my swollen ankles, I'm sure I've never looked better."

"I love this belly," he said, placing his hand over it. "I love our baby, and I love you."

I couldn't help but melt when he said things like that, and he smiled warmly back at me before his eyes got that wicked glint I knew so well. "Do you want me to rub your ankles? Or do you want me to rub something else?" he asked as his hand glided down past my belly.

"Mason," I protested, prevented from escaping by my size and my sprawled position on the couch.

This was another thing I hadn't expected from him. This far along into my pregnancy, I didn't feel attractive at all, but Mason still couldn't keep his hands off me. One slipped past the waistband of my maternity shorts and inside my underwear, while the other lifted my maternity top to expose my breasts, which had also grown bigger.

"So luscious," he said as he stared at them.

I moaned as his finger rubbed the pleasure spot between my legs. He brought it out and sucked it into his mouth. "Mm, you taste so good," he told me.

Using both hands to unhook my bra and bare my breasts, he then returned his hand to where he had left me throbbing and leaned in to suck my nipple into his mouth as he stroked me with his finger. I was so sensitive, and the dual sensations of pleasure brought on my climax quickly.

Yet the wetness between my legs exceeded what was normal. Mason jumped up. "I think your water broke!"

"I think you're right," I told him and extended my hand. "Help me up. I need to take a shower."

"A shower!" he exclaimed. "You need to get to the hospital!"

"Calm down. There's plenty of time. I'm not even having contractions yet."

I felt my first one in the shower while Mason stood anxiously in there with me. "It's happening!" I exclaimed excitedly. "I just had a contraction!"

Mason went into a panic as he quickly got out of the shower but had to reign in his urge to rush while helping me to get out. My assurances that we still had lots of time to get to the hospital did nothing to calm him down. He hurriedly dried me off with a towel and helped me get dressed.

I watched him in amusement after he walked me to the garage and sat me down in the car. "Aren't you forgetting something?" I asked.

He glanced around wildly as he tried to think of what it could be but quickly gave up. "What?" he questioned me.

"I'm sure a lot of ladies at the hospital would love to see you in your birthday suit, but it might be too much for them to handle."

He glanced down at himself and swore. "Shit! I'll be right back."

I laughed as he ran into the house to put on clothes. The fun of being with him was the most unexpected part, and I loved it just as much as everything else about being with him. Now there would be even more to love since we were about to have a baby.

Mason came running back after having thrown on a t-shirt and shorts. When he yanked his door shut after sitting down in the driver's seat, I placed a hand on his arm. "Hey."

He turned his head to look at me. I gazed at him as I tried to find the words to convey everything I was feeling in that moment. His own gaze softened. "I know," he said. "It's amazing."

And it was.

The End